About the Author

Pauline Wilson lives in North East Victoria on the banks of the Murray River. She is a writer and family historian who loves learning and research. She writes historical fiction inspired by true stories of her ancestors. When she is not writing or researching she likes to read and take long walks. Family & Fortune is her third novel.

Connect on Instagram (@paulinemareewilson) of Facebook (@paulinewilsonauthor) or sign up for my newsletter at www.paulinewilson.com.au/news

Also By

Pauline Wilson

Conflict at Hanging Rock

Breaking Free

To stay updated on my latest releases and all my news, sign up to my newsletter
www.paulinewilson.com.au/news

FAMILY & FORTUNE

PAULINE WILSON

Boughyards Press

Chapter One

Mary Ann Turner, Wilden Bedfordshire, 1845

Two formidable figures loomed over the assembled children; the silence was heavy in the room. Ten-year-old Mary Ann stared wide eyed, her body rigid. She glanced at her friend sitting next to her and at her classmates in front of her. Like Mary Ann, they all sat with backs straight and heads up, mimicking the posture drilled into them. Their wooden desks were placed in precise rows facing the blackboard, suspended on its wooden frame at the front of the schoolroom.

Their teacher, Mr Harvey, was a stern-looking man whose mere presence sent fear into Mary Ann's heart. He stood motionless, his thin lips pressed into a tight line. As if that wasn't enough, the man standing beside him raised her anxiety to another level again.

Lord Robotham was the owner of the largest estate in the parish, the Lord of the Manor and patron of the school. Most of the children's parents, including Mary Ann's father, worked for Lord Robotham, so she knew she needed to be on her best behaviour when he visited the school.

'Now, children. You all know Lord Robotham, I am sure. Please say good morning,' said Mr Harvey.

'Good morning, Lord Robotham,' chanted the children in unison.

Lord Robotham was an imposing figure, dressed as he was in a velvet frock coat and striped trousers. His white shirt had a high collar adorned with a sleek cravat and he wore a rich brocade waistcoat under his coat. His silken top hat shone in the sunlight seeping into the room through the multi-paned windows, which lined one side of the classroom.

Lord Robotham removed his top hat and carefully set it on the teacher's desk before resting both hands on his cane. 'Well, well, well,' he said, fixing the students with a steely glare. 'What a dense looking lot of children. I wonder whether you know anything at all.'

Mary Ann sat quietly, trying to make herself as small as possible. Her mother had neatly combed her curly brown hair and coaxed it into tidy plaits before she left for school. She wore a simple dress with a high neckline, long sleeves, and a full skirt. A white apron kept her dress clean. Her feet were clad in stockings and sturdy, though slightly worn, leather boots.

Lord Robotham was a frequent visitor to the school room so Mary Ann knew he would soon fire questions around the room. On his last visit, one of the boys answered a question incorrectly. After Lord Robotham left, Mr Harvey punished him with five strokes of the cane on the palm of each hand. Mary Ann thought he was a bit dull not to be able to answer the question, but she still felt sorry for him and didn't think he deserved to be punished so severely. She had never been subjected to the cane and although she felt quite sure she would know the answer to any question Lord Robotham might ask, she did not want to be singled out. What if her nerves got the better of her?

Despite her best efforts not to attract attention, Lord Robotham raised his cane and pointed at her. 'You at the back.'

Mary Ann's hazel eyes widened. Oh no, was he really pointing at her?

'Yes, you girl, with the plaits.'

Her legs didn't seem to want to work. Eventually, she was able to get to her feet, her hands tightly clasped to stop them shaking. She bobbed a quick curtsy.

'Yes, Sir.' Her voice quivered.

'What is the capital city of Scotland?'

Mary Ann froze. She should know this. It wasn't a particularly difficult question, but fear overtook her, and she felt like her tongue had grown to twice its size.

'Well?'

Suddenly, Mary Ann had a flash of inspiration. 'It's Edinburgh,' she declared, triumphantly.

Lord Robotham looked displeased that she knew the answer. Mary Ann was sure he was more interested in catching the children out than encouraging their learning.

'Hmm, perhaps you are not as dull as you look. Sit down.'

Mary Ann dropped back into her seat and again made herself as small as possible as Lord Robotham continued pointing his cane, firing questions at the hapless children.

She felt her face glow with pride. It made her even more determined to learn everything she could. Geography and mathematics were not her strong points. Her mother said she was a bit of a dreamer, which Mary Ann was convinced was a good thing. She would much rather read stories of fairies in the garden and tales of far-off places, than learn all the boring facts the teacher assured them they must know. She loved reading, although the books at school were so dull. Not like her treasured copy of *Tales of Mother Goose* which contained magical stories of princesses and fairies. Mary Ann breathed a sigh of relief as Lord Robotham left the room. She couldn't wait for the dreadful day to end so she could go home and escape into the land of Mother Goose.

Mary Ann's spirits soared as the school bell rang out, signalling the end of the school day. She had never been happier to escape with her classmates into the narrow streets of the small market town of Wilden. She loved the rolling countryside of gentle hills and valleys, which provided a picturesque backdrop to the village. The surrounding farmland, bordered by hedgerows and woodlands, and dotted with flocks of woolly sheep, provided plenty of space for the adventures of small children. The sun shone warmly on this late summer afternoon.

Mary Ann raced towards home with her brothers, Charles and Josiah. Charles was two years older, and Josiah was her baby brother, who was now nine years old. Sometimes Charles tried to boss her around, which made her cross. But she loved him all the same. Today, as most days, she was starving. Mary Ann hoped their mother would offer them at least a portion of bread to make do until dinner was ready.

As they tumbled through the front door of the small stone cottage, their mother gave each child a warm hug. Ann Turner was a small, demure woman who dressed in simple, practical clothing and spent the best part of her days in the kitchen. Mary Ann rarely saw her without her apron, except when they attended church on Sunday. Her mousy brown hair was worn in a tight chignon at the nape of her neck.

'Can we please have something to eat, Mother?' said Mary Ann.

'After you have done your chores,' replied her mother.

'Oh, but I wanted to read before it gets dark.'

'Not until the chores are done. If you stop arguing and get on with it, you'll still have time to read.'

Charles gave Mary Ann a quick poke in the side. She glared at him, but as much as she hated to admit it, he was right. Arguing with her mother would only mean bed and no supper and definitely no reading time. She ran out with Charles to get the chores done as quickly as possible.

Though Mary Ann grumbled about the splinters in her fingers, she actually enjoyed helping Charles chop the wood for the stove, before stowing it in the scuttle beside the fire. Josiah was responsible for feeding the chickens, which scratched around in the backyard. Scattering their feed in the chicken coop encouraged the chickens to return to their roosts for the night. Once they were all back in and pecking at their feed, Josiah closed the door. The next chore was to put out hay for the cow. The children fed the pig with scraps from the kitchen. At this time of the year, they could also gather acorns falling from the gigantic oak tree at the back of the house. Mary Ann took great delight in watching the pig devour these nutty morsels, which were a rare delicacy in the pig's otherwise mundane diet.

Once the chores were done, they raced back inside. Their mother set a plate of bread and dripping on the table together with a glass of milk, fresh from the cow.

'Thank you!' said the children in chorus.

Mary Ann knew many of the other children in the village were not as lucky as her. Her family always had enough to eat and lived in a small, but comfortable, two bedroom cottage. Like all the tenant farmers who were employed by Lord Robotham, part of their compensation for working the land and minding the livestock was the allocation of a cottage. The main room was the centre of activity, with the stove in one corner for heating and cooking and a large sturdy oak table in the centre of the room, surrounded by wooden chairs. A bench lined one wall where the food preparation was done and where they washed the dishes. Cupboards held the kitchen and eating utensils, and there was a pantry cupboard for the food.

Their parents slept in one bedroom, and Mary Ann shared the other bedroom with her brothers. The only other room was the scullery, where they stored their work boots, tools and firewood. Next to their home was a small allotment, where they grew vegetables and kept their animals.

Their father, Samuel, worked as a bailiff, a privileged position, which held a lot of responsibility as he was required to supervise the other tenants and make sure all the work was completed. This meant their family was well off, compared to many of their neighbours.

Today, Mary Ann could smell something delicious cooking on the stove and despite quickly finishing her bread and dripping, she was still hungry, and her mouth watered as she smelt the stew. 'Do you think Father will be home soon?'

'How should I know?' Charles finished the last of his bread and drained his glass of milk. 'Father works long hours and he'll come home when he's ready. Can't you ever be patient?'

Mary Ann scowled at her brother and went to fetch her book. She knew her father's job was hard and he was often exhausted. She was only asking about dinner. Charles was so annoying.

By the time their father arrived home the sky was darkening, with the last traces of daylight fading into the horizon. Mary Ann and her brothers gathered noisily around him in the scullery as he took off his boots. He was tall with leathery skin, a testament to the many hours spent outdoors. Hard work had also hardened his muscles, although he was still a good-looking man with thick, dark hair and brown eyes.

'Leave your father alone until he has had his cup of tea,' called their mother. By the time Samuel removed his boots and padded into the kitchen in his soft leather slippers, Ann had poured the tea. The children knew once their father had a chance to rest his weary body for a while and enjoy his evening meal, he would be willing to listen to the happenings of their day, and perhaps even tell them a story. They waited patiently as he sat down at the table and sipped his tea.

Ann moved around the living area, lighting the oil lanterns, which cast a soft glow over the room. 'How was your day, Samuel?'

Samuel frowned. 'The sheep seem well, and the crops are growing quickly, but Lord Robotham has enclosed two more areas of the commons. Soon there will be nowhere left for the tenants to run their flocks. There seems to be no way to improve our lot when the landlords are so greedy.'

It didn't surprise Mary Ann at all to hear Lord Robotham was greedy. She was reading her book while her brothers played jacks on the floor nearby, but she always liked to have one ear open for her parents' conversations.

Ann turned concerned eyes to her husband. 'We'll have grazing pastures for our sheep, won't we?'

Samuel said nothing.

Mary Ann regarded her parents solemnly. She could tell they were worried, but her mother did not make any further comment about the sheep and instead turned to her.

'Mary Ann, can you please set the table? Our meal is ready.'

Mary Ann groaned, put her book down and got to her feet. Charles never had to set the table. It was another thing Mary Ann found annoying, but she would not think about that tonight. Her father looked even wearier than usual and she would do anything to make his night easier.

Mary Ann moved quickly to set a bowl, fork, and spoon for each person. The whole family gathered round the table. Ann ladled a good serve of hearty broth into each bowl and there was a freshly baked piece of bread for each as well. They all waited quietly until Ann sat down, then bowed their heads as she said grace. As soon as the prayer was finished, they ate hungrily. The children chattered happily with the sound of spoons scraping on bowls adding to the din. Mary Ann could feel the unease as her father ate silently. Was she the only one who could see something was wrong?

Once stomachs were full, and the dishes washed, the family gathered round the stove where there were two comfortable chairs for Samuel and Ann. Although the fire was no longer needed, and had been allowed to burn out after Ann cooked the meal, it was still a cosy corner for them to sit with a thick rug on the floor. The children gathered around their parents. Mary Ann looked at her father's face, lined with worry, and decided to try to cheer him up.

'Lord Robotham came to school today,' she said as soon as there was a pause in the conversation.

For a moment she didn't think her father heard her. But then he answered her in a gruff voice. 'Is that so, young Mary Ann? And did you pass muster?'

'He asked me a question. And I knew the answer.'

'Well, it is good to know something is being retained in that fanciful head of yours.'

So much for her quest to please him. Their father still sat looking sullen and saying little else while her brothers talked nonstop about their day. Her mother looked up from her knitting and smiled at her. Mary Ann felt encouraged and was sure her mother appreciated that she was trying to cheer her father up. She returned her mother's smile before turning her attention back to her father.

'Father, could you please play us a tune on your fiddle?'

Often after the evening meal and before the children went to bed, Samuel would take out his fiddle and play some gay tunes.

'Not tonight. I am far too tired.' An impatient glance flitted across her mother's face as her father slumped further in his chair.

'Well could you tell us a story?'

'I said not tonight.' Samuel raised his voice, which he hardly ever did and Mary Ann knew she had gone too far.

'Now children, it is time for bed. Off you go,' said Ann with a sideways glance at her husband.

'But it is only early,' said Mary Ann.

'No arguments, please. If you hurry, I will read you a story.'

Charles and Josiah scowled at Mary Ann as they got ready for bed.

'Why did you have to upset Father?' said Josiah. 'It's too early for bed.'

'You're so selfish sometimes,' said Charles.

Mary Ann threw her pillow at Charles. 'I am not! I was just trying to cheer him up.' But Charles and Josiah still scowled.

'That's enough squabbling,' said Ann.

She helped the children get ready. Once they were all dressed in their nightclothes, Ann watched as they knelt to say their prayers before reading them a story. Charles was pretending not to be interested, but Mary Ann knew that despite being older, he still loved it when their mother spent time with them.

When her mother knelt to give her a goodnight kiss, Mary Ann whispered, 'Why is Father so sad?'

Ann frowned. 'I am sure it is nothing. He is just tired from a long day of work.'

After giving them all a kiss and tucking them into bed, she left the room, taking the lantern with her. The room plunged into darkness and Mary Ann listened to the murmur of her parents' voices as she drifted off to sleep. She didn't believe her father was just tired. It was normal for him to be tired, but he wasn't usually this grumpy. Trying to dispel her fears that something was badly wrong, she imagined her parents were the king and queen of a far-off land who had come to visit her home. She dreamed of fairies and goblins in the garden, sitting cross-legged under a mushroom and coming out to dance in the moonlight.

Chapter Two

Richard Evans, Amersham, 1845

I t was market day and the town square in the tiny town of Amersham was abuzz. Eighteen-year-old Richard Evans mingled with the villagers, watching them milling around, bartering what they could afford in order to secure the wares they needed. His frustration built, knowing he had nothing to barter. The market square was at the centre of the town, surrounded by narrow cobble streets lined with symmetrical Georgian style buildings. St Mary's church and the town hall were prominent landmarks of the town, which nestled in the valley of the River Misbourne. On this mild April day, the surrounding fields resembled a lush green blanket enhanced by substantial early spring rains. But the beauty was lost on Richard as he enviously surveyed the bustling crowd. For him and his impoverished family, this place held nothing but heartache.

Farmers came from miles around to buy and sell livestock. It was like a flock of birds had descended, each individual darting and weaving to get a closer look at the wares that were for sale. On the edge of town, Richard could see the sheep pens were full, watched over by the shepherds holding their crooks. The air was laden with the smell of manure and a cacophony of animal and human noise. As he surveyed the busy scene, Richard felt his anger mount, his fists clenching and unclenching. If only he could get his hands on a small portion of the wealth that surrounded him. Although not very tall at 5'4', Richard was a strong young man. But his strength was of no help to him. He could see no way to improve his circumstances other than stealing. It was not a path he would have chosen, but the poverty his family lived in had eaten away at him for years.

In his mind, stealing was not a choice, but a necessity, driven by desperate need. However, this line of reasoning plunged him into a cycle of offending and caused distress to his loved ones, particularly his mother. If only his father would fight back. Years of oppression had beaten his father down. Richard would not let that happen to him. He was not about to let the greedy landlords dictate his survival. He was determined to fight for what he believed he deserved.

Already he had endured two stints in prison. His first offence was in 1840 when he and his friends James and young Tom were convicted of stealing a measly loaf of bread. He was glad that Tom, who was very young, got off lightly, but Richard and James spent two days in the lockup, having to endure a savage whipping. As he remembered the pain of the whip on his back, his sense of outrage increased. But all this had been before he met up with his good friend and accomplice, George Lee.

But where was George? As he moved between the stalls looking at the wares that he could not afford, his anxiety rose. George had agreed to meet him here, where they could lose themselves in the crowd. What if something had happened to him? Richard glanced around, trying to see any sign of the local policeman. Ezra Taylor would no doubt be stalking around, keeping an eye on him, so there would be no chance of stealing anything today. But he and George had bigger plans.

He finally picked out George's tall lanky body and dark red hair in the large crowd. They met up in front of the market stalls and Richard looked around furtively, before they both left the square and ducked down a side alley where they could talk without interruption.

'How are the plans coming along?' asked Richard.

George grinned as he slapped his friend on the back. 'Everything's in place. We shouldn't have any problems avoiding the law in Beaconsfield. No one knows us there.'

'Right, let's get out of here so we can check out the mansion,' said Richard although he wondered whether his friend was right. They could just as easily be caught in the neighbouring town.

It took them two hours to walk the eight miles to Beaconsfield. When they arrived, George led the way to the manor house. 'This is the place. I've been told this landowner is particularly mean and cruel to his tenants. It will serve him right to lose a few of his possessions.'

Richard shuffled from one foot to the other, his anxiety building. 'It's quite a house.' They both studied the square three-storey house. Richard counted twelve windows across the top two storeys. An ornate portico. which sheltered the enormous front door, was supported by two imposing stone columns. Whilst it pleased him that they would be stealing from someone who could obviously well afford it, he was worried about the consequences if they were caught. They had never broken into a manor house before.

'I have a contact on the inside. One of the scullery maids,' said George with a smug grin.

Richard smiled back. He wondered at George's ability to attract the eye of young women. He was never short of a young lassie to step out with.

'She will let us in at the servant's entrance. I just need to let her know when.'

'What is the plan?'

'The scullery maid will show us the way to where they keep the silverware. But I also intend to steal a gun.'

Richard's eyes widened. This was a fresh development. His friend had never mentioned firearms before. This sounded like major trouble if the law caught up with them. 'What do you want a gun for?'

'A little hunting could help feed our families.'

Despite his hesitancy, Richard did not want his friend to think he was afraid, and besides, George was right. A gun would allow them to hunt small game from the enclosed woodlands. It was forbidden to take firewood, let alone game, but the longer he associated with George, the more brazen he became. Still, he hesitated. He needed to think this through. But George was impatient.

'What's wrong? You in or not?'

Despite his hesitation, Richard knew he was already in too deep. 'Of course. When do we do this?'

'There is apparently a big gala ball at the neighbouring manor on Saturday night. That should give us a good chance to steal into the house when most of the family is not at home. Of course, the servants will still be there, so it will need to be late after they have all turned in for the night.'

Richard could not quite believe he had agreed to such an audacious plan. 'I hope we can pull this off.' George seemed convinced it would all go smoothly. Richard ran his hands through his thick, dark brown hair. He didn't want to look at George in case the fear was evident in his eyes. What if something went wrong? They would be locked up for years if they were caught this time.

The following Saturday night, the pair made their way back to Beaconsfield and waited furtively in the nearby woods until it grew completely dark. Richard felt a thrill of excitement, or was it fear, while they watched as all the lights were extinguished in the imposing mansion.

Suddenly, there was a tiny flash of light.

'That's her,' said George. 'I told her to come out with a candle when all the servants were in bed. Come on.'

Richard followed George the short distance to the servants' entrance to find a pretty girl, who he guessed was very young, perhaps around sixteen years of age, waiting for them. She looked around nervously, but she positively beamed when she saw George.

'Hello, lass.' George gave the girl a disarming smile and a quick peck on the cheek. Richard could see the blush spread across her face by the light of the candle she carried.

'Quickly,' she said. 'We must not waste any time. The family could return at any moment.'

Richard's legs trembled like a newborn foal as they entered the mansion with careful steps. He followed nervously as the scullery maid showed them the way to the dining room where abundant silverware filled the sideboard.

'Don't worry about the silver now,' said George. 'Show us the gun cabinet.'

The girl gasped and Richard could see the fear on her face. He wondered if his own face echoed that fear.

'Do you really think it is wise to steal a gun, George?' She backed away, shaking her head. 'You didn't say anything about guns.'

George frowned. 'Come on, we don't have all day. Just take me to the guns.'

By now the maid was quaking in fear. 'I can't.'

George shoved the girl. 'There is no point trying to back out now. You are in this up to your neck.'

Richard stood stock still during this exchange. 'Come on, George. Perhaps she's right. If we just take the silver we might be less likely to get caught.' By now Richard was wondering whether he had made the right decision joining George in this caper. But like the girl, he was committed now and George wasn't about to back down.

'Don't you chicken out on me now. Come on, let's go.'

The now terrified girl led the way to a huge passageway where a number of guns were stored on racks in a cabinet. Richard looked on fearfully as George opened the cabinet and grabbed one of the guns.

Just at that moment, a man appeared in the passageway, swinging a bright lantern.

'What's going on here?' The man was dressed in a night robe, but his authority was clear. Richard's heart was beating out of his chest as the unlikely thought went through his mind that this was most likely the butler. One of those entitled people who came from the same class as himself but thought they were better than him. The young girl began to cry.

George waved the gun at the man, who stopped dead in his tracks. Richard hoped the servant would believe the gun was loaded. As George ran towards the servants' quarters, Richard stood paralysed by fear. It took a moment before he gathered his wits enough to race after George. Together they ran into the woods and did not stop until they were a good distance from the manor.

Once they were thick in the depth of the woods where they would be out of sight, George laughed softly. 'That was a close one. It was a pity that we didn't have time to grab any silver on the way out. But at least we have this.' He waved the gun around his head gleefully.

Richard wasn't so sure. They might have been able to offload some of the silver for a pretty penny. The gun had the potential to get them into much deeper trouble. But he said nothing, as together they snuck away through the woods and made their way back to Amersham. As the pair parted ways, Richard tried to control his troubled thoughts. They had been seen by the butler. He was convinced no good could come of this. It had been a huge mistake to agree to George's daring plan.

Richard was just about to head out to work with his father when there was a loud insistent knock at the door. He glanced nervously at his mother, who pulled her threadbare cardigan tighter around her bone thin frame. His father, William, went to answer the door. The sight of Ezra Taylor standing at the door sent a wave of dread through Richard.

Richard could feel the tension in the room as Ezra and his father exchanged curt greetings. His mother sat frozen in fear.

No doubt she could guess why the policeman was at their door. Richard could not meet her eye.

'Good morning, William,' said Ezra with a forced smile.

'Good morning, Ezra,' William growled. 'What do you want?'

Ezra's expression turned serious. 'I am sure you can guess that I am here about young Richard. I need to speak to him about a robbery in Beaconsfield.'

Richard braced himself for what was to come.

William turned and glared at him. 'What have you done now? I knew your useless friend George would get you into more trouble.'

'What am I supposed to do?' raged Richard. Although he was feeling ashamed that he was the cause of this awful scene, he felt the need to fight back. 'We can't sit back and starve to death. And don't blame George. I make my own decisions.' As he stared defiantly at his father, he couldn't help wishing he hadn't made this particular decision.

Richard could not look at his mother. He knew his actions would once again cause her great anxiety. He loved his mother and did not want to hurt her.

'I am sorry, Mother,' he muttered as Ezra locked the cuffs around his wrists. His mother let out an anguished moan, increasing his sense of shame.

Richard and George faced court at the County Assizes, Aylesbury on March 10, 1845. Richard could not believe he found himself in this situation again. He and George had spent time in prison for their previous transgressions. Only a year earlier, four years after Richard's first offence for stealing bread, together they had stolen a bolt of nankeen cloth from a market stall and were sentenced to six months hard labour. But Richard knew this was so much worse.

As Richard was led into the crowded courtroom, he looked nervously at the judge, dressed in black robes and seated on a raised platform. His throat constricted as he saw the butler and the scullery maid. They were no doubt here to give evidence against him. But the people he really wanted to see were his parents. He scanned the noisy and crowded public gallery. He hoped his parents would be there to support him, but did not really want to see the shame and disappointment he knew would be reflected in his mother's eyes. As he picked them out in the crowd, tears welled in his eyes. Oh God, he could not cry now.

The butler was called first and took the stand. Richard stared at the man who was about to give evidence against him. The only moment of common sense he had that night was recognising that the man who caught them was the butler. Little consolation that was.

'I had retired early as the family was out for the evening when I heard noises in the hallway. I came down the stairs and saw two men and one of them was holding a gun. He pointed it at me, so

I was not able to take any action and the culprits escaped. After they had gone, I saw that there was a gun missing from the gun cabinet. I then realised that the gun being waved around was, in fact, one of the master's guns.'

The judge straightened in his seat. 'And are these culprits, as you put it, in the court today?'

'Yes sir, those are the two men there.' He pointed at Richard and George. Richard realised there was no hope of getting off the charge now. This man had condemned him with his testimony. Emotions of fear and anger competed for his attention.

The next witness to take the stand was the scullery maid. Her eyes were red rimmed. The judge gave her a withering look.

'Do I understand correctly that you assisted these two scoundrels to enter the manor?'

Her voice was a mere whisper. 'Yes sir.'

'Well, go on girl, tell the court what happened.' Through her tears, she told her story.

'George promised he would take me away with him if I helped him to gain entry to the manor. I had to get away. My master was a tyrant. He withheld our wages so we were always beholden to him. George was my only chance for escape, so I agreed to help. I let them in through the servants' entrance.' She gave the judge a pleading look. 'But I didn't know they would steal a gun. I was only going to show them the silver in the dining room.'

The judge was silent as he wrote on the pages in front of him. Finally, he lifted his head and focused stern eyes on the scullery maid. 'Let this be a lesson to you, young lady, not to be taken in by men such as this. I understand that you have lost your employment, which is perhaps punishment enough for your part in this felony. As you have cooperated and given evidence today, you will not be prosecuted.'

The young girl slumped with relief.

'You're dismissed,' he said. Without a glance at Richard and George, she returned to her seat. Richard felt momentary sympathy for the young girl. But it was fleeting as he knew her testimony was a further nail in his coffin.

The judge's sombre gaze landed on Richard and George. A knot of dread formed in Richard's stomach, knowing the consequences of their actions would be severe.

'I am sure you understand that breaking into a house and stealing a gun is a very serious offence.' The judge paused dramatically. 'I hereby sentence you to transportation to the colony of Van Diemen's Land for the term of ten years.'

Richard felt the blood drain from his face. His shoulders slumped. The weight of the sentence felt crushing, knowing he would never return to his home or see his family again. Van Diemen's Land; a world away. It was a penal colony renowned for its harsh penalties and untamed wilderness. As he was led from the court, Richard stole a last glance at his parents seated in the public gallery. His mother's quiet tears and his father's unforgiving expression revealed their despair. He couldn't bear to think of how much he had hurt them with his reckless actions.

Chapter Three

Mary Ann, Wilden, 1845

The village of Wilden was alive with excitement. The annual hiring fair was in full swing. It was a colourful spectacle, filled with hopeful tenants seeking employment for the year ahead. Shepherds clutched their crooks tightly, while carters and waggoners sported whipcord twisted around their hats. Thatchers displayed woven straw fragments pinned to their chests. The landlords could tell at a glance the type of work each man sought from these badges of their profession.

The terms were simple; a year's board and lodging, and a small yearly stipend in exchange for services rendered. A single shilling given at the time of hiring sealed the agreement.

Mary Ann and her brothers followed their father to the fairground, having to run to keep up with his long strides. Their father needed to speak with Lord Robotham. Mary Ann overheard her parents discussing the meeting. It was something to do with his contract as Lord Robotham's bailiff. But she wasn't worried, even if her father seemed to be. He worked hard so he was sure to be hired for another year. Whilst their father was busy, the children would be left to explore the fair on their own. Samuel stopped as they approached the fair ground.

'Now Charles, you're the oldest. Mind you keep an eye on Mary Ann and Josiah.'

'Of course, Father,' said Charles. 'No harm will come to any of us.'

'You have the money I gave you?'

'Yes, Father.' Charles held up his hanky with the coins tied into the corner.

Mary Ann could see his sense of self-importance grow before her eyes. It wasn't fair. Charles was only two years older and yet he was to be put in charge of her. She could look after herself.

As their father strode off, the three children looked around, wondering what to do first.

'Can I have some money to buy a sweet?' Mary Ann asked.

'You heard Father, he gave me the money so I will decide what we spend it on.'

'You're so bossy, Charles.' Her eyes were drawn to a nearby stall. 'Can we at least watch the Thimblerigger for a while? Or is that too much to ask?'

'I want to do that too,' said Josiah excitedly.

Charles sighed but led them towards the stall. They all watched with wide-eyed fascination as a young man placed a coin down to have his guess at which small cup the pea was hidden under.

The thimblerigger drew in the coin and placed it safely into a pouch on his belt. His hands blurred as he moved the cups around at lightning speed. 'Watch closely, my friends. Can you follow the pea?'

The pea appeared and disappeared, flitting between the cups. The children and other onlookers watched, mesmerised by the speed at which the thimblerigger moved. Mary Ann's eyes flew from cup to cup as she tried to determine where the pea was.

'It's time to guess,' the thimblerigger finally called to the young man as the cups stilled. 'Which cup is the pea under?'

The young man pointed to the cup furthest to the left. He didn't look confident, and Mary Ann wasn't surprised. She didn't know which cup she would pick either.

'Aha,' said the thimblerigger. 'You are wrong, I am afraid.' And with a flourish, he lifted the middle cup to reveal the pea. The disappointed man stalked away, red faced, and the next lucky gambler stepped up.

'Come on, I'm hungry,' Charles said, shortly after.

Mary Ann was about to argue until she realised she was hungry too.

They moved on, looking around at the variety of stalls. Soon they came to a food stall and watched on for a few minutes as a haggard elderly woman added grain, milk, raisins and currants to the pot which hung over a charcoal fire. Vessels, holding all the ingredients, sat on a makeshift table that stood within easy reach. She paused in her stirring of the pot of furmity when she noticed Charles pull the handkerchief from his pocket and untie the coins their father had given him.

'What can I get you, young ones?' she said with a grin, which exposed a gap where her front tooth should be. Charles handed over the coins and each of the children was handed a bowl of the woman's steaming furmity. The three children sat down on a patch of grass to eat the delicious bowl of sweet, spiced food.

'Do you think she is a witch?' whispered Mary Ann.

'Your imagination is running away with you again,' replied Charles, giving her a scornful look.

'But her pot looks like a cauldron,' agreed Josiah. 'She could be a witch.'

'Witches are from fairy tales,' said Charles. 'You two are such babies.'

'We are not,' spluttered Mary Ann. 'You just have no imagination.' She smiled at Josiah, glad he also thought the old woman could be a witch.

Charles finished his food quickly. He looked around the fair. 'I'm going to have a look at the waxworks.'

'We don't have enough money,' Mary Ann reminded him with a scowl as she scraped the last bit of delicious furmity from her bowl.

'I can just peek in through the opening in the tent to get a bit of a look. Stay here.'

They had barely finished their food when their father found them.

'Come along,' he said gruffly. Then he noticed Charles was missing. 'Where is Charles?'

Charles came running up looking rather out of breath. 'Here I am, Father.'

'I told you not to leave the others alone. Hurry up, we are leaving.'

'Oh Father, must we leave so soon?' said Mary Ann. 'There is so much more to see.' Her father glared at her, so she said no more, but hurried after him and her brothers. Mary Ann wondered what had happened during her father's meeting with Lord Robotham to put him in such a mood. She really hoped it wasn't anything too bad.

But by the time they arrived home, Mary Ann was sure that something was terribly wrong. Her father had rushed them away from the crowded fair and despite her and the boys trying to tell him about their time at the fair, he said very little. Eventually, they fell silent.

Once they arrived home, her brothers stayed outside, getting their chores done. Mary Ann, curious to know the cause of her father's mood, followed him inside, where Ann was waiting for their return.

'Go to your room, Mary Ann,' said her father. Mary Ann did as she was told but stood quietly near the doorway, out of sight, so she could hear her parents talking.

'What is wrong, Samuel?' asked Ann the moment Mary Ann disappeared from view.

Samuel sat down heavily and rested his head in his hands. 'Lord Robotham has hired a new bailiff. He has kept me on as a labourer, but it will mean greatly reduced wages.'

'How can he do that?' asked Ann.

'I don't know, but it is done now and there is no point discussing it further.'

Mary Ann frowned. She noticed the looks that passed between her parents more and more often since the addition of her brother, John, who was now three years old, so it sounded like this labourer's wage would not be enough for all the mouths they had to feed.

'It's all because of that blasted Enclosure Act,' Ann retorted. Mary Ann wasn't used to hearing her mother sound so angry. 'It's alright for him, reaping the benefits of those new farming machines, but what about the community? He's taking all the land back to make himself richer and leaving us to starve.'

Starve? Mary Ann clapped a hand to her mouth. Surely, they wouldn't starve.

'It is the way things are now, Ann. There's nought we can do about that.'

There was silence for a moment, as though both her parents were lost in their woes. Finally, Mary Ann heard her father say, 'I'll have to sell the sheep. They should raise a good sum as they are still in good condition. I hope anyway. There are a lot of sheep on the market at present.' He paused. 'We are not the only tenants needing to sell. And even if we get a decent price for them, the money can't last forever. Then we will only have my wages as a labourer.'

Mary Ann listened quietly to this disturbing news. She knew things had gotten increasingly tougher for her family. Would she soon be like some of her friends at school whose families had to leave Wilden because there was not enough work for them?

'Perhaps I could get work making lace,' suggested Ann. 'That would bring in some extra money.'

This definitely sounded serious. Mary Ann knew she had to offer to help. She entered the living room.

'I could help to make lace. I am sure I could learn how.'

Samuel and Ann looked up, startled.

'Oh Mary Ann, you mustn't worry,' said her mother with kind eyes. 'You are still at school.'

Mary Ann hadn't thought about that when she suggested it. Would working mean she would have to leave school? She didn't want that. Her glance slid over to her father. He had never looked so grim.

'I could leave school,' Mary Ann said impulsively.

'No.' Ann came to wrap her arms around her daughter. 'You are not even eleven yet. It is up to your father and I to look after you and the boys. It will all work out.'

'Your mother is right, Mary Ann,' said her father, though he looked less certain. 'I am sure we will cope if your mother can start making lace.'

Mary Ann was ashamed that she felt relieved she wouldn't have to leave school. She couldn't help but worry that this might be the end of her fortunate life.

Chapter Four

Richard, Convict Ship Marion, 1845

Richard shuffled up the gangplank with careful steps, his shackles clinking with each step. He raised his head as he set foot on the deck of the Marion, taking in the vastness of the ship. His mind was racing. Where were they going? What kind of life awaited them in the colonies? But even as the uncertainty gnawed at him, there was a flicker of excitement as the smell of salty sea air filled his senses.

After sentencing, they had taken him to Aylesbury prison and then a month later, he was transferred to Millbank. The three months Richard spent there felt like an eternity. His paranoia was rampant, as he was under constant surveillance. The prisoners were in single cells surrounding a central area where the guards were always watching. He was forced to wear a mask when exercising or working at menial tasks, which prevented any form of communication, adding to his sense of isolation and despair. Disease was rife in the swampy grounds on the banks of the Thames River. Although Richard avoided any serious ailments or punishments, his rebelliousness was being quashed whether or not he liked to admit it. They had been shackled for the several days that it took to travel the seventy-five miles from Millbank Prison to Portsmouth. But now at last they were boarding the convict ship.

'God, it's cold,' moaned George.

'At least we are out of that godforsaken hell hole,' said Richard.

'You are right there, my friend,' replied George. 'I wonder what is in store next for us.'

Any sense of hope that Richard had felt was soon dashed as their shackles were removed. Guards barked orders and shoved them towards the hatches into the ship's prison in the bowels of the ship. It took Richard several minutes to adjust to the gloom in the dark unventilated space between decks as the hatches were closed and locked behind them and his sense of despair deepened as he realised this was to be their prison for however long the voyage would take. He soon discovered how crowded their quarters were going to be, sharing the smallest of spaces in which to lie down on the double bunks. The prison was about fifty feet long and fifty feet wide to accommodate all 298 convicts. The air was thick, almost suffocating and the stench was overpowering. Despite his short stature, Richard struggled to stand upright in the confined headroom of only five foot six inches.

'This is worse than I imagined,' said Richard, his voice trembling. George kicked out at a rat that scurried past his feet. 'How long do you think they will keep us locked down here?'

'No idea,' Richard replied, his voice tight with anxiety. 'But I don't like it. It feels like a coffin.'

Richard grappled with the reality of their current situation as days passed in a blur of darkness and despair, the ship rocking at anchor in the harbour. He tried not to focus on what lay ahead. Right now he just wanted to escape this abominable prison. Surely they would let them out soon.

'What do you think, young Roger?' asked George. 'Do you think we will ever leave this hellhole?' Richard turned to the young convict they had befriended when he claimed the bunk next to them. Roger Jackson was only seventeen years old and had been convicted of stealing a few coins from his workplace. They had sentenced him to transportation for seven years, which seemed to Richard even more unfair than his own sentence.

Roger's eyes reflected his fear. 'They can't keep us locked down here forever, can they?'

Richard felt sorry for the young lad. He was only two years younger, but Richard could tell that Roger was much less experienced in criminal life. This was his first offence.

'I'm sure they can't, Roger. They will have to let us out once we are at sea. Not like we can escape then.'

Just as despair was beginning to suffocate him, Richard heard commotion from above decks. The sound of the anchor chains rattling as the crew hoisted them aboard sent a wave of relief through him. The crew could be heard shouting orders to each other, and the convicts felt the motion as the ship began to move.

Not long after the ship left the harbour, the hatches were flung open.

'Right, you lot,' came the guard's voice. 'Up you come.'

Richard was relieved to be among the first group to scramble out of the bowels of the ship. The guards herded them into a cage at one end of the deck. The bright sunshine bit into his eyes, but he was grateful for the fresh air and open sky after weeks in darkness and filth.

As the ship sailed away from the English coast, the seas turned treacherous. Richard was stunned at the might of the ocean. Living as he had in a landlocked county, he had not seen the ocean before, let alone felt its power. The ship was tossed about like a toy and pitched violently beneath his feet.

It wasn't long before they were relegated back to the ship's prison. They were only allowed on deck for short periods each day. Most of their time was spent below decks where many of the prisoners succumbed to seasickness.

'God save us,' whimpered Tom, huddled in the corner of his bunk as seawater seeped into their prison hold. It mixed with the filth and vomit, intensifying their nightmarish conditions.

'Aye, lad,' Richard murmured 'We're all in this together. We'll get through. Just hold on.'

The younger man nodded weakly, taking some comfort in their shared misery as he braced himself for another wave.

But the journey had just begun. The ship soon settled into a routine. At 6:00am the cooks were directed to light the fires to cook breakfast. The prisoners were allowed on deck, one group at a time. The remaining convicts cleaned and scraped that section of the prison and then the entire process was reversed. Meals consisted mainly of meat and peas with a ration of wine and lime juice to prevent scurvy.

As they approached the equator, the ship was becalmed in the doldrums. The air hung heavy with heat and humidity and no breeze made it below decks. Richard was relieved when it was his turn to go on deck but, although it meant escape from the torment of the ship's prison, there was no respite from the relentless onslaught of the sun, which hung in the sky, a blazing orb, from daylight to dusk.

'Feels like we're being cooked alive,' grumbled Richard, his face slick with sweat as he squinted against the harsh sunlight.

George sighed heavily. 'Aye, not even a whisper of wind to cool us.'

Eventually, after what seemed an eternity, the ship approached Cape Horn. Eight weeks had passed since their departure. Remarkably, though, despite their uncomfortable journey thus far, the health of the convicts remained surprisingly good. Richard, Roger and George were on deck when they overheard a discussion between the Captain and the Surgeon General.

'Not a single case of scurvy among 'em,' noted the Captain.

The Surgeon General nodded approvingly. 'Excellent stock,' he murmured under his breath before making his decision known. 'No need to stop at Cape Town then,' he announced decisively. 'We press on for Van Diemen's Land. Let's get them there as soon as we can.'

Richard and George scowled at each other. That meant they would be confined to the ship right until the end of the journey.

As the ship rounded Cape Horn, the prisoners were soon wishing they were back in the doldrums. The roaring forties took hold of the ship and tossed it like a piece of flotsam from one wave to the next. Richard was overcome by seasickness as their prison filled with vomit to go along with the excrement and general odour of men crowded together with little sanitation. The waves washed over the ship and water flowed into the bowels of the ship. Although the bilges ran all day, the level of water and excrement was never below ankle deep. Would this torturous voyage ever end?

The convicts were laying on their bunks when a commotion was heard overhead.

'I wonder what's up,' mused Richard. At that moment, the hatch was thrown open, and a guard called down.

'We need some volunteers up here.'

Richard thought quickly. 'What about it, George? Any excuse to get out of here for a bit.'

'Sure, why not? You coming, Roger?' By now, Roger had great faith in Richard and George. He followed them up the ladder.

'Lower the longboat,' called the captain as the group of convict volunteers stepped on deck.

They looked out on the heaving ocean where the sailor indicated. There was a ship being thrown around at will. Its mast was down and the remaining sails were torn and ragged. It was obviously in a lot of trouble.

'This looks like high adventure,' said George with his usual bravado. Richard was not so sure and he noticed Roger had gone pale.

The rope ladder was thrown over the side and the convicts climbed down into the boat together with two of the ship's crew. They grabbed the oars and rowed towards the stricken vessel. As they approached, Richard could see that the ship was sinking.

'Row faster, boys,' yelled the sailors.

A rope ladder slid down the side and men started appearing over the side of the sinking ship, six in total making it into the longboat.

'Is that the lot?' asked one of the crew. 'Where are the rest of your party?'

'Some were swept off the decks and others escaped in the longboats. But that was hours ago. Lord only knows where they are now. We're all that are left,' replied one sailor, looking haggard after his ordeal. He sat down in between Richard and

Roger as they began rowing back to the ship through the turbulent seas.

'You look done in,' said Richard to the young sailor. 'How long have you been trying to save your ship?'

'The storm was ferocious when it hit. We worked for hours, but we knew we were in trouble when she started to tilt and water was coming in faster than the bilge could pump it out. I tell you it was terrifying seeing men being swept overboard. There was nothing more we could do. A better sight has never met my eyes than when I saw your ship come into view.'

As they rowed the crowded longboat back towards the Marion, they watched the beleaguered ship sink slowly below the waves.

'There she goes,' said Roger.

Eventually the convicts, sailors and shipwreck survivors were all safely back onboard. The young sailor reached out to shake Richard's hand. 'Thank you,' he said. 'I am not sure I will want to continue as a sailor after this.' Richard gave the man a rueful smile. 'At least you have a choice to be at sea. I'd rather be back in England.'

But Richard had no time to find out more about the young sailor as the overseer started brandishing his cat o' nine tails. 'Righto, you lads. Don't think because you have done your good deed for today that you can loiter on deck.'

When they were back in the ship's prison, George grinned at his friends. 'Well, that was a bit of excitement to break the monotony. No thanks for risking our lives though.'

Richard was less impressed and the colour was only just now returning to Roger's face. 'It was an adventure I could have done without.' George seemed to think this was all a bit of a lark. Richard was realising that falling in with George and his risky behaviours could have him ending up dead.

Richard, Van Diemen's Land, 1845

Early on the morning of September 16, 1845, the Marion arrived at Hobart Town. Richard shivered in his threadbare clothes as he joined the other prisoners on deck. It might be spring in the southern hemisphere, but it was still freezing here in Van Diemen's Land. An icy wind blew from the south. Richard, like all prisoners on board, was bone thin, dirty and dishevelled. But the contractors would be well paid for this voyage, as there had only been three burials at sea.

'It is good to see land, is it not?' said Richard.

'Yes, indeed, it is. I wonder how long it will be before we can go ashore?' replied George. 'What do you think awaits us on these shores?'

They would not find out their fate until seven days later when, on September 23, Richard and the other convicts finally set foot on Van Diemen's Land. They stumbled down the rope ladder into the waiting boats and under the instruction of the overseers, took up the oars to row into the dock.

As they rowed, George whispered to Richard. 'We will soon find out what we are in for now, my friend. Here we are on the other side of the world. There's no looking back.'

'I don't doubt that it will be hellish,' replied Richard, gripping the oars until his fingers turned white. He couldn't help but think of his family again and it filled him with despair, knowing there was little chance of ever seeing them again. He had been overwhelmed with relief when his mother visited him in Millbank. Not that he had expected her to. But in the hope that she might, he had taken the advice of other convicts and made a love token from a cartwheel penny for her. After smoothing the surface, he engraved a message.

Dearest Mother, please forgive me and remember me always, as I will you.

It felt like a small consolation when she accepted the token with tears flowing down her cheeks and hugged him tightly.

Soon the boats pulled into the docks and the guards herded the convicts into the prison yards, wielding whips and guns to ensure none were adventurous enough to take the opportunity to escape.

'Come on, keep moving, you dogs,' yelled a guard, and Richard felt the sting of a whip as he shuffled past.

Blacksmiths awaited them in the prison yard.

'Looks like we are going to be back in leg irons,' groaned George.

The overseer overheard and sneered. 'Very astute, lad. They will help you remember you are a government man now and there is no escape.'

Richard felt the bite of the leg irons as they were fitted to each ankle, the blacksmith making sure that they were not so big that he could pull his foot through but not so tight as to cause immediate injury. He flinched as the blacksmith's hammer secured the irons with a strong rivet, the short chain between his ankles only enabling him to walk with a shuffle.

A pile of prison issue clothing was shoved into Richard's hands. As he dressed in the half black and half yellow garments printed with the broad arrow – a further sign that he was government property – he felt the coarseness of the roughly woven wool. The trousers buttoned up the sides to accommodate the leg irons.

For the first month Richard endured the harsh conditions on the road gangs before he and George found themselves on another boat.

'I wonder where we're heading?' mumbled George.

Soon they were struggling onto land, severely limited in their movements by the leg irons.

As they disembarked on Maria Island, off the east coast of Van Diemen's Land, Richard looked around at the green countryside, the farm like appearance, and the grazing sheep. He couldn't help but wonder aloud, 'This place doesn't seem as harsh as they made it out to be, does it?'

George, looking around in awe, replied, 'Aye, Richard, it's not what I expected. Could be better than the road gangs, at least.'

The two friends exchanged a brief, hopeful smile, unaware of the harsh reality of their new lives as prisoners on Maria Island.

Richard soon found out that he and George were to be separated. He would be stationed at the Long Point probation centre whilst George was to spend his probation at the Darlington centre, on the other side of the island. Richard was disappointed that he would not have his friend to look out for him. He would now have to rely on his own wits. But there was a tiny niggle in his mind that this might not be such a bad thing; George was probably not the best companion if he wanted to stay out of trouble. Despite his earlier tendency to rebel against authority, Richard was coming to the conclusion that there was no point trying to fight the system in this environment. Keeping his head down might be the best way to survive. He looked around at the convicts who would be stationed at Long Point and was pleased to see young Roger amongst them. Roger had become a good friend during the long voyage from England. Richard found him to be loyal and steady, unlike George, who would probably be in trouble wherever he ended up. A break from George might be the best thing. Richard wondered if this might be a chance to rebuild his life.

'Right, you lot,' shouted the guard. 'Now's your chance to show what you are made of. Don't expect an easy time of it here. You will be working hard on the land, growing wheat, hay, vegetables and attending to the stock. As you can see, there are sheep and pigs to raise.'

They worked hard for long hours, still in leg irons. Although Richard had vowed to keep his head down, he felt fury mount every time the cat o' nine tails flicked his back. But at least there was usually enough to eat, with the harvest of vegetables and tough, stringy meat from sheep that were nearing the end of their useful lives. Their quarters were bare, but the overseers ensured that they kept them clean.

They were also forced to attend classes and go to church on Sundays, not that Richard minded. He could read a little, but was pleased to be able to work on his letters.

One morning, when he fronted up for the day's work, he noticed there were blacksmiths in the yards.

'Line up,' shouted the overseer, his cat o' nine tails flicking around his head.

'What's going on?' muttered Richard to the convict next in line. 'Surely they are not going to remove our leg irons?'

But it seemed that was indeed what was going to happen. As each prisoner came to a blacksmith, the rivets were struck off the shackles with a chisel and for the first time in many months, the convicts were freed from the chains. After the initial pain of the rivet being hammered out, the relief Richard felt was intense. Although his ankles had become tough and calloused, it felt good to be able to move more freely again.

They were then assembled into their work teams for the day's work.

'Right, I am sure you are all pleased to have more freedom,' said the overseer. 'But be warned. Don't think you can now do as you please. Any man who takes the slightest liberty without shackles will soon find himself chained again.'

As they carried out the backbreaking work, they spoke quietly amongst themselves so as not to alert the guards.

'It is good to be able to move a bit more freely now that we don't have the leg irons to contend with,' said Richard.

'Surely is,' said Roger. 'Do you think anyone will try to escape?'

'Not me,' replied Richard. 'I plan to get on with it and keep my head down.'

Richard, Maria Island, 1846

The sky was dark and ominous as the convicts went out to work. Light rain was falling and a bitterly cold wind was blowing off the southern ocean. Richard had been at Long Point for nearly a year. The convicts got to work pulling turnips. Richard did not find this particularly hard work as the turnips were released easily from the sandy soil, but it was back breaking, having to be constantly bent over. The guards never let up, wielding their whips on anyone who took a moment to stand up to stretch their backs. One guard had taken a particular dislike to Richard and seemed determined to rile him up. Every chance he got he would use his whip on Richard.

'Stop lagging, you dog,' yelled the guard. 'What do you think you are doing? Get moving.' The whip cracked on Richard's back and suddenly he could take no more. He turned to glare at the guard, his fists clenched. 'Leave me alone,' he yelled. The guard raised the whip again, but this time Richard moved forward and snatched the whip out of the guards hands. The guard's anger matched his own.

'Put that down you scoundrel, I will have you before the superintendent.'

Fear rose in Richard's belly and, without thinking, he dropped the whip and scampered off into the scrub at the side of the paddock.

'Let him go,' yelled the overseer, as other guards started off to chase Richard. 'We need to get these men back to the station. We will track him down soon enough. He has nowhere to go.' He gave a harsh laugh. 'I don't suppose he can swim.'

Richard found himself in the wilderness. He could not believe he had let his temper get the better of him after having been so determined to keep his head down. With no bush skills and no way to feed himself, he immediately regretted his impulsive decision to run.

After two nights in the bush, he was starving. Under the cover of night, he approached the potato fields, hoping to find some food. He knelt and dug through the sandy soil with his hands until he unearthed a potato. He was just about to take his first bite when he felt a gun in the small of his back.

'I wouldn't do anything foolish if I were you,' said the guard. Richard felt almost relieved. He put his hands on his head and allowed the guard to march him back to the camp.

The guard took him to the superintendent's quarters. The superintendent sneered at him.

'So, you are back. Now you know there is nowhere to go, perhaps you will think twice before attempting to escape again.'

Richard remained silent. He knew better than to argue. The blacksmith was called to fit leg irons and he was thrown into solitary confinement.

Four days later, weak from hunger, Richard was led out into the bright light which assaulted his senses after the black darkness of the cell.

He was brought before the superintendent, trying to stand straight and tall.

'You are charged with absenting yourself from your post for a period of two days and stealing potatoes,' said the superintendent. 'What do you have to say for yourself?'

'I know I have been foolish. I have learned my lesson, and I will never try to escape again.'

The superintendent peered at him over the top of his glasses and made some notes in the book in front of him.

'As you appear to show some remorse for your actions and have, to date, been well behaved and you have already spent time in solitary confinement, I see no reason to add to your sentence at this time. However, you will be given hard labour and kept in leg irons until such time as I see fit to have them removed. But be assured, any further misdemeanours will be dealt with severely.'

Richard was astonished. He sighed with relief. His biggest fear of an extension to his sentence was not going to happen. What's more, he escaped the lash as well. He had put up with leg irons before and he would do it again gladly, now that he knew he had not ruined his chances of ever completing his sentence.

Chapter Five

Mary Ann, Wilden, 1847

Christmas was approaching. Mary Ann knew that her family were fortunate to have a pig, which they had fattened up for an entire year ready for slaughter when the weather was cold enough to preserve the meat. The pig, a veracious eater, had grown quickly. Mary Ann marvelled at the amount of scraps it could consume, not to mention the acorns, when they were available. However, she had become attached to the pig. It was the closest thing she had to a pet and her stomach clenched every time she thought about the pig being killed.

Mary Ann and her brothers were outside doing their chores on a wintry afternoon. The sun was setting quickly. She turned to Charles, who was piling up the wood he had just cut.

'It's nearly time to kill the pig.'

Charles grunted at her. 'And?'

'Well, don't you feel sad? I am going to miss feeding him and looking at his funny face as he eats his food.'

'Don't be silly, Mary Ann. You know why we have a pig. You shouldn't become so attached to it. In any case, this might be the last time we have one. You should just be grateful that we will have something delicious to eat this Christmas.'

Mary Ann stared at him in horror. 'What do you mean?'

'Well, I don't think Father will be able to afford to buy another pig. I heard him telling mother that the money from the sale of the sheep is running out.'

This was news to Mary Ann and bad news at that. She had complained about being hungry lately and often her mother had not been able to give them anything to eat when they came home from school. Her parents told her not to worry, but she could not help it. She saw the lines of worry on their faces, and it scared her. What if they all starved to death? And now there was another mouth to feed. Mary Ann loved her baby sister, Susan, who was born last year. She had wanted a sister forever and she delighted in helping her mother to look after the doll-like creature. But she couldn't dismiss the thought that more babies just added to their problems.

Her mother had set up her lace-making in the main room of their home and the family was making a small income from the lace, but they still struggled to survive. Charles had been forced to leave school and now went to work each day with his father. He spent his days picking up stones and scaring birds from the crops. But there was less and less work for them as the enclosed lands spread further.

The day of the slaughter had come. Mary Ann was torn. She wanted to be brave enough to watch, but she wasn't sure she would be able to. Her father sharpened his knife on the stone and Mary Ann felt a sick feeling in her stomach. Her hands flew to her face to cover her eyes as her father killed the pig. Despite her horror at the sight of all the blood, she knew it meant they would have fresh pork that day and would eat well. Her mother would cook up the pig's liver with some flour and onion. That was the first dish they all looked forward to.

Once slaughtered, Samuel doused the pig in boiling water to remove the bristles. Charles was standing nearby to help his father.

'Right Charles, make sure you collect up all the bristles.'

'Why are they collecting the bristles, Mother?' Mary Ann asked.

'I will tie those together to make a brush. We mustn't waste anything. After Father has finished butchering the pig, I will salt and smoke most of it, so we have meat to last through winter and spring.'

'Will we have some for Christmas dinner?'

'Yes, of course. There will certainly be a leg to be roasted for our Christmas feast,' called Samuel with a smile, listening whilst he carved the carcass into chunks.

They used every part of the pig. The offal was used in meatballs. Mary Ann's mother boiled the pig's head to make brawn. Some of the skin was saved to bake as a delicious crackle treat, but most of it would be used to make leather. The blood was used to make black pudding. But the most surprising part for Mary Ann was when all the work was done her father filled the bladder of the pig with air, and they had a ball to play with.

The Christmas of Mary Ann's twelfth year was a bright and happy occasion.

'Do you want to help me find a Christmas tree?' asked Samuel.

'Ooh, yes please,' said Mary Ann. She and her brothers pulled on their coats and boots and went out into the snowy fields. They found a branch, which had fallen from a towering pine tree and Charles and Samuel dragged it back to the cottage. The makeshift Christmas tree was propped up in the corner of the living room.

'Now we need to make some decorations,' said Mary Ann, feeling the excitement bubble up inside her. They decorated the tree with paper chains. Then their mother brought out a box containing a few precious shiny baubles. The children were not allowed to touch these special ornaments that their mother carefully unwrapped and hung on the tree. Ann's mother had given them to her, and they were one of her few treasured possessions. Mary Ann's eyes shone as she watched her mother hang the ornaments.

Christmas morning came at last. Each member of the family had a small gift under the tree wrapped in brown paper and tied with string. They opened these gleefully.

Mary Ann's parcel contained a tiny doll her mother had made from scraps of material and some of her beautiful lace.

'Oh, thank you, Mother. She is perfect.' Tears of joy glistened in her eyes as she hugged her mother. She noticed that her mother's eyes were also welling with tears. But she couldn't tell if they were happy or sad tears.

Ann roasted the leg of pork with potatoes and turnips in lard rendered down from the pig. Added to the feast was a plump chicken Samuel had slaughtered the day before. The delicious aromas of the Christmas feast made everyone's mouths water. After the main meal, there was plum pudding with custard. Mary Ann's joy was complete as she knelt to say her prayers that night. When she got into bed, she placed the tiny doll next to her on her pillow.

But the joy was not to last. One morning, not long after Christmas, Mary Ann was lost in her book when her mother called her.

Mary Ann looked up and noticed the anxious looks on her parents' faces. She put her book down and rose slowly to her feet. As she approached the table where her mother and father were sitting, she became more anxious. Surely there was not more bad news. Her father twisted his hands together.

'I am sorry, Mary Ann. But your mother and I have decided that you must leave school. We need the extra income.'

Mary Ann could not believe what she was hearing. When she had offered to leave school, to her relief, they said no. But now it seemed they had changed their minds. Mary Ann stared at her mother, hoping that what her father had said was not what her mother really wanted. She was not quite able to comprehend what this would mean.

'You must learn how to make lace so that you can help me,' said her mother.

'But I love school.' How could they do this to her? 'How will I learn everything I need to know?'

'It is not what we would have wanted,' said her mother, her eyes glistening with tears. 'We have no choice.'

'But if I stayed at school, I could learn more and perhaps I could get a position as a governess. I could earn more.'

'You have enough learning. We can't wait any longer,' said her father, his tone becoming stern.

'It's not fair. You can't make me leave school.' She gave her father a hostile glare and tears brimmed in her eyes.

'That's enough, Mary Ann. There will be no further discussion.'

Mary Ann could contain her tears no longer. She buried her head in her hands and sobbed. After a few moments, her chair scraping loudly as she rose from the table, Mary Ann ran from the cottage, slamming the door. She kept running, past the neighbour's cottage and into the darkness of the nearby woods. She ran and ran, her heart beating in her chest and her breath becoming ragged. Finally, when she could run no more, she slumped down against a large tree. She sobbed bitter tears. How could this be happening to her? She could not imagine her life without school. Her tears spent, she got to her feet and retraced her steps. As she arrived back at the neighbour's cottage, she noticed that their garden was full of weeds. It was so different to their own garden, where her mother worked hard to grow their vegetables in neat rows. One of the windows was boarded up and there was no smoke coming from the chimney, even though it was a freezing cold day. Her mother said that the family was struggling, as Mr Price had been unwell and unable to work. Suddenly her friend, Alex, came around from behind the house, pushing a broken-down wheelbarrow. Guilt surged through Mary Ann. She couldn't meet his eye as she hurried on, wanting to get home as quickly as possible.

Mary Ann had an empty feeling in the pit of her stomach as she opened the door and saw her parents still sitting as she had left them. She realised how selfish she had been. Her mother's eyes were red rimmed, and her father sat rigid, regarding her with a stern look. She leaned in to hug her mother. 'I am so sorry. I didn't mean to make you cry. I love you all so much.' She glanced at her father. 'Of course, I will leave school and help with the lace making.'

'That's my girl,' said her father. 'I know this is hard for you. But the family must come first.'

'Of course.' Feeling her eyes beginning to well again, Mary Ann went to her room, where she could hide her tears. It felt devastating to have to leave school. What would her life be like now, stuck at home without the ability to gain answers to all the questions that plagued her curious mind? But she simply must come to terms with it. Surely her future held something good. But right now, she couldn't imagine ever being able to escape poverty and boredom.

Soon there was another lace making station set up in their now cramped living room where she worked alongside her mother. Each day, as she sat down to weave the lace, she thought about what might have been.

She missed going to school each day. The overbearing teachers no longer intimidated her, and she learned that if she had kept her head down and worked hard, her teachers would barely notice her. She had a quick mind and was able to retain a lot of knowledge. Now that she was at home all day working on her lace, she often became bored. Her only source of solace were the few books that were in the house. It was a lonely life for a young girl and Mary Ann often felt sorry for herself, but she knew there was no alternative. She must play her part in the family

Chapter Six

Richard, Fingal, 1847

After a gruelling eighteen months at the harsh Long Point station, Richard finally received the news he had been yearning for. The probation period was over, and he was to be reassigned to work for a private employer. He was promised a modest wage, seven pounds per annum, to be precise. It was hardly a king's ransom, but to Richard, it seemed like untold wealth after years of not having a single penny to his name.

Back in Hobart Town, grim-faced soldiers on horseback greeted them. The soldiers would accompany them on their next journey.

'We're headed north,' a soldier barked out as they began their trek towards Fingal; a notorious convict station nestled deep within the rugged wilderness of northern Van Diemen's Land.

The distance stretched an intimidating 120 miles ahead of them. While the soldiers rode horses with saddles creaking under their weight, Richard and his fellow convicts trudged along on foot.

'Hey Roger, what do you think? We are going to be paid a wage. I have never seen that much money.'

Roger adjusted the pack on his back. 'It all seems unbeliev-able. I suppose we need to wait and see to find out what really is in store for us.'

They lugged rations of flour, sugar and tea in their packs. To supplement these rations, the soldiers hunted. On a good day, the party would enjoy a feed of kangaroo stew or quail roasted over the open fire. On days when no meat had been caught, the party had to be satisfied with damper cooked in the ashes of the open fire and boiled stinging nettles, which left a peculiar taste in their mouths.

Exhausted and hungry and with blistered feet, they eventu-ally reached Fingal. Their journey had taken ten arduous days. Richard slumped down on a rock and took a swig from the water bottle that was being handed around. The tepid water felt good sliding down his parched throat. He took a moment to survey the surrounding landscape. The chill of winter gripped the valley. The surrounding hills, some of which were crowned by snow caps, were blanketed by dense forests which loomed around them on all sides. Closer to the town, the countryside was a vibrant canvas of lush greenery, punctuated by towering gum trees.

Initially, Richard was assigned to work on a road crew. The days were gruelling and he spent the freezing nights in cramped cells.

'I can't wait till we're out of these cells,' Richard muttered under his breath one night as he and Roger lay shivering, trying to get some sleep.

'When do you think we will be assigned?' asked Roger, as usual deferring to Richard.

'Your guess is as good as mine.' Richard turned over, hugging the thin blanket close and tried to get some sleep.

By February, summer had taken hold in Fingal. Compared to the cold of winter, the heat was relentless when they were working, but the nights were pleasantly cool.

Richard was assigned to Mrs Brown, a widow with seven children ranging from ages seven to sixteen. Her husband had died five years ago, but with the help of her older children and convict labour, she had prospered on her small farm. She farmed sheep and grew potatoes and other vegetables. Richard arrived at the farm under military escort and was introduced to Mrs Brown.

'Hello Richard, welcome. We are pleased to see you. There is plenty of work to do.'

'Thank you, Mrs Brown,' answered Richard, taking off his hat and bowing his head.

'This is my overseer, Hugh Bates,' said Mrs Brown. 'He is a fair man, as I am sure you will discover, if you work hard and do the right thing.'

Richard just nodded. He wondered what this man was really like. So far, he had not met a fair overseer and was not looking forward to finding out if this dour looking man was any better than the rest. Once again, he silently vowed to keep his head down and not come under scrutiny.

'Mr Bates, please show Richard to his quarters and introduce him to the other men,' said Mrs Brown.

It was late in the day and as Richard entered the rough living quarters in an old slab hut, he saw four men, whom he assumed were also convicts, about to sit down to their evening meal. His mouth watered as the smell of stewed mutton drifted to his nostrils. The men looked up as Richard and the overseer entered.

'This is Richard. He will be working here with you ruffians. Get him something to eat and show him where he will be sleeping.' With that, the overseer left the room, slamming the door behind him.

'Good day, Richard,' said a well-spoken man. 'I'm Amos West. Very pleased to meet you. We could use some extra help around here.' The other three men nodded their assent but didn't comment.

Richard nodded back to them and, taking a seat at the table, began to eat the satisfying plate of food. After a long day of walking to his new posting and with nothing to eat since breakfast, he was too tired to focus on anything except his gnawing hunger. But once he had eaten, he decided it would be wise to get to know these men he would be working with.

'What is it like to work here?' he asked. 'Mrs Brown seems like a pleasant woman.'

'Aye, that she is, but mind out for the overseer,' said Amos. 'He has a high opinion of himself and will take it out on us if anything goes wrong about the place. He is not one to take the blame himself. Young Clarence here felt the sting of his whip just last week for no good reason.'

The young man called Clarence winced as he nodded his head. Amos continued. 'And he is not afraid to call in the magistrate so that our time as government men can be extended.'

Early next morning, Richard rose with the other men and after a breakfast of porridge, tea and surprisingly fresh bread, he started work on the farm. As he walked towards the paddock where they would be working, the sun was rising, and Richard took the chance to survey the surrounding country. Mrs Brown's farm was set between two ranges rising on either side of the valley. Despite a long hot summer, rainfall was plentiful in this region, so the countryside around was still green and lush. Sheep grazed lazily in the pasture.

Soon this idyllic landscape became the setting for Richard's first torturous day on Mrs Brown's farm. After the recent harvest, the ground now had to be ploughed, ready for the next crop. There were no mechanical aids here, not even a horse. Richard and another man were hitched up to a plough and toiled away for several hours without respite, with Hugh Bates overseeing their work to ensure they did not slow their pace. If they did, they would feel the bite of his whip on their backs. Each time he felt the flick of the whip, Richard could feel his old anger rise, but although it took all his resolve, he pushed his anger down and continued working.

The men made their way back to the farm accommodation, exhausted, thirsty and hungry. As Richard lay down on his bedding, which comprised a hessian bag covering a layer of straw, he thought about what opportunities this land might offer once he had served his time. He had heard many stories of convicts who had been granted conditional pardons and land grants and were now doing very well for themselves. One day, he resolved, he would be one of those men.

Chapter Seven

Mary Ann, Wilden to Bedford, 1850

Despite their best efforts and Mary Ann's lace-making contributing to their income, it was not long before the family was in a state of abject poverty. Every morning, Mary Ann awoke with a pit of dread in her stomach, knowing the day held nothing but the same hunger and hopelessness as the last. Her clothes felt shabby, despite her efforts to mend the holes in her stockings and patch the thinnest parts of her clothing. She knew her mother often went without anything to eat so that there was more for the rest of them. Mary Ann wondered what was to become of her family.

One cold October evening, the family sat down to another meal of watery soup. There wasn't even any bread to supplement the meal. Samuel sat at the head of the table. Mary Ann glanced up sadly, seeing the lines of worry clear on his face. He cleared his throat.

'Your Mother and I have decided that we will need to move to Bedford. There is nothing left for us here.'

'We are leaving?' asked Mary Ann. 'Do you mean we have to leave our home? Do we really have to?'

Charles gave her a withering look. 'Honestly, Mary Ann, don't be so selfish. You know Father and Mother only want what's best for us.'

Mary Ann glared at Charles but hung her head. She knew she was being selfish, but why did Charles always have to point out her transgressions? He always thought he was better than her. But she could not hide her trepidation at leaving what had been the only home she had ever known.

'Where will we go?' asked Charles, his eyes downcast.

'I will need to find work, so I will go into the town and see if I can secure a position. Bedford is becoming something of an engineering hub, so I am told. The brewery is also likely to be looking for workers. There seem to be better opportunities in Bedford, and it is not that far from Wilden. I think we could easily make the move,' explained Samuel. 'We will be best placed to wait until November when our yearly stipend is paid.'

Mary Ann fought back the tears that threatened to spill. She did not want to cry in front of Charles. It would only make him more annoying. He was so smug and self-righteous sometimes. The family ate their meal in silence.

Later, when Mary Ann was helping to clear the dishes, her mother gave her a quick hug, looking at her with sympathy in her eyes. 'You mustn't worry, Mary Ann. Everything will work out. No matter what happens or where we live, we will always have each other.' Mary Ann attempted a smile, but her mother's kind words only added to the likelihood of her tears spilling over.

As the year drew to a close and with their year's wages in hand, the family gathered their few possessions together and set off for Bedford. Although the town of Bedford was only six miles from Wilden, the difference was marked. Mary Ann watched from her seat amongst their possessions in the cart, as they left the green fields of the surrounding countryside where livestock grazed and crops grew. Soon she noticed the gradual buildup of the town. The streets became narrower and were hemmed in by buildings. The market square emerged as a bustling hub of activity, encircled by an array of shops, welcoming inns, and the imposing town hall. They continued on until their borrowed horse and cart trundled across the bridge over the River Great Ouse which ran through the town. In 1850, like most other large towns, Bedford was crowded and noisy. A thick pall of smoke hung over the town as the family rode towards their new home; their cart loaded with all their worldly possessions. Smoke belched from the chimneys of the factories and the gutters ran with waste. The smell was overpowering.

Despite the smoky atmosphere and the stench, Mary Ann felt a surge of excitement as she looked around at the crowded streets filled with noise and activity. This was so different from Wilden, and despite her earlier trepidation, her sense of adventure caused her to imagine that life would be better in this town.

She looked forward to meeting new people and getting to know her new home.

She nudged Charles. 'What do you think? It looks so different, doesn't it?'

'It certainly is different to Wilden and the smell is shocking,' replied Charles, looking around with a frown.

'Well, I think it will be exciting living here. And I am sure we will hardly notice the smell after a while.'

Charles only grunted. The family had rented rough accommodation in a small cottage on the south side of the river. As they sat down to eat their first meal in their new home, Samuel was the first to speak.

'What do you think, children?' he asked with a tight smile for Ann.

'I think it is exciting,' said Mary Ann.

'It's a new start. I am pleased that you can see the promise of our new situation. You and your Mother can continue your lacemaking, and I have been fortunate to secure a position in the brewery.'

'What am I to do Father?' asked Charles. 'The only thing I have ever done is work in the fields.'

'Well Charles, that is a good question. I have secured an apprenticeship for you. The local shoemaker was looking for a lad to work for him. You will go to live with his family.'

Charles looked shocked. Mary Ann stared at him, wondering why he didn't say anything. Their parents expected him to leave home and learn a new trade.

'But Father, do you really mean Charles will not be living here with the rest of us?'

Samuel looked downcast. Mary Ann knew how much her father relied on Charles to help with the chores. But yet he was sending him away.

'That is correct, Mary Ann,' said Samuel. 'None of this is easy for any of us. I will miss having Charles around. But we all have to do our bit to make the most of our new situation. I am sorry, Charles, but I know you understand.'

'Yes, Father,' replied Charles. 'I am sure I can make a go of it as a shoemaker.' Mary Ann could not believe how brave Charles was being. But she knew how much he loved and respected his father.

The next day, Mary Ann watched on as her big brother packed his belongings and set off to learn his new trade. Tears filled Mary Ann's eyes as she hugged him farewell. He waved sadly to them all as he hitched up his bag and set off.

Mary Ann, Bedford, 1851

Although life had been hard for the Turner family, they were finally getting back on their feet in their humble home at 21 Priory Street, Bedford. The move had proved successful. The whole family was working hard. Mary Ann and her mother continued to work side by side, making lace. Charles was by now an accomplished shoemaker, a strong young man, seventeen years of age. Josiah worked as an errand boy whilst John and Susan went to school each day. John was now aged nine, so Mary Ann felt sure he too would probably be forced to leave school soon.

Mary Ann felt a wave of irritation as she sat in the corner of the small living room. She was an accomplished lace maker now and spent many hours each day weaving the intricate patterns. She enjoyed her trade except for the simple fact that it kept her locked inside all day whilst her brother was able to go out to work. Josiah would come home late each night, tired and hungry after long days running errands for a surly factory owner. But he always had stories to tell about the goings on in the city and the people he met whilst doing his deliveries. She hardly ever saw Charles, which caused her further sadness. Although he was often abrupt with her when they were growing up, she missed his teasing. She knew that he did love her as much as she loved him. If only they could go back to those carefree days in Wilden, when they were young and trouble free. Susan, the sister she had longed for, was the only thing that brightened Mary Ann's days. She spent time playing with the little girl whenever she could.

Mary Ann looked up from her work as her mother came in from outside after hanging yet another load of washing on the clothesline.

'Would you like a cup of tea, love?' asked her mother, wearily.

Mary Ann sighed and put aside her bobbins. 'Yes, please.'

Her mother put the washing basket down and turned to her with a look of concern. 'What is it, Mary Ann? You sound quite forlorn.'

'Oh, I am sorry, it is just that I sit here all day with only you to talk to. The others get to go out each day and mix with people. I guess I am lonely.'

'Well, that's a woman's lot, Mary Ann,' said her mother, putting out cups and saucers. She then added two teaspoons of tea to the pot. 'Many women work in the home and their days are so full that they have little chance of seeing other people.'

Mary Ann felt chastened. Of course, her mother also rarely left the house. 'I'm sorry. But at least you have a husband. I do not have any friends at all.'

Her mother sighed. Mary Ann could see that her mother had some sympathy for her. But that was no help.

'At least we have food on the table again now. You must be grateful for what you have.'

But loneliness was not Mary Ann's only concern. She was worried about her father. He was no longer a young man and had taken up a job as a labourer on a farm. He had worked at the brewery for a time, but soon decided that he was too old to learn the modern ways of factory work, so had returned to farm work. Despite the industrialisation of Bedford by this time, there were still pockets of farmland scattered throughout the area. Once again, Samuel had returned to his role as a shepherd, where he spent countless frosty nights tending to the flock. The physical labour took its toll on him, causing him to appear much older and more fatigued than his actual age.

Mary Ann was also worried about the downturn in the lace making trade now that more and more lace was being made in factories with new machinery. It might not be long before she was out of a job. She could marry, of course. But she was only fifteen and what was more to the point, she did not know any men, let alone one who she might fall in love with. When she mentioned this to her mother, she was met with a short, ironic laugh.

'Mary Ann, you are such a romantic. Not every woman will marry a man who loves her. You must be satisfied with what you have.' Mary Ann stared at her mother, then quickly lowered her eyes. Surely her mother would prefer that she married someone she loved. She would not just be satisfied. She wanted to fall in love. Taking a sip of her tea, she sighed deeply. 'Well, it doesn't matter anyway. I won't meet any man locked up in here all day.'

'You are young, Mary Ann. You have plenty of time to worry about finding a husband. Your Father will know of young men who you will be suited to.'

'Surely, you don't mean Father will choose a husband for me?'

Her mother waved her hand dismissively before picking up the cups and taking them to the sink. 'That's enough silly chatter. Get back to your work.'

Mary Ann sighed again and picked up her bobbins, feeling the comfort of the soft, silky thread running through her fingers. It didn't matter what her mother said, Mary Ann was determined that if she was to marry, it would only be to a handsome man whom she had fallen in love with.

Chapter Eight

Richard, Fingal, 1850

The magistrate looked at him sternly. 'Richard Evans, having served five years of your ten-year sentence, with only....' He paused to look down at the register in front of him, 'one misdemeanor. Your good behaviour has served you well. I can tell you that you have been granted a Ticket of Leave.'

Richard stared at the piece of paper the magistrate handed him. When he had left the Burnsford farm that morning to travel to Fingal for the monthly convict muster, he had just been glad for a reprieve from the backbreaking work. He couldn't believe his good fortune. His heart lurched in his chest, a sudden, jarring thud that left him momentarily disoriented, as if the ground beneath him had suddenly shifted. Finally, he had a ticket of leave after enduring five long years of slavery, doing whatever paltry work the authorities had seen fit for him to do and often feeling the bite of the cat o' nine tails. But it seemed he was one of the lucky ones

'This means that you can go about your business and find work for yourself,' the magistrate continued. 'But remember, you cannot leave Van Diemen's Land. You must continue to report to the muster every month.'

Richard understood he wasn't entirely free, but the sense of relief that swept over him was immense. He did not know what to say, so remained silent. The magistrate was still speaking.

'Be warned, Richard, should you commit any offence, however small, you could be right back where you started. Your Ticket of Leave can easily be withdrawn. If that happens, you will have to serve the remaining five years of your sentence.'

As Richard left the office, he inhaled deeply, savouring the cool, clean air that filled his lungs, each breath a reminder that the worst was finally over. But he knew he must heed the magistrate's warning. Given that he was a known convict, any small misdemeanor could get him into trouble again. He took a silent vow that he would never let that happen. For now, he revelled in the freedom the ticket of leave afforded him.

After three years at Mrs Brown's farm, he was pleased to see the back of Hugh Bates and move on to the new posting. For the last two years, he had been posted to another farm in the Fingal area. Mr Burnsford was a kindly master, and his overseer was a vast improvement on Hugh Bates. He had worked hard to please Mr Burnsford and was grateful for his kindness.

It was a long walk of seven miles back to the farm, but Richard spent the time rejoicing in his newfound freedom and pondering his future. He wondered what to do. As he walked, he thought carefully. Perhaps Mr Burnsford would keep him on as a Ticket of Leave fellow. He thought he would at least ask.

When he arrived, he went straight to the farmhouse and knocked at the door.

Mrs Burnsford opened the door which led directly into the living room of the small cottage.

'Ah, young Richard, how can I help you?' She smiled at him, and Richard felt a wave of pleasure, uncommon over the last few years. He felt reasonably sure that Mrs Burnsford had rather a soft spot for him.

'I would like to speak to Mr Burnsford, if he is available,' said Richard, removing his hat and inclining his head slightly.

'Well come in and take a seat. I am sure you could use a cup of tea after your long walk.'

Richard looked at her with surprise. Did she already know that he had a Ticket of Leave? This was the first time he had been invited into the Burnsford home.

'I'll just fetch Mr Burnsford,' she said as she left the room. Richard was astonished. She must know. Otherwise, she would never have trusted him to sit alone in the house.

'Hello Richard,' came the strong but kindly voice of Mr Burnsford.

He sat down at the table opposite Richard as Mrs Burnsford took out three cups and made a pot of tea.

'I believe you have your freedom. I suppose you will be leaving us now?'

So, they did know!

Richard drew in a deep breath. 'Well actually, no. I have enjoyed working for you and I wondered if you could see your way clear to continue to hire me as a free man.'

Mr Burnsford rocked back in his chair. 'That is a lot to ask. I am sure you are aware that I would be obliged to pay you substantially more than a convict's wage.'

Richard was downcast, but he noticed the look that passed between the farmer and his wife. He felt sure that Mrs Burnsford was sending an unspoken message to her husband.

'Hmm, the farm has done well over the last couple of years, and that is partly down to your hard work, Richard. So, I would be foolish to let you go and I am sure we can come to some arrangement about your wages.' Mrs Burnsford beamed as she placed the steaming teacups down in front of the two men, who were now, if not exactly equal, certainly on more equal terms.

'Thank you, I am extremely grateful.' Richard picked up the cup and took a sip, smiling at Mrs Burnsford over the rim of his cup.

Another two years passed quickly. Richard had worked hard to repay the Burnsfords for their generosity, and he developed a good working relationship with Mr Burnsford. It was possibly the happiest two years of his life so far. Yet every month he still had to trudge the seven miles into Fingal to report at the convict musters.

Today he set out on a bright but chilly spring morning to make his way to the convict station. As usual, he lined up with all the other convicts and reported to the magistrate.

'State your name,' barked the Magistrate, his tone gruff.

'Richard Evans.'

'Well, it seems it is a good day for you, Richard Evans,' said the magistrate. He was not in the habit of talking kindly to the convicts. Richard tried to hide his impatience. He just wanted to get this done and be on his way.

'It seems that you have been granted a Conditional Pardon.' Richard was stunned. He couldn't believe this could really be possible. He stood silently, shifting his weight from foot to foot, as he waited for the magistrate to continue.

'Here is your paperwork. You are now a free man. You have the right to leave the colony of Van Diemen's Land should you wish to do so, but you must not leave the colonies altogether. That is, you are not permitted to return to England.'

With trembling hands, Richard accepted the paper from the magistrate. He looked hard at it. Yes, it actually had his name on it. He could barely believe that after all these years of being imprisoned and controlled, he was finally a free man.

'Thank you, sir,' he said gratefully, flashing the magistrate a wide grin.

'Very well, now move on. I have many more convicts to process.'

With that simple exchange, Richard's entire life changed. Thanks to his time at the probation station on Maria Island, he had learned how to read and could decipher his official paperwork. He saw his name printed several times, as well as the words 'Conditional Pardon.' A sense of freedom and possibility washed over him as he stepped out into the bright spring sunshine. He started on his return trip to the farm in somewhat of a daze. He felt almost weightless, his steps light and effortless, buoyed by an exhilarating sense of triumph.

As he began the long walk, he paused. The thought occurred to him that, in fact, he did not need to return to the farm. He could do whatever he wanted. But he was indebted to the Burnsfords and besides, his few possessions were there and after seven years being told exactly what to do, he was unused to making his own decisions. He really needed time to think about his next move.

He hurried back to tell the Burnsfords of this promising news. As he walked towards the farm where he had worked hard and, dare he say it, been happy for the last three years, he looked out over the lush green valley and at the tiny bush home where Mr and Mrs Burnsford lived. He had come to trust the couple and felt a twist in his stomach as he thought about his future. It was exciting, but also daunting to think about going out in the world by himself again. So many of the men he had come across during his incarceration had been cruel and had mistreated him. But what would it be like in this rugged country when he had only himself to depend on? Who would he be able to trust? He had spent most of his adult life bowing to the will of authority. So many questions raced through his mind.

He knocked at the door and Mrs Burnsford opened it with a smile.

'Good day, Richard,' she looked at him quizzically. 'You look right pleased with yourself. What are you so happy about?'

'Ah, you know me too well, Ma'am,' he said with a grin. 'I have been granted a Conditional Pardon. I am a free man!'

Mrs Burnsford beamed and threw her arms around him, pulling him into a tight hug. Richard tensed. Mrs Burnsford pulled away.

'Sorry, young man, I guess you are not used to being hugged, but I am just so happy for you. Come in, take a seat. I will make tea.' As she moved around the kitchen, she called out to her husband. There was a spicy aroma in the comfortable room and Richard's mouth watered. He was hungry after his long trek into Fingal and back.

'Good news. Richard has been granted his pardon,' she said when Mr Burnsford entered the room.

'Well, that is indeed good news, Richard. What do you plan to do with yourself?'

'I have not yet had time to think. You know, I was not expecting this to happen so quickly. I have only served seven years of my sentence. I am not at all sure what I should do.'

Mrs Burnsford beamed as she placed steaming cups of tea and a plate of freshly baked biscuits in front of Richard and her husband. Mr Burnsford took a bite of a biscuit before he spoke.

'Well, you are welcome to stay on here until you make up your mind.'

'Thank you, I would like that very much. It is very generous of you. I need time to think.' The two men sat in comfortable silence for a time whilst Mrs Burnsford bustled around the kitchen.

'I hear they have discovered gold in Victoria, so maybe I should try my luck there,' said Richard.

'You are a young man with no commitments, so that might be an excellent way to start your new life. I hear they are picking up nuggets the size of your fist.'

But Richard's anxiety at the thought of making his own way meant that he could not bring himself to leave the farm. It was several months before he built up the confidence to leave the security of his position with the Burnsfords. Eventually, he decided that if he was to start a new life, he must set out on his own. As the cold weather set in on Van Diemen's Land, he packed his few belongings and said goodbye to the Burnsfords.

Chapter Nine

Richard, Victoria, 1853

Richard made his way north to Launceston, where he booked a passage on board the coastal steamer Clarence. It felt like a momentous day when on July 25, 1853 he set sail for the newly independent colony of Victoria.

He stood on the deck staring out at the dark churning ocean, the briny scent filling his nostrils. The sky was black and ominous. Richard hoped there would not be a storm. He had terrible memories of storms at sea whilst on his voyage to Van Diemen's Land eight years ago. Another traveller came and stood by his side.

'Where are you bound?' asked the stranger.

'I'm going to the goldfields,' answered Richard.

'Aren't we all?' said the stranger. 'Which fields are you headed for?'

'I'm not sure, but I hear there are rich pickings at Mt Alexander.'

'I'm heading for Bendigo. There have been plenty of new strikes out that way. It's a bit further than Mt Alexander but worth the extra miles I hope.' Richard had been searching the man's features as they talked.

'Don't I know you?' said Richard, his brow creasing in thought. The stranger looked at him, but before he could comment, Richard continued. 'I know. You're one of the sailors we rescued from that shipwreck.' Richard couldn't quite believe that this could be the same man. Yet here he was. It was a strange coincidence.

The stranger looked at him in surprise.

'I was in the longboat that came to rescue you and the others,' continued Richard, feeling a glow of pride that the man was standing in front of him due in part to his bravery. He had little to be proud of in his past.

'Well, it seems I owe you.' He extended his hand for Richard to shake. 'My name is Walter Allen. After that episode, I decided a sailor's life was not for me. I have been working all sorts of odd jobs in Van Diemen's Land for the last few years. But now that gold has been discovered, I have decided to try my luck.'

'I could use some company getting to the goldfields. Perhaps we could team up. Name's Richard Evans.'

The two men fell into a companionable silence, deep in thought, as the steamer ploughed its way through the increasingly high waves. Richard felt a slight uncertainty. Was he wise to trust this man, who he barely knew, in what he imagined would be an unpredictable and harsh environment? Still, the benefit of having a companion would probably outweigh his doubts. As he leaned on the rail of the ship brooding, he decided to be cautious with his new friend, but at the same time, he would embrace the opportunity.

It was a rough crossing of Bass Strait on the notoriously dangerous stretch of water, but the crew did not seem concerned. Richard was very pleased to set foot on dry land in the colony of Victoria at the end of the short voyage.

He felt on edge as he took in the vibrant energy of the port and the city. Both were in stark contrast to his quiet and isolated life in Fingal, causing a faint sense of unease to wash over him as he and Walter struggled to navigate the bustling streets and the constant press of bodies around them. The scent of saltwater mixed with the stench of raw sewage, and the odour of many bodies, created a pungent aroma so strong that Richard could almost taste it. He was glad that he was only passing through this bustling city and was grateful that he had met up with Walter and had a companion on the trek to the goldfields.

After finding accommodation in a boarding house, the two men sat eating a hearty meal prepared by the buxom hostess.

'So, what do you think about travelling together?' asked Richard.

'I think it would be grand to have some company,' replied Walter. 'I have heard it is a long, tough trek. But good things await us. I can feel it in my bones.' Richard began to feel more confident in the trust he was placing in Walter. Perhaps it really was a good plan to team up. Maybe they would have better luck together.

The pair stayed in Melbourne just long enough to gather the tools and equipment they would need to make their way to the goldfields. Soon they were on the muddy rutted road with hundreds of other men, women and children, who were hoping to make their fortune on the goldfields.

Winter in Victoria was harsh. Although not as cold as Van Diemen's Land, there had been substantial rainfall, which made travelling tedious and backbreaking. Richard carried all his belongings on his back and although it was a heavy load, he was glad that he had chosen not to use any type of push cart or wagon. There were many along the track who struggled in the mud and got bogged in the deep ruts made by the steady stream of travellers.

Although Richard had no real idea where they were heading, he supposed all they needed to do was keep moving with the rest of the crowd until they found their way to the diggings at Mt Alexander. The shadows were lengthening when, after several days of travel, they crested a small rise. Richard stared in amazement at the scene before him. It looked like an anthill, with hordes of men toiling away in the mud and mullock heaps on the banks of Forest Creek. The air was thick with the sounds of men calling to each other and the clanking of tools. The creek was muddy brown, and the land was scarred; turned over in the quest for gold. The scent of sweat and rancid mud filled his nostrils. Makeshift tents and shanties were clustered in haphazard rows all along the creek. Richard turned to his new friend.

'What do you think? It's pretty crowded. Do you think we are too late?'

'It might be a good sign that there are so many prospectors here. I had thought to keep moving on to Bendigo, but perhaps we should try our luck here first.'

'I suppose it can't hurt to spend a few weeks here,' replied Richard.

Whilst there already seemed to be too many men on the creek, they would soon become participants in the chaos. They must find a piece of land to lay claim to. Richard struck up a conversation with a burly looking man who was resting on his shovel, wiping the sweat from his brow.

'I wonder if you can help us, sir,' he began. 'We are new here and we really don't know where we can stake a claim.'

'Well, there are not many rules, young man. Not as far as claiming a piece of land anyway. You can stake your claim for eight square feet anywhere there is space.' The man spoke in a thick Irish accent. 'But once you make a claim, you will need to work it every day except Sunday. If anyone gets wind of you not working the claim, they can take it from you. You can be sure there are plenty of claim jumpers around watching for ground that appears to be yielding well.'

'Thank you for your advice,' said Richard, holding out his hand. 'My name's Richard, and this is my friend Walter.' The Irishman had a firm grip as he shook hands, first with Richard and then with Walter.

'Joseph,' came the reply. 'Glad to help.' Joseph nodded towards a piece of earth not far away that seemed to be unoccupied.

'That looks like a likely piece of ground to stake a claim. I haven't seen anyone on it for a while. Of course, that could mean it wasn't yielding and has been abandoned. But there is no way of knowing for sure.'

Richard and Walter turned to look at the piece of ground, noting the signs of someone else having already tried their luck there. 'It is as good a place as any to start, I suppose,' said Richard.

'Don't forget to buy your mining licence. The traps are always on the lookout. It's highway robbery, but still safer to have one than not, if you can afford it.'

'Good advice. Thanks again.'

Richard and Walter picked up their packs and wandered over to the piece of dirt that Joseph had indicated. They pegged out their claim and soon had pitched their tents and stowed their belongings. Having set up camp, they found their way to the Commisioners Camp where they were able to purchase mining licenses. Once all that was done, they lit a fire.

'It's been a big few days. I am glad we decided to try our luck here,' said Richard as they cooked damper and boiled the billy.

'It was quite a trek, wasn't it?' said Walter, stretching his legs and yawning. 'It might be a good idea to get an early night so we can start at daybreak.' He left Richard sitting by the fire and retired to his tent.

As dusk fell, Richard sat drinking his tea and surveying the surrounding camps. He felt a thrill of excitement and wondered if this new beginning would end in good fortune. Surely, now that he had done his time, he deserved a bit of good luck.

The next morning, the two men rose with the sun and began work. Richard filled his mining pan with dirt and swirled the water, watching as the layers of dirt washed away, hoping to see the glimmer of gold in the rim of his pan. He filled the pan repeatedly, without the slightest sign of gold. Walter also had no luck.

It was hard work, but that was something Richard was well accustomed to. He slaved away for long hours every day, working from sunrise to sunset, his back aching and his hands callused and sore from the constant digging and handling of the dirt. The smell of dust and his own sweat filled his nostrils, his mouth constantly dry from thirst. Yet after a few days, he had very little to show for all his hard work. Frustration and doubt plagued his mind as he wondered if he was doing something wrong.

As the days turned into weeks and the weeks turned into months, Richard continued to work tirelessly on his claim. Summer came and the sun beat down on him. Water was becoming scarcer, which made the work even harder as all the miners jostled to access the diminishing creek. Over the months, though, Richard and Walter had started to see a glimmer of hope and their luck changed. Each day, they found small amounts of gold and as time went on, these amounts grew larger.

Richard was overjoyed with his newfound wealth. He had never imagined that he would have so much gold in such a short amount of time. He was careful with his money, opening an account at the Bank of Victoria to deposit the bulk of his earnings.

With each deposit he made, Richard felt a sense of pride and accomplishment. He had worked hard and now it was finally paying off. With so much gold in hand, Richard couldn't help but wonder what he would do with it all. He had never been a wealthy man before, and now he had a small fortune at his disposal.

Richard had been at Forest Creek for some time when he began to look for entertainment. He had worked hard and had not spent a lot of time in any of the places of leisure that attracted the lonely men of the diggings. Not that there weren't plenty of opportunities. Despite being illegal, sly grog shops sprang up everywhere on the goldfields. Walter had spent some time in the now thriving settlement of Castlemaine, and he encouraged Richard to spend some of his hard-earned money.

'You should go into town and see what's on offer,' said Walter. Being older than Richard, Walter was more experienced in the ways of the world. 'You should visit Fanny Finch's establishment.' He showed Richard a notice in the local newspaper.

BATHS. BATHS. BATHS.

MRS FANNY FINCH begs respectfully to inform the Inhabitants of Castlemaine and Diggers generally, that she has taken the undermentioned extensive premises, which she has furnished as a Bathing Establishment.

In offering this great summer luxury to her friends, Mrs F. begs to assure them that no expense has been spared and that every regard has been paid to the comfort and convenience of bathers and hopes to meet that encouragement and support which such an undertaking deserves.

A Refreshment and Reading Room is attached, where all the leading periodicals will be found. Ladies and children carefully attended to by Mrs F. personally.

Hot, Cold, and shower baths always ready at the following moderate prices Hot Bath, 5s. Cold ditto, 4s. Shower ditto, 3s.

Note the address— Templeton-street, next door to Messrs. Pye and Co.'s Lemonade Manufactory.

Richard read the notice through several times, taking his time to be sure he understood what was on offer. It had been a very long time since he had had a hot bath. His luck had been in, so perhaps he could afford himself the luxury of a bath and a good meal. He told Walter that he would think about it. Perhaps he would pay a visit next time he was in town.

His gold was mounting up again, so it was time to sell it and put the proceeds into the bank. He made his way into the fledgling town of Castlemaine. As he passed the shops on the main street, he savoured the smells of wood smoke and freshly baked bread. His first stop was, as usual, at the gold dealer's tent. The dealer watched with interest as Richard emptied his pouch onto the scales and then he deftly weighed the gold.

'A good haul, Mr Evans.'

Richard's chest swelled with pride. He pocketed the payment and headed to the bank. Keeping aside a small amount for his planned entertainment, he banked the rest and watched with satisfaction as the teller's stamp recorded his deposit. The State Bank of Victoria was still a temporary building, although it was rumoured a more permanent structure was being planned. Richard marvelled at the growth of the small town. Barely two years ago, this area had been nothing but bush and scrub.

After completing his banking, Richard headed out onto the bustling street again. There seemed to be more people in the town every time he came and there were several new traders since his last visit. New buildings were springing up everywhere. The miners could now buy everything they needed in the growing township.

Richard decided to follow Walter's advice. He pulled the crumpled newspaper clipping from his pocket and read the address. As he approached his destination, his pulse quickened, a mix of excitement and apprehension coursing through him. He had heard many tales of Fanny Finch's legendary establishment, a place where fortunes could be won or lost at card games and a man could slake his thirst.

It was said that Fanny had been at the diggings since the very beginning, when Forest Creek was nothing more than a collection of tents in the bush. She had often earned the ire of the traps, who were always on the lookout for sly grog establishments. They went around the diggings, burning down the tents of anyone they suspected. However, Fanny was such a popular hostess that every time her tent and business was ransacked and burned, the diggers would help her set up again. She had recently moved her business from Forest Creek into Castlemaine and set up a more permanent and respectable establishment.

As he approached the address, a raucous burst of laughter spilled into the street. He hesitated with his hand on the door handle, then taking a deep breath, he entered Fanny Finch's domain.

'Good morning, young man,' came a loud voice as Richard stepped through the door of the new establishment. 'And how can I help you today?'

Richard was tongue tied. This vision of a woman standing before him must be the notorious Fanny Finch. She made an immediate impression on him. He had never seen a woman like her, dressed as she was in bright blue silk, with her raven black hair adorned with flowers.

'I would like to take a bath and then partake of some refreshments,' he stuttered. Fanny smiled at him knowingly. Richard was aware that she had easily deduced that he had little experience with women, and particularly a strong and unusual woman such as Fanny. He felt the colour rise up his neck and into his face.

'Come right in. What should I call you?'

'Name's Richard,' he said. It was all he could manage.

'You must be new around here. I haven't seen you before.'

'My first visit.'

Soon Richard had bathed and sat at a table, eating a delicious meal and looking around him at the fascinating women who were serving ale and hearty meals to the hungry diggers. They were certainly a sight for a young man with little experience with women.

In the weeks that followed, Richard found himself drawn to Fanny's establishment often. The bustling restaurant, once a mere distraction from his gruelling work, had become the place to visit when he ventured into town.

One evening, as he and Walter sat at the bar, nursing their drinks, his eyes followed Fanny as she served the men, her laughter ringing out over the din.

'Quite a sight, isn't she?' said Walter.

Richard nodded, a wistful smile tugging at his lips. 'She something else alright.'

'Careful lad,' chuckled Walter. 'She won't be interested. Many have tried to catch her eye.' But Richard was not to be put off. As Fanny returned to the bar, he took his chance.

'Another, boys?' asked Fanny.

Richard straightened in his seat and ran his hand through his hair. 'No thanks, Mrs Finch. But could I have a moment of your time?'

'Surely, Richard. What can I do for you?'

'I wondered if you might like to take a walk with me someday. The weather has been warm and I thought you might like to get some fresh air away from all this.'

'Why, that's awfully kind of you, Richard. But I am afraid this place keeps me very busy.'

Richard's face fell, but he quickly masked his disappointment with a polite nod. 'Of course, but the offer stands, if you ever find yourself with a free afternoon.'

Fanny gently touched his hand before turning to serve another customer. Well, it hadn't been an outright refusal. Maybe with time and patience, he could win her over.

Chapter Ten

Samuel Turner, Luton, 1855

S amuel trudged along the dusty road. He had risen early that morning to cover the last few miles of his journey. The morning was icy cold, the ground white with frost. He pulled his kerseymere greatcoat closer and buttoned it up to the neck. Dust caked his boots and gaiters.

Ever since Lord Robotham had dismissed him from his bailiff position all those years ago, he had been desperately seeking another suitable position. But so far, no opportunities had presented themselves and he had been forced to work as a general farm labourer, doing any menial task that presented itself. Sometimes he had no alternative other than to take on the poorly paid jobs that the young children did, like scaring the birds off the grain, picking up stones or weeding. It was humiliating. There had to be a better way. When he first moved his family to Bedford, Samuel had high hopes that he might be able to work happily in a factory, but the brewery work had stifled him. The long days shut up indoors, surrounded by noise and unpleasant smells, left him cold. He longed to work in the open air again. So, he returned to the fields. The work was just as hard, but at least he could see the sun and breathe the fresh air. But he was getting tired. Now at 56 years old, half a lifetime of backbreaking manual work had taken its toll on his ageing body. Desperation gnawed at his insides as he realised that something had to change soon.

The hiring fair in Luton presented an opportunity. It was a good distance from Bedford, but he would be prepared to move his family if he could find a position as a bailiff. He had kissed Ann goodbye and, taking only the bare essentials necessary for his journey, bundled up in a worn pack slung over his shoulder, headed off on the long walk to the hiring fair. It took him three days and by the time he reached Luton, his legs were bone tired, but his spirit was buoyed by what he saw.

Luton appeared to be flourishing. The streets were teeming with people, their faces flushed with well-being. They moved with purposeful strides that spoke of success and contentment.

He took in the sight of well-dressed men haggling with street vendors over shiny trinkets, while women draped in elegant gowns chatted animatedly. A sense of satisfaction washed over him as he navigated through the throng. Luton had indeed become a hive of activity and wealth, much more so than his hometown of Bedford. But he knew all this. News had reached Bedford that the population of Luton was over 10,000 and the hat industry had meant that the town was prosperous. Straw plaiting and the production of straw hats was a major industry, supplying hats all over the country.

A wave of energy surged through Samuel. It seemed to be an excellent decision to come to the hiring fair. Entering the town covered with dust and looking untidy, he knew if he wanted to gain employment as a bailiff, he would need to look respectable, like a man used to being in charge. His first order of business was to find himself lodgings so that he could wash and remove some of the dust from his clothes before making his way out into the field where the hiring fair was in full swing.

Feeling refreshed after a bath and a meal, he ventured out to the fairground. He looked around him at the other men and women who were also looking for work. Although the major industry in Luton was hat making, there was still a need for other occupations. It was obvious the sort of work each man was looking for. The shepherds, carters and thatchers milled around, all wearing or carrying the badges of their trade. Unlike at hiring fairs he had attended in other towns, there were many women with pieces of plaited straw pinned to their bodices to indicate their skill in hat making.

Samuel started asking around for bailiff positions. But it soon became apparent that luck was not with him today. He tried to hide his deepening frustration as each query got a negative response. His jaw tightened as he realised Luton was not the town for him after all. Agriculture was taking a back seat to the new industry of hat making. He groaned audibly at the thought that he would have to return home, having wasted his time. He would have to continue as a labourer and rely on the other members of his family to help provide for them all.

He returned to his lodgings at the inn as the sun was sinking. Entering the crowded room, he ordered a meal and a tankard of ale. As he sat drinking his ale, in a morose state, and waited for his meal to arrive, a man wandered up.

'Do you mind if I sit here?' he asked. 'There doesn't seem to be another seat available.'

'Surely, no I don't mind at all,' replied Samuel, surveying the stranger and deciding quickly that he seemed a likeable enough fellow. 'I could do with some company after a long and worthless day. Samuel Turner.'

'William Evans,' said the stranger. 'Where are you from?'

'Bedford, and back there I'll be going.'

'Were you hoping to secure work here today?'

'I was hoping to be hired as a bailiff. Work I have done before.' Samuel proceeded to relay his entire story to William, although he wondered at his loose tongue in the presence of a complete stranger.

William listened patiently, nodding and making noises of understanding.

'It seems to me that you have been wronged by Lord Robotham. I came here looking for better prospects today as well.'

Samuel looked properly at William for the first time, realising that because of his own melancholy, he had been monopolising the conversation.

'Where are you from?' he asked.

'Amersham. It is only a small town and it's in decline. Many do not have enough work and are leaving for the cities, hoping to secure work in the factories. But I am trying to keep my family together in the country. I still think it is a better life. Although we have not been without our troubles.'

Samuel nodded and took another draught of his ale.

'Can I buy you a drink?'

'Yes, let's have one more.'

For some reason, which Samuel could not really understand, he felt a strange connection to William. He liked him and it felt as if their lives had taken similar paths. Soon he was listening to William talk about his son.

'My oldest son Richard has been sent to Van Diemen's Land for 10 years. He was a good boy but got mixed up with some bad types. At first, he was convicted merely of stealing a loaf of bread because of his hunger. But it didn't stop there and now he is gone forever. My wife has been devastated by the loss.'

'When was this?' asked Samuel.

'Ten years ago, in 1845,' replied William. 'He's a free man now, having served his sentence. It seems unlikely that he will ever return, as he has built a life for himself in the colony. We received little correspondence from him in the early days, but since he earned his pardon, we have had several letters. He is working in the goldfields. He tells us he is doing very well and would like to marry, if you can believe it.'

'Is that so? It sounds like he has made a good life for himself.'

'Well, yes, it does seem so. He has been regularly sending small amounts of money home, which has been of significant benefit in recent times. I think we may have all ended up in the workhouse if not for Richard.'

'How old is your son?' asked Samuel, the kernel of an idea forming in his head. If Richard was indeed as well off as William said, he might make a good match for Mary Ann.

'He is 30.'

It was getting late, so the two men retired to their rooms.

The next morning, they met again as they were preparing to leave for their respective homes. Samuel, having given his idea much thought overnight, decided to broach the subject of a match between William's son and Mary Ann. After all, he had nothing to lose.

'My daughter, Mary Ann, is a lace maker. But the trade is dying as a cottage industry. Machines are making much of the lace now, so she is getting less and less work. She is 21 and needs to marry. I thought that perhaps your son Richard might make a good match for her.'

William looked stunned. It was obvious that the idea came as a complete surprise to him. But Samuel could see that he was thinking it through.

'Well, that is a very interesting proposition,' said William. His brow furrowed as he contemplated the proposal. 'I suppose there would be no harm in writing to Richard to see what he thinks. His letters so far have indicated that there is a shortage of women in the colonies, so he might be pleased to consider the idea. But what of your daughter? It would be a big thing for her to consider. You would probably never see her again if she was to go to Richard on the other side of the world.'

'Of course, that is all very true, but Mary Ann's prospects do not look good and she is 21, so is running out of time to find a good match.'

'Very well, I will write to Richard and see what he thinks of this wild idea. If you will write down your address, I will let you know what he says.'

Samuel took the piece of crumpled paper and a pencil, which William had fished out from the pocket of his breeches, and wrote his address. The two men shook hands and parted ways, walking quickly off in opposite directions.

As he walked, watching the sun rise higher in the dull cold sky, Samuel wondered at his actions. What had he done? Did he really want to marry Mary Ann off to some ex-convict in a land on the other side of the world? And what would Ann say? He knew she thought him impulsive in many of his decisions. She had not been in favour of him taking this long journey to try to find work in the first place. What would she think of his latest plan?

Chapter Eleven

Richard, Castlemaine, 1855

Richard had amassed a modest fortune over the two years he had been in Mount Alexander, and his friendship with Walter had also flourished. The population of Castlemaine had grown to around 25,000. Richard marvelled at the grand buildings that now dotted the town, all financed by the riches of the goldfields. The town was moving quickly from tents to bricks and mortar, and Richard felt he was moving with it. He was still carefully banking the proceeds of his labour and he watched with a sense of pride as his balance at the Bank of Victoria grew along with the grand new building that housed the bank.

But despite his successes, a gnawing feeling began to creep in. He longed for companionship and yearned for a wife. His attempts to court Fanny had been fruitless, and he couldn't shake the thought that she wasn't interested in him. It pained him to admit it, but it seemed it was time to look elsewhere. At 30 years old, Richard felt he would soon be past his prime and desired nothing more than having a family of his own. However, he knew finding a suitable partner on the goldfields would prove challenging. He refused to settle for the ladies of the night who frequented the sly grog shops. He wanted someone better, someone who could match his ambitions.

Feeling dejected after these thoughts had been plaguing his mind constantly for many weeks, he decided he needed some cheering up. He took his bar of tallow soap down to the creek and had a thorough wash. Refreshed, he put on clean clothes, a new set of dungarees and a smart-looking shirt he had purchased recently. He knew he looked well turned out in the new clothes as he set off for town.

The first place he went was Fanny's restaurant. It was always his preferred option when he wanted some down time, despite the fact he could not get any more than a friendly smile and a quick chat from Fanny. But there was always an ale and a good meal on offer at her establishment. Fanny was there to greet him as usual.

'Hello there, Richard. You are looking very well to do in your fine new clothes. The mine must be paying well.'

'Well yes, Fanny. I have had to work hard, but it is paying off.'

'What's wrong?' asked Fanny. 'You look far too glum for a man with a thriving gold mine.' Richard gave her a bemused look. Fanny rarely gave him more than a quick welcome.

'I think I am lonely. I have been thinking about taking a wife. The problem is good women are hard to find in the colonies. There are many more men than there are women.'

'That's true,' replied Fanny. 'Perhaps a trip to Melbourne is in order. You may have more luck in the city.'

Richard mulled over the idea. 'Perhaps.' As Fanny turned away to serve another customer, he thought about the one woman who really interested him. He shook his head to dismiss that thought. He really must accept that she would never welcome his advances. Perhaps he should take a trip to Melbourne and see what the city offered.

With renewed energy after some of Fanny's excellent food and before he had drunk enough liquor to make himself too maudlin, he left Fanny's and headed out for a walk around the town. Although the peak of the gold rush was over by now, and many of the diggers had moved on as new gold fields opened up in other districts, the population was still large and new industries were being established.

He hadn't checked his mail for a while, so he called in at the Post Office. He was mildly surprised to receive a letter from his father. Richard thanked the Postmaster and left the Post Office wondering what the news from home would be. As he left in a contemplative mood, he looked out over the view that was afforded by the position of the post office on a hill. The diggings were spread out before him. Although the main town was moving from tents and canvas to more permanent buildings, there were still a lot of makeshift canvas dwellings over the rough, pockmarked ground. Richard headed back to his camp so that he could read his letter in private. He still was not the most confident reader, even though he had continued to work hard to improve his reading whenever he had the chance.

The shadows were lengthening by the time Richard had stoked his fire and he sat down to read his letter before the darkness fell.

15th September 1855

Dear Richard

I hope this letter finds you well. Although times are tough, we are managing, thanks to the money you have been sending home from time to time. Your mother, brothers and sister are all well.

I have a proposition for you. I had a chance meeting with a fellow at the hiring fair in Luton and we got to talking. He has a daughter, Mary Ann, who is twenty-one years of age and wants to marry. In our last correspondence, you said that you had not yet found a wife and I know you are eager to do so. Perhaps you would consider writing to Mary Ann to see if she might be interested in becoming your wife. She is an accomplished woman who has a trade as a lace maker, but that trade is dying out as machines take over. She needs some form of support.

Please consider this carefully and send a letter for her. I will make sure that it gets to her. If you have the slightest inclination to accept this suggestion, I would think that a small purse might help to convince Mary Ann's father that this would be a good match.

Your mother sends her love.

Your father.

Richard was stunned. This was indeed a coincidence, having just been discussing the matter with Fanny. What could this mean? Was he just supposed to propose marriage to a young woman half a world away? Would she agree to come all this way to be his wife? He certainly was not going back to live in his home country, so if they were to marry, she would have to come to Australia. It appeared that their fathers had arranged for this to happen. He needed to think this through. Maybe Fanny could help. He valued her advice and she was the only woman he really talked to. But it was getting late and anyway, he needed more time to think this through before speaking with Fanny. Perhaps he could talk to Walter about it, too. The sun was sinking below the horizon and fires glowed outside every tent as he sat by his campfire, considering what seemed such a preposterous idea.

After a restless night, Richard had decided. He had to finally admit that Fanny had no romantic interest in him; with the lack of women in the colonies, if he wanted to marry, this might be the best opportunity available to him.

He and Walter worked side by side through the morning. When they stopped for a meal at midday, Richard broached the subject with Walter.

'I have had a letter from home. I haven't had one in a while. But my father has come up with a scheme I would never have dreamed of.'

'That sounds interesting,' replied Walter, without looking up from his meal.

'He has met a man who has a daughter of marriageable age who may be interested in becoming my wife.' Walter fixed him with a bemused stare. Now he had Walter's full attention.

'Really? That seems a hair-brained idea. Would you really consider marrying someone you have never met?'

'I really don't know. I am going into town to talk to Fanny. I know she will give me good advice.'

'You have developed quite a relationship with her,' said Walter with a sly grin.

'I am sorry to say that she gives me the time of day, but that is all.' Richard wanted to convince himself, as much as Walter, that he was not interested in Fanny romantically.

The next day, he once again left his claim and headed into town. He wanted to see Fanny early before her main trade started for the day, so that he could seek her counsel privately. As soon as he slipped through the door, he spotted Fanny sitting at a table, sipping a cup of tea. He wandered over to her, wondering if he was disturbing her. Fanny was an imposing figure and he was always nervous in her company. But, as usual, this morning she gave him a warm smile.

'Good morning, Richard. What brings you here this early in the morning?'

'Hello Fanny, I was hoping to talk to you for a moment.'

'Well, in that case, it was good that you came early. I hear there has been a big new strike over on the Forest Creek diggings, so I am sure it will get rowdy in here soon as some will have gold to spend.' It pleased Richard that Fanny seemed disposed to spend some time with him this morning. She was a naturally kind and friendly person, but he had felt many times that she did not want to develop close relationships with any of the men. She was her own woman and had shunned his advances frequently.

'Yes, I heard tell of that yesterday evening. It is much further along the creek than where my claim is.'

'What is it you wanted to talk to me about?' asked Fanny, the intense look in her eyes indicating she was indeed curious about what Richard had to say. It made him feel more confident to tell her his news.

'I had a letter from home. My father still writes to me occasionally with news of the family. But this letter had some rather surprising but perhaps welcome news, I think.'

'That sounds intriguing. Go on, tell me more,' said Fanny, her eyebrows raised, giving him her full attention.

'The letter said there is a young woman living in England who might be willing to become my wife. It seems so unlikely, but apparently our fathers have arranged the match.'

'Well, that is a coincidence after our talk yesterday. What do you think? Would you consider such a strange idea? Of course, you should have a wife. You have been alone on the diggings for years now. What do you know of her?'

'That's the thing. I know nothing other than that she is 21 years old and is a lace maker. Apparently, she has so far been unable to find a husband, which in itself raises some questions. But would she really come all this way to marry a man she has never met anyway?'

'You won't know until you ask. I think you should see this through. You must send a reply at once. There are very few young women around here and this sounds like a chance to have a wife.'

Richard looked at Fanny, feeling torn. He had hoped he might finally attract her attention as more than a friend by mentioning another woman. But here she was, encouraging him to marry a stranger. Whilst he felt some stirring of emotion at the thought of meeting Mary Ann, he was saddened that he really was putting an end to any chance he may have had with Fanny. It was clear he must put his feelings for Fanny aside; he resolved to write the letter to Mary Ann straight away.

Chapter Twelve

Mary Ann, Bedford, 1856

Mary Ann Turner sat working diligently in a corner of the kitchen, weaving her dozens of bobbins, crossing over from left to right, twisting from right to left, pinning her design to create the delicate lace patterns. She loved the feel of the silk thread between her fingers and seeing the beautiful lace patterns come together under her hands provided her with great satisfaction. But in the present circumstances, it also helped to calm her turbulent thoughts.

She still lived with her parents and three of her siblings at 21 Priory Street, Bedford. Her family relied on the income from her lace making to supplement their income and she was pleased that she was able to contribute.

But all that was about to change. A marriage had been arranged. She was 22 years old, and she knew it was time she had a husband. But why did it have to be like this? She was petrified that the man she had been told she was to marry would not be what she had hoped for since she was a young girl. She was not averse to getting married; it was what every young girl longed for. But in her romantic mind she had hoped that she would have the chance to fall in love with the perfect man who would be kind to her and return her love, like the fairytales she had so enjoyed as a child and secretly still enjoyed.

It had shocked her when her parents told her the news. The family was eating their evening meal when her father cleared his throat and began to speak.

'Mary Ann, there is something your Mother and I would like to talk to you about.'

'Really, Father. What is it?'

Samuel looked at Ann, his eyes pleaded for her to continue.

'Well, Mary Ann, it is a young man,' said her mother. Mary Ann could only stare. She knew her parents wanted her to marry. They had spoken to her many times about how she would be an old maid if she didn't marry soon. But she had not met the man she wanted to marry yet. Actually, she had hardly met any men at all as a consequence of her trade, which kept her in the house most of the time. Was this someone her parents wanted her to meet, a prospective suitor? Her throat constricted as she tried to swallow her concern.

'He has made a good life for himself in Australia, and he wants to marry a good strong woman who would join him on his gold mine,' said Ann.

Mary-Anne gasped. The world seemed to freeze around her. She could only stare, eyes wide, as her mind struggled to grasp what her mother had said.

'Australia? What do you mean? Surely, you are not expecting me to take up with a man I have never met and to go to the other side of the world with him?'

'Now, Mary Ann, please be reasonable,' said her father in a stern voice.' There is a letter here for you. His name is Richard, and his father has assured me he has made a good life in the colonies. You must at least read the letter.'

She looked at her siblings around the table and saw they had all lowered their heads and appeared to be in deep concentration on the food they were eating. They knew when their father spoke, he would brook no argument. No one was going to stand up for her. Mary Ann was on her own.

Mary Ann was horrified as she took the letter her father handed her. She stood up and left the table, not able to finish the remainder of her meal. In her tiny space in the house, partitioned off by a canvas curtain, she stared at the letter. Her hands shook as she slowly lifted the seal and began to read.

Dear Mary Ann

You don't know me, and I know that this will come as a shock to you. But I wish to propose marriage. Our fathers have arranged this, and I am very keen to proceed.

I have been in Australia for over 10 years and have made a good life for myself. I am a gold miner and have amassed some wealth. I have to be honest and tell you what you may have already guessed. The reason I am in Australia is that I was transported here after being convicted of larceny. But I have served my time and am now a completely free man. I have lived an honest life since gaining my pardon.

Please consider my proposal. I promise I will treat you well and I know you will soon adapt to conditions in Australia. It is a magnificent country with excellent prospects. I know we could do well.

Best regards

Richard Evans.

Mary Ann could not believe what she was reading. Surely they had all gone mad. She could never just leave her family and home to marry this man. Her family meant everything to her. She remembered her distress the day that Charles had been forced to leave and he had only been leaving to take up his apprenticeship. This was worse than anything she could imagine. Australia. It was the other side of the world. She would never see any of them again.

She lay down on her bed and wept. Her hands clenched on her bedclothes. But it would do no good to be angry. She knew if her father was determined, she would have no say in this decision. What was she to do?

The next day she rose early and went to her work bleary-eyed, hoping that the repetitive action of weaving her lace would soothe her. Her father rose soon after her and gave her a small smile as he entered the living room.

'I hope you have considered this proposal carefully, Mary Ann.'

'I don't know what to think, Father. How can you want me to leave you all?' Mary Ann paused in her work and looked at her father. It was as if he didn't care about her at all. She knew this wasn't true. They had always been close. She simply couldn't understand why he was insisting on this marriage.

When her father did not respond, she continued through gritted teeth. 'This is not fair, Father. You cannot do this.'

The colour rose in his face. 'It has all been arranged. The young man is on his way by sea and should be here within the month.' Despite his words and his forbidding demeanor, it felt like he was having second thoughts. Perhaps she could change his mind. 'You can't mean that. Don't I have any say?'

'I am sorry, Mary Ann.' His eyes were downcast, as if he couldn't bear to look at her. 'We would have preferred for you to make your own way, but at 22, you are running out of time. We cannot support you forever.' He made her sound like a burden!

'But my lace brings in some income. How will you manage without that?'

'It is not enough. We need the money this young man has offered for your hand.'

'You are selling me off?' Tears sprang to Mary Ann's eyes as she came to the realisation that she truly had no say in this transaction. He might be having second thoughts, but it was clear he would not change his mind. She could not believe that she was apparently being sold to the highest bidder. Her heart contracted and the sick feeling in the pit of her stomach increased. It was clearly pointless to argue further. She collapsed backwards into her chair.

Just at that moment, her mother entered the room. Without looking at Mary Ann, she went to the stove and stoked the fire. Maybe there was still a chance to enlist her mother's help.

'Mother,' Mary Ann took a step towards her, fighting with the urge to throw herself at her mother and beg. 'Surely you do not want me to leave?'

Mary Ann could see the sympathy in her mother's eyes, but she made no reply. Mary Ann knew then that her mother would not go against her husband's wishes. She stood up, fled from the room and flung herself on the bed as her tears flowed freely again.

Chapter Thirteen

Richard, England, 1857

S tepping back onto English soil, Richard was flooded with a mix of emotions. On the one hand, he had yearned for this moment after spending over ten years in Australia. But now that he was here, he couldn't help but feel conflicted. England was the place of his birth and he had lived here for the first nineteen years of his life. His family was here. But Australia had become his home.

The voyage on board the Medway, whilst exceedingly more comfortable than the voyage to Australia on the convict ship all those years ago, was still long and crowded. He was glad to make dry land again, but the noise and degradation that he saw around him in Portsmouth made him long for his country home in the Australian bush. Despite this feeling that he no longer belonged, he was eager to see his family. From Portsmouth, he caught a train to London and then on to Watford. From there, he would walk the final miles to his home in Amersham.

Once in Watford, he shouldered the few belongings he had brought with him and walked down the dusty road, allowing thoughts of his bride-to-be to fill his mind. He did not know what she looked like or what nature she would possess; he could not help but wonder if she had some affliction, given that she had not already found a husband. But that was of little consequence. The longer he had thought about the idea of marrying Mary Ann, the more it had appealed to him. He wanted a wife to share his life and give him a son. His advancing age made him wonder what his legacy would be if he did not have a son and heir to the modest fortune he had amassed.

He arrived at Amersham after trudging the last few miles. As he walked the familiar streets, he could not shake off the feeling of being torn between two worlds. It was market day and although the town looked much the same as when he had left ten years ago, the atmosphere at the market was completely different from what he remembered. The number of sheep and other livestock had diminished significantly as other industries had taken over. So many questions filled his racing mind. What would the town be like? How were the residents of the small town coping? It wouldn't be long before he found out. His family's plight would be a good indication. As he approached the small, thatched cottage where he had grown up, he couldn't help feeling anxious at what he would find behind the closed door. His muscles were wound tense as he lifted his hand to the latch to open the door, but then he stopped short and knocked instead.

Within moments, the door opened, and his father was standing there. They had not set eyes on each other in twelve long years. His father grabbed the hand Richard extended and wrapped his other arm around Richard's shoulder and called to his wife.

'Matilda, it's Richard. He's arrived.'

Matilda appeared in a rush and hugged Richard tightly. 'Oh, my boy, let me look at you.' She held Richard at arm's length and explored his features hungrily. 'You look well. How are you?'

'Hello Mother,' he said, grinning broadly, suddenly realising just how much he had missed his family. He felt like a small boy again. 'I am well. It is so good to see you. Where are the rest of the family?'

'We are on our own. Isaac and the girls have their own lives now. But they are all well and they will join us for supper tonight,' said his mother. 'Come in, you must be hungry after your long trip.'

The feelings that flooded through him upon reuniting with his parents overwhelmed Richard. He looked tenderly at both and saw tears of happiness welling in his mother's eyes and the huge smile on his father's face. The small dwelling where he grew up had changed very little. His family seemed to be coping quite well and his chest swelled with pride that the money he had sent had obviously made a difference.

Soon the three of them were gathered around the kitchen table enjoying the meal that Matilda had prepared, exchanging stories and catching up with each other's news. Richard talked little about his convict years but focussed on the good fortune that he had found once he had gained his freedom and headed to the goldfields.

'Australia has been good for me. I am far from rich but have made a good living,' Richard told his parents.

'We are very proud of you, son,' said his father. 'And we are exceptionally thankful for the money you have sent to us.' His mother smiled at him, and Richard felt a warmth flow through him. He knew that his actions as a young boy had hurt her, and he was glad that she now seemed proud of him.

'When will I be able to meet Mary Ann?' he asked.

'You will need to travel to Bedford, so I suppose it is up to you,' said his father. 'Apparently the young lady has agreed to meet you, although her father says she was quite upset when she first found out what he had agreed to on her behalf. You may have to take some time to convince her it is in her best interest to marry you.' Richard frowned. Surely he hadn't come all this way, only to have his proposal turned down. If she didn't want to marry him, but was being forced to by her father, then the relationship might not be off to a good start. He must leave at once to ensure that he could convince her he was a worthy husband.

'Very well, I will set off tomorrow. Whilst I am pleased to see you, I do not want to be away from my claim for too long.'

That evening, the entire family gathered in the small cottage. Isaac was now a fine-looking young man who had managed to get some work and still contributed to the family. As he stepped into the living room, he greeted Richard with a warm handshake.

'Well, we meet again. I did not think this would ever happen. I am so pleased to see you. You look well.'

'As do you, Isaac. I am pleased that you have made your way without following in my footsteps.'

'Yes, I learned that lesson quickly when they sent you away.'

'That's enough talk of the past. We have a bright future to look forward to,' said their mother. 'Look, here are the girls.'

There were hugs all around as the family became reacquainted. His sisters had married well and between them had borne several children. It was certainly a full house that evening, but Richard was overjoyed to reunite with his siblings and to meet his brothers-in-law and his nieces and nephews.

The next day, he bid his parents farewell and set out to meet Mary Ann. He had a long walk to St Albans, a distance of some eighteen miles, but from there he could catch a train to Bedford. The journey would take less than two days. Richard spent much of that time wondering what this enormous step he was about to take would have on his life.

Chapter Fourteen

Mary Ann, Bedford, 1857

T he day that she was to meet her future husband came all too soon for Mary Ann. After the initial shock of finding out that her father had promised her to a man she had never met, Mary Ann began to wonder whether this might indeed be the adventure she had waited for all her life. In her very early years, when her father was a bailiff and the family was reasonably well off, she and her brothers had run free and played adventurous games. But as time had gone on and her family's circumstances had changed, she had always felt there was something missing in her life. Now she had a chance to have her own life-changing adventure.

But it was all so daunting. She oscillated between great excitement and overwhelming fear. Marrying a man she had not even met was one thing, but going with him to the other side of the world was quite another. But she had no choice. Her father had made the decision, and after all, perhaps that was a good thing. But she was still angry. This was her life. Her father had no right to make her decisions. She thought about rebelling against him and not marrying Richard. But then what would she do? Her father was a good man, but his word was law. He had said that she must go through with this or make her own way in the world. And that was much more frightening than the alternative. She knew she would not last long without the support of her family and would soon end up in a workhouse or somewhere worse. So, she steeled herself and tried to forget the fear and embrace the sense of adventure that sometimes found its way to the top of her emotions.

That morning, she dressed carefully, hoping that she was suitably attired in her best dress. It was simple enough, brown checked calico lined with thicker calico for warmth. The bodice buttoned to the neck, with long sleeves and a full skirt gathered at the waist. She had added some of her handmade lace to the cuffs and collar. She rarely had the opportunity to dress up, so as she glanced in the mirror that morning, she felt a glow of plea-sure as she realised she looked quite well, perhaps even pretty. Now she sat with her parents nervously waiting for Richard to arrive. Susan, who had recently turned eleven, was also waiting somewhat impatiently and had been warned that she must be on her best behaviour. She sat on the settee, her hands folded in her lap, barely able to contain her excitement. Mary Ann gave her sister a reassuring grin, but underneath, she felt quite nauseous as the butterflies tumbled around in her stomach.

There was a knock at the door. All four of them jumped. Mary Ann realised her parents were probably every bit as anx-ious as she was. Susan jumped off the couch, but as she caught the look her mother gave her, she quickly sat herself down again.

'Very well, Mary Ann,' said Samuel. 'You should answer the door.' But Mary Ann was frozen to her chair. Whilst she had become used to the idea that she was to marry since hearing the alarming news, meeting this man for the first time filled her with trepidation. What would he be like? For all she knew, he could still be a criminal and might not treat her kindly. A long moment passed before she took a deep breath and went to open the door. Standing before her was the man she was to marry. With a start, she realised he was a good few years older than her. Of course, she knew he had been in Australia for over ten years, but it just had not occurred to her that the man she was to marry would be so much older. Her first impression of Richard was that he was not very tall, only slightly taller than her, but he had a kind face and after having looked her up and down, was now smiling widely at her. She wondered what his first impressions of her were.

'Good morning, I'm Richard,' he said.

'Hello, Mary Ann,' she replied in hushed tones. 'Won't you come in?' She led Richard through to the living room where her parents sat waiting. 'This is my Father Samuel and my Mother Ann.'

'Hello Mr and Mrs Turner. It is good to finally meet you. It has been a long journey.'

Samuel rose and shook hands with Richard, looking him over with a wary eye. 'Please take a seat. Mary Ann will make tea.'

As she moved around making tea and cutting generous slices of the plum cake she had made for the occasion, Mary Ann glanced at Richard. He was quite handsome, his brown hair falling forward over his brow as he sat talking to her parents. She listened as her father questioned Richard.

'I understand you've made quite a fortune for yourself on the Australian goldfields?' Samuel's tone was probing yet respectful.

'That's correct, Mr Turner,' Richard replied confidently. 'I've been fortunate enough to find success there.'

'And I assume that would mean you're capable of providing my daughter with a comfortable life?' Samuel continued, his gaze never wavering from Richard.

'Yes, sir,' Richard answered earnestly. 'I assure you I can give Mary Ann the life she deserves.'

At this response, Mary Ann saw her father nod slowly in approval. His unsmiling expression softened slightly as he seemed to acknowledge that Richard might indeed be a suitable match for his daughter.

After they had finished their tea, Ann motioned to her youngest daughter. 'Come Susan, the vegetable garden needs watering.' Susan and her mother left the room. Mary Ann suddenly realised her family was about to leave her alone with Richard. 'Would you like another cup of tea, Father?'

'Thank you, but I think I will join your Mother in the garden and leave you two to get acquainted.' Left alone with Richard,

Mary Ann felt her chest constrict, as if a band was slowly tightening around her ribs.

Richard tried to make small talk for a few moments. Mary Ann sat uncomfortably on the edge of her chair. She struggled to respond to Richard's questions, her nerves getting the better of her. Suddenly, Richard appeared to lose patience. He looked at her with piercing hazel eyes.

'Mary Ann, you know why I have come. I would like to marry you and have you return to Australia with me.'

Mary Ann felt the colour rising from her neck right up through her face. She looked at Richard from under her eyelashes. He was very forward, which did nothing to allay Mary Ann's concerns. Although she knew she had little choice in this transaction, she would like a chance to get to know this stranger a little more before she was forced to marry him. But she had to admit he was quite handsome and seemed nice enough.

Richard noticed the blush and gave her a kindly smile. 'I promise I will be kind to you. I know we can have a good life together. Australia is growing fast and is not so much the colonial outpost it was fifty years ago. I live in a town called Castlemaine and I have a piece of land on which I mine for gold.'

Mary Ann still did not feel able to answer him. Her mind was racing. This was really happening. She had so many questions, but did not feel able to ask any of them. He continued talking about his prospects for a few more minutes whilst she sat silently listening, trying to take it all in.

'So, Mary Ann, will you agree to marry me?'

Mary Ann's throat was dry, and her voice came out as a squeak. 'Yes, I will marry you.'

She really had no choice other than to agree and could only hope he would keep his promise to be kind to her and that she could make him happy. He seemed like a gentleman. She hoped her first impressions were correct. At the back of her mind, despite her nervousness and lack of experience with men, excitement was beginning to bubble. She had always wanted an adventure, to do something with her life, and she did think she felt some attraction to him. But this was a lot to take in, a man she didn't even know, a far-off colony, leaving her family, probably never to see them again.

As soon as Richard took his leave, her parents came hurrying back into the room, followed by Susan, who was bubbling with excitement.

'Well, Mary Ann, what did you tell him?' asked Samuel.

'I agreed to marry him, as I really had no choice.' She still felt some anger towards her father for arranging all this without her consent and was not going to let him think she was pleased with his interference.

Susan let out a little squeal and hugged Mary Ann. 'That is so exciting. I think he is very handsome.' Mary Ann looked at her little sister with concern. In her excitement, Susan didn't seem to realise that Mary Ann would be leaving for good and that Susan would never see her again. She dreaded having to say goodbye to her baby sister.

'Look, I know you are angry, but I am sure you see the good that could come of this,' Samuel continued, looking at his daughter fondly.

'Yes, Mary Ann, you know we will be distraught when you leave us, but I really think this is a good idea,' added her mother. 'Now that we have met Richard, he seems a fine young man. And you can't argue that he has not done well for himself.'

Mary Ann softened as she heard her mother's words. 'I know, Mother. Perhaps this really is for the best. But I will miss you all dreadfully.'

Suddenly Susan seemed to understand what this meant. 'Are you really going away?' whispered Susan, tears brimming in her eyes.

'It certainly looks that way,' replied Mary Ann, trying to be positive for her adored baby sister. 'But you mustn't be sad. I will write to you to tell you all about my adventures.'

Chapter Fifteen

Mary Ann, Luton, 1857

Mary Ann woke on the morning of her wedding feeling a mixture of excitement and anxiety. Her heart fluttered like a caged bird at the thought of what was to come. It was October 13, 1857, the momentous day when she must give herself to Richard. She rose quickly and pulled on a warm coat against the cold, frosty air. It was early and no one had risen to light the fire yet. Her aunt and uncle's cottage was small, but they had made room for Mary Ann and her family to stay with them so that the wedding could take place in Luton, midway between the homes of her and Richard's families.

Mary Ann felt hemmed in, in need of some fresh air. She buttoned up her coat and ventured out onto the street, walking quickly towards the wooded area nearby. As she entered the canopy of the trees, she admired the beauty of the colourful autumn leaves still hanging on, although many had fallen and now carpeted the ground. She breathed in the crisp morning air deeply. *What had she agreed to? Could she really go through with this?* She sat on a fallen branch and thought about everything that had happened since the first day she had met Richard.

It was all such a rush. Richard was very keen to get back to his mining claim as soon as possible so there had been no time to really think about what she was committing to. Her dress, borrowed from a family friend, had been hastily altered and refashioned to make it her own, with some of her own handmade lace to adorn it. Then there were the arrangements to be made about where the wedding and reception would be held. Thanks to the generosity of her aunt and uncle, Luton had proven to be a good option.

The sun was peeking through the trees and casting a golden light on the path that led back to the house. She knew she should be getting back. As Mary Ann reached the house, she saw the windows were open and smoke was rising from the chimney, indicating that the household was awake and preparing for the wedding.

Her mind was still racing with thoughts of what life would be like after today. Before she could enter the house, her mother came out and beckoned Mary Ann to sit on the garden seat with her.

'It is rather chaotic inside. Perhaps we could have a moment alone. My darling, the day has arrived. How are you feeling?'

Mary Ann clasped her mother's hand. 'Oh Mother, I am so nervous. What if he turns out to be not such a good man as he seems?'

'Now, Mary Ann, you must not worry. I am sure, despite his past, he will be good to you.' But Mary Ann wondered if her mother truly believed what she said. Why had she again brought up Richard's convict past? She looked into her mother's eyes. Ann turned away, but not before Mary Ann saw the tears welling.

'I am sorry. I am sure it will be fine. Please don't worry about me.'

'I know, my darling. It is just that you will be so far from home. You must promise to write often. And if Richard continues to do well in his mine, perhaps you will be able to come home for a visit some day.'

By now, both mother and daughter had tears in their eyes. They realised that the likelihood of ever seeing each other again was slim. They sat holding hands for some time until the chilly morning forced them inside. It was time to start preparations for the wedding.

Once Mary Ann was dressed, her mother took out a velvet jewellery case. 'I have something for you.' She opened the case to reveal a beautiful string of glistening pearls. Mary Ann was stunned. She had no idea that her mother owned anything so beautiful.

'They were my Mother's,' said Ann, as she fastened the pearls around Mary Ann's neck. 'They will be something borrowed on your wedding day.'

'They are so special,' she exclaimed, hugging her mother tightly. 'I promise to take good care of them.' She fingered the pearls and let her hands run over the skirt of her dress, smoothing the soft folds. Her mind was racing. This was really happening. There was no backing out now. She was getting married and going to Australia. It was all so hard to believe. She gave herself a little shake and turned to her mother. 'I am ready. Shall we go?'

At the appointed time, a horse and cart decorated with white fabric and flowers pulled up at the front of the house. Samuel assisted Mary Ann, her mother and her sister, Susan, to climb into the cart and they moved off at a slow pace. Samuel, the boys and Mary Ann's aunt and uncle and cousins walked alongside. They made their way the short distance to the church. The family entered, leaving Mary Ann standing with her father, her hand clinging to his elbow. Samuel patted her hand and smiled at her.

'Mary Ann, you look so beautiful. Any man would be proud to be your husband. Are you ready?'

Mary Ann breathed in deeply. 'Yes Father,' she replied, attempting a smile as they entered the church. Mary Ann's eyes took a moment to adjust to the dimmer light provided by flickering candles and the soft glow of the sunlight filtering through the stained glass windows. Her family and a few close friends were seated at the front of the church on either side of the aisle. She raised her eyes to the grand arched ceiling at the front of the church and saw that Richard, dressed in a dark formal suit, was standing at the altar alongside the clergyman. The air was heavy with the scent of candles and fresh flowers.

Mary Ann saw Richard turn to look at her and hoped that she met with his approval. She lowered her eyes.

At the altar, the clergyman cleared his throat. 'Who gives this woman to be married?'

'I do,' replied Samuel. He took Mary Ann's hand and placed it into the hand of her husband-to-be, fixing him with a steely look. Mary Ann raised her head and looked directly at Richard. He gave her a nervous smile. *He is probably just as nervous as I am,* she thought. They both turned to face the clergyman.

The simple ceremony was soon over. As they exited the stone church, the sound of pealing bells echoed in Mary Ann's ears, a stark reminder of her new reality.

Richard, now her husband, whilst still somewhat of a stranger to her, took her hand gently. He led her towards his parents and siblings. Their names were familiar from Richard's occasional mentions, but they remained as unknown as the man she had just married.

Her heart pounded in her chest as Richard introduced each family member. She offered them timid smiles, battling the overwhelming sense of uncertainty that clouded her mind.

To her relief, they all returned her smile with genuine warmth. It was an encouraging sign that eased some of the tension knotting up inside her. She felt a glimmer of hope that maybe she could build a new life with Richard, despite the unconventional circumstances of their marriage.

The wedding party proceeded to the home of Mary Ann's aunt and uncle for the wedding breakfast. A small feast had been prepared. The table was piled high with cheese and bread, roast potatoes and turnips. They were fortunate that the annual slaughter of the fattened pig had taken place just days earlier, so there were delicious pork pies made from the fresh meat. There was plum pudding and jellies for dessert. Plenty of ale and cider was provided for all. The guests filled the small living area and spilled out onto the verandah, balancing their plates on their laps. Mary Ann moved around the room, speaking to the guests nervously. She merely nibbled at her food, her stomach churning with thoughts of what was to come.

After everyone had eaten their fill, the table and chairs were cleared from the living room and Samuel took out his fiddle. His brother joined in with his accordion and soon there was dancing and merriment. Richard and Mary Ann were still unsure of each other, but as the music began, Richard took her hand, and they led the guests in a merry jig.

Soon it was time for Richard's family to leave, as they had a long journey back to Amersham. Mary Ann stood by Richard as he farewelled his family. William gripped his son's hand firmly, knowing this would be the last time he would see him before the couple sailed for Australia.

'I am proud of you, son,' he said with a quiver in his voice. 'It has been so good to see you again and to know that you are well and have made your way in the colonies. Take care of Mary Ann and she will be good to you.' With that, he turned and strode over to the wagon, waiting to assist Matilda to climb in.

Matilda hugged her son tightly for a long moment but was not able to say more than a quick goodbye as tears ran down her face. 'I love you, my boy. Make sure you write often.' Then she turned to Mary Ann and gave her a quick hug as well. 'I am so pleased my son has found such a lovely wife.'

Mary Ann smiled at her new mother-in-law, feeling Matilda's warmth and realising that Richard's family had accepted her. 'Thank you. I will do my best to make your son happy.'

William helped his wife climb into the wagon, where the rest of the Evans family were waiting. He jumped up himself and flicked the reins so that the horses moved off. As they waved goodbye, Mary Ann wondered whether she and Richard would ever see her new family again.

***

Richard and Mary Ann spent their wedding night in lodgings in Luton. At the conclusion of the festivities, Richard took Mary Ann's hand and led her from her aunt's home.

'Come, Mary Ann. It is time we left. We have lots to do in the next few days.'

The time had come. Mary Ann cringed slightly but managed to smile, knowing that she had given herself to this man she hardly knew. Her stomach turned over and over as Richard helped her into the buggy to travel to their lodgings. She did not know what to expect. But she did not want to show her nervousness.

She had tried to talk to her mother, but it was such a sensitive subject that all her mother had told her was that she must accept Richard's advances and try to please him and that she must fulfil her obligations as a wife. She wanted very much to make Richard happy, hoping that if he was happy, he would treat her kindly.

Richard opened the door to their room and ushered Mary Ann in. He followed her and placed their bags on the bed. 'Well, did you enjoy your day?'

Mary Ann looked at him nervously as she opened her bag to find her nightgown. 'Very much, thank you. It was very special. I was pleased to be able to meet your family.'

'I think they liked you, not that there is any reason why they shouldn't.'

He came closer and took her face in his hands. Her body tensed as he brought his lips to hers. This was the first time he had kissed her. In fact, it was the first time any man had kissed her. She tried to relax and soon realised that it felt rather nice to be kissed in such a gentle way. An unfamiliar heat emanated through her body.

As he drew away from her, he smiled. 'I am sure you are feeling a little nervous. I will wait in the sitting room whilst you prepare for bed.'

'Thank you.' It was all she could say as he turned and left the room. She undressed hurriedly and pulled her nightdress over her head. Not knowing how long it would be before he came back, she quickly climbed into the four-poster bed and pulled the blankets up to her chin.

Richard returned to the room and got into bed beside her. She felt vulnerable and exposed. But she hoped this intimate time together might help to build a bond with Richard.

When she awoke the next morning, she felt the colour rise in her cheeks as she remembered what had passed between them the previous night. Her dominant emotion was one of relief, tinged with happiness. When she had looked to Richard for reassurance, he had been patient and understanding.

Now it was time for the next part of the long journey. They must make final preparations for the voyage to Australia.

The next day, Mary Ann and Richard, together with the rest of Mary Ann's family, bid goodbye to Luton and Mary Ann's aunt and uncle and travelled back to Bedford, where they would make the final arrangements for the return trip to Australia.

Over the next few days, Mary Ann packed a trunk with her belongings. She would not be taking her lace making tools with her and she knew she would miss the calming effect of working with the bobbins and the silken thread. But there would be no place for lace making where she was going. In her trunk she packed her clothes, which didn't take up a lot of space as for the last few years the family had not had the means to buy fabric for new dresses. But she did have some linen and a precious tea set that she had been gifted during more prosperous times. As she packed, Mary Ann's anxiety increased. Richard had been kind and gentle with her so far, whilst they were in the company of her family, but would she be able to please him when they were in the harsh mining town environment that Richard had told her so much about?

The day of their departure dawned. It was a freezing morning in late November, and there was a sprinkling of snow on the ground. Mary Ann was up early and dressed warmly in her travelling clothes, ready to leave.

Richard had packed her trunk into the hired horse and cart that would take them to the train station in Bletchley. Charles and Josiah were there to say goodbye, as were her younger siblings, John and Susan.

'Oh Mary Ann, I shall miss you so much,' said Susan as she hugged her sister tightly. She and her little sister had always been so close. Mary Ann didn't know how she could bear to leave her.

'And I shall miss you too, my darling little sister.' Mary Ann felt the tears pricking at the back of her eyes as she turned towards her mother. But she was determined not to cry. She knew this was hard on her family, too.

'Take care, my darling girl,' her mother whispered in her ear as she hugged her. As her mother released her, she pressed something into Mary Ann's hand. It was the velvet jewellery case containing her mother's precious pearls.

Mary Ann stared. 'No Mother, I couldn't. They are so special to you.'

'Yes, they are, but I want you to have them so that you never forget me.'

'I could never forget you.' She gave her mother another quick hug, fearing that her determination not to cry would be lost if she did not turn away now.

Finally, she turned to her father. She wondered how he was feeling, whether he regretted having taken money for the hand of his oldest daughter. But she knew that, in reality, it was probably for the best. She could have a good life with Richard, despite having to leave her family, probably forever.

Her father had no words for her, but she felt the strength of his hug and concentrated on the feeling. She took a deep breath, planting the feel and the scent of her father in her memory, hoping it would last forever.

Richard was waiting for her beside the cart. He helped her in and climbed up beside her. As the horses moved off, Mary Ann turned and waved. Tears glistened in her eyes as she realised she really was on her own now. For the first time in her life, she would be without the support of her family. She must now make a new family with the man at her side. As her family faded into the distance, she looked sideways at Richard. He was a powerful man who had been through so much. She prayed he would look after her.

Chapter Sixteen

Mary Ann, England to Australia, 1858

By the end of the long train ride from Bletchley to the port of Liverpool, Mary Ann was slumped in her seat, exhausted. The journey had drained her, leaving her feeling raw and weary. But this was only the beginning. She climbed aboard the cart that was to take them on the last part of their journey before they boarded the ship. As they approached Waterloo dock where the Oceanica was moored, Mary Ann got her first view of the ocean, having never travelled to the seaside before today. She stared in amazement at the bustling harbour, her senses alive with the newness and energy of the scenery. She smelt the tangy, salt laden air and the sounds of the harbour filled her ears. Waves lapped against the dock, seagulls called to each other overhead, and she could hear the creak of ship ropes in the distance. Ships of all shapes and sizes rocked at their moorings. There was a constant flow of movement as boats sailed in and out of the harbour.

'Here we are, Mary Ann, let me help you down.' Richard held out his muscular arms and Mary Ann jumped down from the cart. 'Now, just let me get your trunk unloaded.'

Too overwhelmed to respond, Mary Ann waited as he unloaded her trunk and his luggage and put them on the ground next to her. 'Stay here whilst I find out where we board the ship.'

She stood by the luggage and waited nervously until Richard returned with a trolley and took Mary Ann's trunk to the harbour crews so they could take it onboard the ship.

'Let's get something to eat.' Richard smiled kindly at her. Despite her fatigue and uncertainty, she managed to reply. 'That sounds good. I think I am hungry.' Although she wasn't sure how she felt, maybe the feeling in her stomach was more to do with anxiety than hunger.

They found a small inn close to the harbour. Mary Ann ate the bowl of steaming broth and fresh bread that was placed before her. She found she was indeed hungry after the long journey. Taking a sip of cider, she hoped it would calm her nerves. Although she felt better after eating, the crowds and the hurried activity that surrounded the busy port only added to her dismay.

The couple made their way back to the ship, which was now ready to board.

'This is the ship we will sail on, Mary Ann. Isn't she magnificent? The Black Ball company has an excellent reputation for safety and the Oceanica is a relatively new clipper. She should get us there in about three months.'

Now that they were standing there looking up at the ship they were about to sail on, the reality of it all actually began to dawn on Mary Ann. She was leaving her home and family, the people who meant everything to her, forever.

'How are you feeling?' asked Richard, his brow furrowed as he examined her. 'You look a little peaky.'

'I must admit to feeling quite anxious,' she replied. 'This is all so new to me. But I am sure I will be fine once we are settled in our quarters.' Mary Ann tried to give Richard a reassuring smile.

Before they boarded the ship, they had to undergo a medical examination to ensure they were well enough to travel. They were both in good health, so this was quickly accomplished.

They were to travel steerage. Mary Ann stared in horror as she took in the small space they would occupy below decks. 'Is this all the space we have? How will we manage?'

The wooden bunks, three rows high, were crowded in with only enough room for a single person to move between and she wondered how she could sleep with Richard in the single berth they had been allocated. The burlap covered mattress filled with straw did not look particularly clean.

Richard looked at her with concern. 'I know it seems cramped, but it's not as bad as it seems. We only need to be here to sleep. The rest of the time we can spend on deck. It is not like the voyage I had as a convict, where they locked us up below decks for days on end.'

Mary Ann realised Richard had been through far worse than this so he would not find the voyage such a hardship. But to her, it seemed unbelievable. She could not imagine having to sleep in the confined space below decks – actually, below the waterline -for three entire months. Just the smell of so many bodies sharing the small space was enough to turn her stomach.

Once they had found their quarters, they returned to the deck. The crew were scurrying around preparing for the departure, loading cargo and supplies.

'Now we just wait until the weather conditions and tide are right for the ship to leave the harbour,' said Richard. This did not quell Mary Ann's fears. She was already feeling slightly queasy as the ship rocked gently. She hated to think what it would be like when they were out on the open ocean.

It was two days before they eventually saw the pilot come on board with his compass and charts, and the ropes were untied from the dock and the ship was underway.

'Here we go,' said Richard. His grin was infectious, and Mary Ann smiled despite herself. She hoped the voyage would go as well as Richard seemed to think it would. The sails filled with air and the boat moved swiftly. Mary Ann gasped; it was such a strange sensation.

'We are finally on our way,' said Richard. 'I hope you will be happy in your new home.'

Mary Ann smiled again. Despite the cramped quarters where she would live for the next three months, she was starting to feel the excitement of it all now that they were moving and there was nothing more for her to do. The sense of adventure was overriding her nervousness now. She was also getting to know

Richard better and so far he had treated her with kindness and respect.

The ship sailed out of the harbour and they were on their way down the Mersey River. Mary Ann was on edge as she watched as the huge clipper manoeuvred its way between the large array of ships, barges and other smaller boats. She clung onto the ship's railing. 'The river is so crowded. How will the ship ever manage not to collide with one of these boats?'

'The pilot will take care of everything. The other boats are the least of his worries. There are other dangers lurking beneath.' Mary Ann could not hide the look of horror that settled on her face. Richard smiled. 'Don't worry, he is an experienced sailor who knows how to contend with the tides, shifting sandbanks and all the other vessels. He has done this many times. I can assure you that we will be safe.'

The pilot left the ship at the Point of Ayr, negotiating the rope ladder down into a small pilot boat. Now they had really begun the long and perilous journey to Australia.

Mary Ann was awed, and not a little frightened, the first morning she came up on deck and could see nothing but the horizon. There was no land in sight in any direction. Just the enormity of the sea and the sky. The boat had seemed gigantic when she had first seen it at the dock. But now it felt so small and she felt even smaller being tossed around on the vast seas. There might not have been land in sight, but there were other sights to astound Mary Ann.

'Look,' cried Richard one morning when they had ventured on deck. He pointed out a pod of dolphins frolicking beside the ship.

'What are they?' asked Mary Ann. She had never seen anything like these creatures.

'Dolphins. They love to play in the ship's wake.'

On another occasion, Mary Ann was stunned to see albatrosses flying overhead with their huge wing spans.

As the days rolled by, the air grew thick and heavy with heat as they crossed the equator. Suddenly, the wind seemed to hold its breath, leaving them becalmed. Mary Ann and Richard spent as much time as possible on deck, hoping to catch any whisper of breeze that dared to stir. Mary Ann waved her fan in front of her face. 'Is this usual?'

'Actually, yes, it happens on many voyages, I am told. It is called the doldrums. I have experienced it on both of my voyages to and from Australia. But be assured, it will end, and we will be underway again soon.'

Mary Ann did not share Richard's confidence as she squinted against the sun's glare, watching the lifeless sails hanging listlessly in the faint breeze. The heat was unrelenting, unlike anything she had ever felt before. The deck offered little respite from it, despite some canvas being strung up as makeshift shades.

Finding a spot under one such shade, Mary Ann removed her straw hat and began using it as a fan. The relief it provided was minimal, but still preferable to being trapped below decks where the heat was suffocating.

'Never thought I'd miss the cold of England,' she muttered to herself.

A soft chuckle came from nearby. Another passenger, Mrs Higgins, sitting close by on a deck chair and also trying to escape the worst of the heat, smiled sympathetically at Mary Ann.

'Indeed,' she responded with a nod. 'This heat is merciless.'

Mary Ann glanced at the older woman and returned her smile weakly. 'I suppose this is just one of many new experiences waiting for me in my new life.'

Mrs Higgins patted her hand comfortingly and replied with warmth in her eyes, 'Yes dear, but remember, not all new experiences are hardships.'

It was nearly two weeks before the wind blew again, and the ship continued on its path towards the Cape of Good Hope. Mary Ann's heart sank as the seas became mountainous. She and Richard were relieved when the ship anchored at Cape Town to take on supplies and they could go ashore to get some respite from the heaving decks. Stepping onto land, they marvelled at the fresh fruits and vegetables, knowing it would stave off scurvy for their long journey ahead. As they set sail once more, they felt a glimmer of hope, relieved that they had maintained good health thus far, unlike some of the other passengers. Perhaps they could remain that way until they reached their destination.

But there was worse to come. As the ship sailed into the Southern Ocean, the weather became rougher and the temperature dropped markedly. A tremendous storm hit the ship. Mary Ann was terrified as the gigantic waves washed over the ship and the crew scrambled to batten down the hatches, trapping the steerage passengers below decks. Despite the hatches being closed, water still leaked through and although the bilges worked overtime, the water was never less than ankle deep.

Mary Ann and Richard sat on their narrow bunk, wet and freezing. Richard held the shivering Mary Ann as they bounced about on the heaving ship. Mary Ann was feeling queasy, which was not helped by the stench of vomit that filled the suffocating air.

'I am so afraid, Richard, we might all be drowned.'

'I am sure the captain and crew have been through storms such as this many times before and probably worse. They will steer the ship to safety.' Mary Ann moved closer to get the most possible warmth from Richard's body. 'I do hope you are right.'

When the storm abated and Mary Ann was able to come on deck, she stared in wonder at the night skies as the clouds finally cleared. She was used to the skies in the northern hemisphere, but now she was seeing a whole new range of constellations. Richard pointed to the south.

'Look, can you see those five bright stars that look like a cross?'

'Yes, I think so.'

'That is the Southern Cross.'

It was a momentous day when eventually they sighted the Australian shore.

'Land Ahoy,' called the sailor perched in the crow's nest, high above the deck.

Richard's face was alight with pleasure and excitement. 'The west coast of Australia. Can you see it?'

Mary Ann had to squint, but eventually she could see what she hoped was land. As the ship sailed closer, the outlines of the brilliant white sandy beaches and the vegetation became clearer. It certainly was a wonderful sight to see.

'The beaches are so white, not like in England,' said Mary Ann.

'You will soon see that many things are different and, in many ways, better than in England.'

But there were still days of treacherous sailing as they continued through the rough seas along the south coast of Australia. Eventually they sailed into Bass Straight.

Richard gave Mary Ann a concerned look. 'I don't want to alarm you, but you should be prepared. This last bit of the voyage can be extremely rough. Even though we are now close to our destination, the waves and currents are very strong in this thin strip of water between Victoria and Tasmania.' Soon Mary Ann found out how right he was as the ship was battered yet again by high winds. Ominous rock outcrops lined the coast and tales of shipwrecks were told amongst the passengers. Lighthouses shone their bright beacons to assist the ships to navigate away from the worst rocky hazards. Richard had also apparently been right about the experience of the captain because the ship negotiated this last dangerous leg of their journey to sail through the rip and into the relative calm of Port Phillip Bay.

Chapter Seventeen

Mary Ann, Victoria, 1858

T he moment had finally arrived when Mary Ann would set foot on land in Australia. As their ship made its final approach towards the harbour on March 11, 1858, her feelings tripped over each other as she tried to make sense of all that had happened. So many conflicting thoughts clashed in her mind. She felt a sense of adventure, but also of trepidation, homesickness and worry that she might not prove up to the task of being a good wife to Richard. The sky seemed so big, so far away, a distant and intimidating vastness that swallowed up everything beneath it. She looked out over the railings as the harbour slowly came into focus, buildings and docks starting to take shape on the horizon. Beside her, Richard's face lit up with a wide smile.

'We are home. Can you believe it?' he said, wrapping one arm around her waist.

Mary Ann tried to mirror his enthusiasm but found herself lost for words. Her heart pounded heavily in her chest as a mix of emotions washed over her; fear, excitement, apprehension and a tiny flicker of hope that struggled to shine through. She simply nodded and managed to give Richard a small smile in return. Her hands tightened on the worn wood of the railing as she silently braced herself for this new beginning, in a world so vastly different from anything she had ever known before.

Once the ship docked and the crew lashed the huge ropes to the jetty, the surgeon general was able to report that there had been no serious outbreaks of contagious diseases on board the ship. There was no need to quarantine, so it was not long before disembarkation could take place. The gangplank was lowered, and the passengers began their descent onto the jetty.

'Mind your step, Missus,' said one of the crew as Mary Ann cautiously moved between the gang plank and solid ground. She felt unsteady, her sea legs needing to adjust to the solidness of the ground after so long moving in time with the rocking and rolling of the Oceanica.

She stumbled but thankfully, Richard was there to take her arm. 'I am sorry.'

'Don't worry, that won't last long,' he said, trying to reassure her.

But she did not feel reassured. Apart from her shaking legs, the heat that hit her in the face, as the sea breeze evaporated now that they were on dry land, was something she could never have imagined.

The crowd jostled around them as they waited for their baggage to be unloaded. Richard hired one of the carriers that lined the wharf to transport them to an inn where they would spend the night before heading back to Castlemaine. Whilst Mary Ann was used to the busyness of the market town of Bedford, she was not prepared for the burgeoning city of Melbourne. The stench of the open drains and horse manure overtook her senses as soon as they cleared the wharf. Melbourne had boomed since the gold rush and services had not kept up. As their cart moved through the crowded streets, Richard pointed out the broomies, employed by the Melbourne city council to sweep up the horse manure. Unfortunately, their efforts did little to lessen the odour. Mary Ann swatted at the flies that continually landed on her face, as persistent as her feelings of unease.

Eventually they arrived at an inn. They entered the bar where the female proprietor served tankards of ale to rowdy patrons. Seeing Richard and Mary Ann enter, the proprietor left off serving and came over to greet them.

'How can I help you?' Her broad smile disclosed several gaps in her teeth.

'We would like a room for the night,' replied Richard, smiling at his wife. 'My wife is quite overcome by the heat, so perhaps we could have some water to bathe. Then we will want something to eat.'

'Right you are, sir. If you will follow me.' The proprietor led them up a narrow flight of stairs. She showed them to what appeared to be a clean and comfortable room with a double bed and washstand with a dish and jug.

'Someone will be up directly with water.' She left them, closing the door behind her. As soon as the door had closed, Mary Ann slumped onto the edge of the bed.

'Oh Richard, it is so hot. I was close to fainting.' Richard gave her a look of concern, making her regret her complaints.

'I know, my dear, it is quite a shock when you first arrive here. But you will get used to it.' Not long after, there was a knock at the door and a young lad appeared with a bucket of water.

'I will leave you to freshen up, and I will see about getting us something to eat.'

As Richard left the room, Mary Ann leaned forward resting her head in her hands. *What have I done? How will I ever get used to this place?* Getting slowly to her feet, she poured the cold water into the porcelain dish and splashed her face. The cold water felt so good and despite her anxiety, she felt slightly revived by the time Richard returned.

'You look refreshed, Mary Ann. Are you ready to eat?'

The couple made their way back down the stairs and sat down to the meal that had been prepared for them.

'We leave for Castlemaine tomorrow,' Richard stated with pride in his voice. 'I have purchased a horse and cart, so we will travel in style.'

Mary Ann looked at Richard and attempted a smile. *He has a strange idea of travelling in style*, she thought, not looking forward to the final part of the trip, which she knew would take several days. It was going to take her some time to get used to the hot, dry weather and the thought of sitting in the sun in an open cart was daunting.

After a fitful sleep with no reprieve from the heat, Mary Ann arose and prepared for the final leg of their journey. Richard was buoyant but she could not help feeling apprehensive, thinking about what would be in store for her when they arrived at the goldfields. Her trunk, with everything she owned carefully tucked away within its wooden confines, was piled into the cart along with supplies that Richard had purchased.

Although Mary Ann wore a broad brimmed straw hat to protect her from the relentless rays of the autumn sun, she soon felt the milky skin of her face turning pink and her lips felt parched and dry.

The roads they traversed were also dry and deeply rutted from the countless trips taken on them previously by other travellers to the goldfields. Mary Ann held on tightly as each bump in the road sent a jolt through the cart, causing their belongings to rattle ominously. Dust clouds billowed up from beneath the wheels, covering everything in a fine layer of earthy grit. Mary Ann's throat was constantly dry. She felt as though she was eating dirt.

After three long days of travelling and sleeping under the stars, they finally arrived at the Mount Alexander diggings.

'Here we are, Mary Ann,' said Richard triumphantly. Mary Ann stared in amazement. It was nothing like she had imagined. As they approached Richard's claim, she could see the frown creasing his brow.

'What is it?' Mary Ann was looking for some sort of cottage. *Where were they to live?* All she could see were mounds of dirt surrounding holes in the ground. Everywhere men were work-ing feverishly and the only sign of anything resembling a home were makeshift canvas dwellings. Richard scowled.

'Claim jumpers.' His voice simmered with barely contained anger. 'It looks like men have been working my claim whilst I have been away. Stealing my gold.'

But there were more immediate problems on Mary Ann's mind.

'Where will we be living?' she asked.

'No need to worry about that. We will soon have a comfort-able tent set up for the time being until we can build something more substantial.'

'A tent? You didn't tell me we would have to live in a tent.' Mary Ann was becoming more alarmed by the moment.

Suddenly a man came running up from the creek. He looked at Mary Ann with interest and, feeling shy, she lowered her gaze.

'Walter, it's good to see you, old friend,' said Richard.

The two men shook hands, but Walter looked worried. 'I'm glad you're back. I'm afraid I haven't been able to protect your claim.'

Mary Ann could see that Richard was trying to control his anger.

'I'm sure you did what you could. I just hope there is still some gold left.' Walter was gazing at Mary Ann. 'Oh sorry, this is my wife, Mary Ann. Mary Ann, this is my friend and partner, Walter.'

'Pleased to meet you, Mary Ann. It's a tough life out here but there are other women, so you will soon find your way.' Mary Ann wondered how that could ever happen.

Over the next few weeks, Mary Ann was to discover how hard her life would be. Richard rigged up a makeshift canvas dwelling, propped up by timber that he cut from the surrounding bush. He built a low bed for them. Mary Ann dug through her trunk to find her needle and thread to fashion a mattress from hessian and stuffed it with dried leaves, making it up with threadbare blankets.

Mary Ann's mother had taught her to cook, but she felt totally inept when confronted with the idea of cooking outdoors over an open fire. Each night, Mary Ann slumped into the makeshift bed, totally exhausted from the rigours of her new life. She thought wistfully of her precious tea set still packed in her trunk, wrapped in some of her finer linen. Her life back in England had been hard, but at least they'd had a solid roof over their heads. She hid bitter tears from Richard as he snored beside her in those first few weeks.

It wasn't long before the consequences of Richard having left his claim for the voyage to England became clear. Night was falling and Richard was stoking the fire, ready for Mary Ann to cook the evening meal. Richard stood up and stretched his back.

'Those claim jumpers stole all the gold. We are barely getting enough to buy food, let alone the other supplies we need to keep going.'

'What are we to do?' asked Mary Ann as she chopped up a small piece of mutton that she would cook in a stew with some vegetables. Richard had rigged up a canvas covering for the stone fireplace, so at least she was shielded from the drizzling rain that was falling now.

'I just don't know. But we will have to come up with another solution soon.'

Alluvial gold was no longer being found in any quantities. Their situation was becoming dire. Richard's savings had dwindled due, in part, to the cost of the trip back to England. He needed to come up with another plan.

Mary Ann was mending a pair of Richard's threadbare breeches when he returned from a trip into Castlemaine. She was surprised to see he had a bounce in his step and was grinning broadly. He began speaking in an excited rush.

'Mary Ann, I have news. I visited Fanny Finch's establishment whilst I was in town. She told me...'

'Please slow down, Richard. Who is Fanny Finch?'

'She runs a restaurant in town. We have been friends for a long time, and she has often given me good advice.' Richard looked sheepish, making Mary Ann wonder if there was more to the story of Fanny Finch. But Richard was racing on.

'I had a drink with a bloke whilst I was there. He told me there has been a new strike at Moonlight Flats. They are digging shafts out there and some are having a good amount of luck. I think that is where we should go. We can get a piece of land and I can build you a proper home.'

Mary Ann sighed. 'If that is what you think best. We are not doing very well here, so surely it can't be any worse.' But she wondered if things really could be worse. Weariness spread through her whole body, thinking about the prospect of packing up and starting all over again. *But what choice did she have?*

'That's my girl. I know this will prove to be a good move.'

Together they packed up their belongings and moved further away from the major rush and settled on a piece of land to the north of Moonlight Flats. Then the hard work really began.

Richard teamed up with a group of miners, including his good friend Walter Allen, and they began digging deep shafts to access the quartz gold underground. The group had set up a small steam powered crushing mill. Each day, Mary Ann helped Richard, winding the windlass to bring heavy buckets of rock to the surface. Then they carried their rock to the crushing mill to reveal the gold within. Richard was buoyant.

'I knew this would be a good move for us, Mary Ann,' he said as they sat waiting for the billy to boil during a break from their work. 'We are starting to get back on our feet again. And you have been such a help. I could not have done it without you.'

Mary Ann smiled, masking the exhaustion she was feeling. She was genuinely pleased that Richard appreciated her hard work. She certainly felt that after the initial few weeks, she had become a lot stronger and was more used to the backbreaking work. 'I am glad to be able to help.' His praise was welcome.

In the months that they had been working closely together, she had developed a strong admiration for her husband's tenacity. Their shared struggles had strengthened the bond between them, causing her to feel much closer to him. He was a good man with a kind heart and despite their harsh life, her love for him was growing. But each night as she lay in her bed, exhausted, every muscle in her body aching, she wondered if this was to be her life forever.

It was not easy extracting the rock from the deep shafts and although the group made a living from the quartz, it was certainly not a fortune. It was very dangerous and there had already been a small cave in. Mary Ann had been at her wit's end until she knew Richard was safe. Fortunately, no one had been hurt, but they both knew that more work would need to be done shoring up the shafts and tunnels as the mine went deeper and extended further.

Mary Ann was glad that Richard had such a close friendship with Walter. He was hardworking and good company. He was single, so often Richard would invite him to their tent for a meal and they would sit by the campfire and share a drink of rum. Mary Ann liked him too, so she was happy to share her hearty stews with him.

One evening, not long after the cave in, the two men sat by the fire as Mary Ann prepared the meal.

'I am very grateful for the work you have put in shoring up the tunnels,' said Richard. Walter looked pleased. 'It was a good idea to use that extra timber to make them safer.'

Mary Ann served up the meal and the three ate in companionable silence. When they had finished their meal, Richard poured all three a generous measure of rum. Walter raised his tin cup. 'To good friends and better fortune.'

'Hear, hear,' replied Richard, clinking his cup against Walter's. Mary Ann smiled.

Despite the exhaustion and the dangerous work that Richard did every day, Mary Ann was becoming accustomed to life on the goldfields. Although she still missed her family dreadfully, she had to admit that most of the time she was happy. Richard was working hard and, except for a few creature comforts that would have made life easier, they really had everything that they needed.

One afternoon, Mary Ann was hanging the laundry outside the tent, humming a song from her childhood. She had not seen Richard returning from the mine.

'It's good to hear you singing,' he said, putting his arms around her from behind.

'I didn't realise I was. I suppose I was thinking of home,' she said, turning to face him and looking deep into his eyes.

'You don't regret coming here with me, do you?'

'No, I really don't. Of course I miss my family, but it feels right being here with you and building our life together.' She could see the love in Richard's eyes as she leaned into his embrace.

Chapter Eighteen

Richard, Moonlight Flats, 1859

'We start today, Mary Ann,' said the ever-optimistic Richard.

Mary Ann sighed. 'What are we starting?'

Richard looked at her with concern. She looked so weary. The past year seemed to have drained every shred of her energy. He felt guilt stirring, not for the first time. Was she working too hard? But he knew that if they were to continue to live in this harsh environment, then they must have a more permanent home.

'I am going to build you a solid stone home. Winter is approaching. I don't want you to have to go through another winter like the last one. Look around you at all these rocks. They will make perfect building material and will insulate us against the cold.'

'But what about the mine?' asked Mary Ann.

'Walter has agreed to keep working the claim until we have the house built. Of course, I will need to help out from time to time. But I think I can take a few days here and there to build our home.'

Richard was trying to be positive, but he remembered only too well when they had first arrived, the effort it had taken to grub the stones out of the ground so that they could level out a smooth earthen floor for their tent. Now the work would begin in earnest. He hoped he was not asking too much of his wife. No doubt, she had been a dependable and fearless partner through all their trials so far. And she had grown physically stronger. But building the house would be a huge undertaking. He pushed his doubts aside.

'We will start by preparing some bark for the roof. It will take some time to flatten and dry. We should do that first, so it is ready when the walls are built.'

Over the course of the next few days, Richard proceeded to cut down two of the huge gums that were standing in the way of where he intended to build the house. But nothing would be wasted. Any timber they did not use in the building of the house would be used for firewood. Once the trees were cut down, the stumps were piled high with dry timber and set alight so that the remains of the gigantic trees would be burnt. The holes that were left would be filled with dirt. Whilst the stumps were burning, Richard took his axe and made cuts around the trunks of the trees that he had cut down, then up the length of the trunk. He prised the bark off and then, with Mary Ann's help, he dragged them to the creek so the bark could be soaked until it was flexible enough to be flattened and spread in the sun to dry. Once the bark was removed, he cut the trunk to a size that could be split for timber for the doors, shelves and anything else they might require. He then sawed the remaining branches into manageable sizes so the fallen timber could be moved away from the site of the house. Mary Ann stacked the remaining wood in piles to dry for firewood whilst Richard cut some stout branches to make a frame for the roof.

'Tomorrow we will get on to the rocks,' said Richard as he laid down his axe and surveyed his handiwork proudly. A tremendous sense of satisfaction washed over him. All the timber components were ready and there was a large space cleared for their new home. He smiled at Mary Ann as she wiped her brow and straightened her back. 'It's coming along well. Maybe we will be finished before winter sets in.'

'You can be sure of that, my girl. You will have a warm comfortable home before you know it.' Grabbing Mary Ann, he lifted her off the ground and swung her around. Richard understood how hard this work was for Mary Ann, so he was glad when she began to laugh happily. He felt his heart surge, feeling renewed admiration and love for her.

Using a mattock and a rock bar, they pried the rocks from the ground. Although the rocks appeared to be lying everywhere, a certain amount of each rock was buried in the soil. Some of them had to be broken up with a pickaxe into more manageable sizes. After gathering a large pile of rocks, Richard began arranging them into a rectangle, beginning to form the outer wall of the house. When he completed the first row, he stood up to stretch his aching back and drew his arm across his brow.

'Two rooms, I think. One for a fireplace and a kitchen table and one for a bedroom. What do you think?'

'That sounds wonderful.'

Richard continued to place the rocks with care, choosing the best shapes to fit into one another to build a sturdy stone wall. Once they had a few rows in place, he turned to Mary Ann. 'Now we will need some mortar to fill the gaps.'

Richard surveyed the ground nearby and found some clay-based soil. Mary Ann fetched water from the creek, and soon they had a slurry of mud mixed in the wheelbarrow. Mary Ann added dried grass, horsehair and some lime. Once the mixture was the right consistency, she started slapping the mud on the stone walls, forcing it into the gaps, as Richard continued to build them. Mary Ann fetched bucket after bucket of water from the creek whilst Richard dug up more of the hard clay soil.

At the end of another long hard day, they stood surveying their hard work. Richard wrapped his arm around Mary Ann. 'We are making good progress.' He took both of Mary Ann's sore chaffed hands between his own. 'I know it is hard work, but I promise it will be worth it.'

Mary Ann beamed at her husband and reached up to plant a kiss on his cheek. 'I can see our home taking shape,' she said. 'I am so happy.'

It was Richard's turn to smile. Despite the exhaustion she must be feeling, she seemed genuinely happy. It was the first time he had seen her so animated since they had arrived at the goldfields. It pleased him to think that he would be able to provide her with a real home by winter.

Within a few weeks, the walls of their new home were standing tall, with gaps left for two windows – one in each room – and a door. A stone chimney stood at one end. Richard and Mary Ann collectively assessed the results of their efforts. Richard could not contain his pride in what he had achieved with the help of his strong, resilient wife. He was so proud of her.

'I can't believe I will soon be able to cook indoors,' said Mary Ann. Richard knew how much Mary Ann was looking forward to some of the comforts the home would bring.

The next step was the roof. The bark had dried straight and strong. Richard erected the framework from the branches he had prepared and then proceeded to tie the bark onto the frame with wire. Then there was only the door and windows to finish. Richard built the door from the timber he had cut and fashioned some shelves inside the house. They would cover the windows with hessian for the time being until the glass they had ordered arrived.

The day finally arrived when it was ready for them to move in.

'What do you think, Mary Ann?' Richard stood with his hands on his hips, his face radiant. He lifted Mary Ann and carried her laughing through the front door.

There was a fire burning in the fireplace with a kettle steaming on the hook above. A partition of wattle branches daubed with mud separated the main room from the small bedroom where their newly made bed stood. Their new home was almost complete and all the effort had been worth it.

'It really is wonderful,' she said, giving Richard a triumphant look. That evening, Richard watched on as she took her precious tea set from its nest in her trunk. Choosing a beautifully embroidered runner, she carefully arranged the delicate china on the shelf that Richard had built specifically for this purpose. It might be a rough stone house with a bark roof and an earthen floor, but it felt like home.

During the first winter of living in their new home, they were warm and cosy. The bark roof smelt mouldy when it rained, but if that was all they had to complain about, they were doing well.

Richard was overjoyed when he discovered a good deposit of slate on the land covered by his mining lease. Before long, they had chosen some of the squarest pieces of slate and had laid them on the earthen floor.

Richard stood back looking at the new floor. 'That should make life easier,' he said proudly.

Mary Ann finished sweeping and leant on her broom. 'I must say it will be wonderful not to have billowing clouds of dust every time I sweep. And now there won't be mud at the front door each time it rains.'

The glass for the windows had been fitted and they removed the hessian coverings during the day so that the sun could warm the home on the cold winter days.

Later that evening, they sat at the table finishing their meal. Mary Ann smiled at Richard nervously. He thought she seemed subdued during the meal and wondered what was on her mind. But he said nothing and now she spoke tentatively.

'Richard, I have news. I think I am going to have a baby.'

Richard could not hide his delight. He had longed for the day when he would have children, and now it seemed that it might be a reality.

'Are you sure, Mary Ann?'

'I wanted to wait until the cottage was finished before I told you. I am not exactly sure. This is not something I am very knowledgeable about, but I think I must be.'

'We will go into Castlemaine tomorrow to see a doctor.' He rose from his chair and pulled Mary Ann up to hug her. 'I am so pleased. You have made me immensely happy.' He looked at her radiant face as she glowed with happiness. He deposited her back on the floor and kissed her deeply and tenderly. His emotions stirred as he felt her return the kiss with equal passion. He wondered if he could ever feel any happier.

Soon the doctor confirmed Mary Ann's confinement. The baby would be born in the next few months. Richard was grateful that they would have a warm comfortable home in which to bring their child into the world.

Chapter Nineteen

Mary Ann, Moonlight Flats, 1859

As well as learning about her impending motherhood, Mary Ann soon discovered more about her husband's infamous friend Fanny Finch. Richard was taking her to dinner at Fanny's restaurant.

'Hello, Richard,' said Fanny as the couple entered her restaurant. 'It is good to see you.' Fanny smiled fondly at Richard. 'And this must be your lovely wife.'

'Fanny, I would like to introduce you to my wife, Mary Ann.'

'Hello Mary Ann, it is good to finally meet you. I have heard a lot about you.'

Mary Ann's brow furrowed. Surely Richard was not sharing his thoughts with this woman. But realising she might appear rude, Mary Ann smiled brightly at this woman, who seemed to know so much about her. 'Hello Mrs Finch, I am pleased to meet you too.'

'Well, I will leave you to enjoy your meal.' As she left, Mary Ann glanced at Richard. His eyes were alight as they followed Fanny into the kitchen. The food caught in Mary Ann's throat.

What was the relationship that Fanny and Richard shared? They certainly seemed close.

As they rode home in the cart across the hills back to Moonlight Flats, she sat upright and silent. Richard turned to her. 'Is something wrong Mary Ann? You have been very quiet.'

She stared blankly ahead, not sure how to broach the subject. 'Richard, please tell me more about Fanny. You seem to know her very well.' Even in the dim light of dusk, Mary Ann could see the colour rise in Richard's face.

'Fanny was very good to me when I first arrived in Castlemaine. She was friendly and offered me advice on occasions. You know it was she who convinced me to write to ask you to be my wife.' This news did nothing to allay Mary Ann's concern and confusion. Her jaw clenched as she tried to contain her rising anger.

'Surely you did not discuss such personal matters with the owner of a restaurant?'

'She is not just the owner of a restaurant, Mary Ann. She is a friend.' Richard was indignant as he tried to explain.

'When I first came to Mt Alexander, she was running a sly grog shop in a tent on Forest Creek,' Richard continued, obviously feeling that he needed to give more details. 'Of course, the traps were always on the lookout for unlicensed premises. They fined her many times and went so far as to burn her tent and belongings to the ground twice. But she was so popular with the miners that they always set her up with a new tent, so she was able to carry on with her business. Even when she moved into her current premises in Castlemaine, she still could not escape the harassment. Edmond Jackson, who owns the hotel next door to her restaurant, is always trying to find ways to put her out of business. She was fined an exorbitant amount of money and is now in debt. Yet she is so kind to her patrons and often allows them to set up an account. She says that if everyone paid just part of the money they owed her, she would be able to pay the fine without any problems. Most of the miners support her although not all can pay their bills. I admit to having owed her money in the past, although not now. One fellow even wrote a letter to the editor of the Argus in support of her. She is very much admired. Do you know she even cast a vote in the municipal elections in 1856? Apparently, as a ratepayer, she was entitled to. But, of course, the authorities disallowed her vote, and they threw it out.'

Mary Ann listened in silence as Richard extolled the virtues of his friend. But doubts plagued her and she could not help but wonder how close Fanny and Richard had been before she married him. She held tightly to the rail of the buggy, her knuckles whitening as she struggled to suppress her resentment.

Thoughts of Fanny stayed with Mary Ann over the next few days. Was she just being silly and overly touchy? If she was honest, her mood had been a bit up and down during her pregnancy. She needed to talk to another woman. Having recently met her widowed neighbour, Mrs Fletcher, who lived in a small cottage not that far from their home, she decided to pay her a visit. Mary Ann liked the older woman and had already confided some of her worries about the upcoming birth.

Despite her advancing pregnancy, Mary Ann enjoyed the quiet ten-minute walk to visit her neighbour. As she knocked at the sturdy door of the slab hut, she wondered how Mrs Fletcher had lost her husband. She had not known her for very long, so she didn't know her story, but her cottage was quite substantial with glass in the windows and a solid bark roof. Mrs Fletcher appeared at the door in response to Mary Ann's knock.

'Hello Mary Ann, this is a pleasant surprise. Won't you come in?'

Mary Ann entered the tidy room. It was sparsely but comfortably furnished with a small table and chairs and two easy chairs by the fireplace. There was a framed portrait of a handsome young man on the wall and shelves that held a range of nicknacks and crockery. A large pot hung over the open fireplace and other cooking utensils hung around the hearth.

'Mrs Fletcher, I hope you don't mind me dropping in unannounced.'

'Not at all. Please sit down. The kettle is boiled. I will make some tea.' Mary Ann sat in the easy chair as directed and watched as Mrs Fletcher poured boiling water into the teapot. She put out two delicate china cups and saucers and a plate of plum cake on a tray before setting them on a little table between the two chairs and sitting herself down in the other easy chair.

'How is everything going?' asked Mrs Fletcher. 'That baby looks like he will be on his way soon. I expect you will be wanting a boy?'

'Yes, certainly Richard would like a boy. You know what men are like about having an heir.'

Mrs Fletcher smiled sadly. 'My husband and I were never blessed with children. He was gone too soon.'

'I am sorry. I didn't mean to bring up sad memories.' Mary Ann picked up her cup and took a sip to cover her discomfort.

'Don't mind me. I am being a sentimental old fool. My husband was a kind man and I loved him very much. But he has been gone for years now. Although I still find it hard when I think about how he died.'

Mary Ann sat patiently, waiting for the older woman to continue. She seemed deep in thought and Mary Ann did not want to interrupt.

'We were in Bendigo at the time. It still pains me to remember that day. There was a mining accident. My Bert and another man were trapped underground and by the time the other miners got to them, they were both gone. I was lucky that the mine owner was a good man and he paid out a good sum of money to compensate for my loss. This allowed me to relocate here and start a new life. But you never forget.'

Mary Ann felt her heart would break. Such a sad story. She couldn't help but think how she would feel if her Richard met with a similar fate. Mining was such a dangerous occupation.

Mrs Fletcher gave herself a small shake and smiled at Mary Ann. 'But that, as I said, was many years ago.' She paused for a moment as though weighing her words. 'I hope you don't think it forward of me, but I know you are a bit isolated out here. Do you have someone to attend the birth with you?'

'I expect the doctor will come,' replied Mary Ann.

'Yes, I would hope so, but he may not be available, you know.'

Mary Ann put her cup back on the saucer with a clatter. 'Oh really? It had not occurred to me that a doctor would not be present. I feel quite anxious about the birth really.'

'Unfortunately, we only have the one doctor and with so many people living in these parts now, he is a very busy man.'

Mary Ann's hand shook as she tried to finish her tea. 'What am I to do if he is unable to come? I have no idea what to expect.'

'Well, you know, despite not having any children of my own, I have attended a few births. I could be there to help, if you like?'

'Oh, would you? That is so kind. I really could use the support of another woman.'

'How is that young man of yours treating you anyway? I hope he hasn't got you working too hard.'

'No, I haven't been needed at the mine of late.' This seemed like an excellent opportunity to bring up her concerns about Fanny. 'I must admit to being a little concerned about his female friendships. Do you know Fanny Finch?'

'Oh, of course, everyone knows of Fanny. She's quite a woman. Why are you worried about her though?'

Mary Ann squirmed in her chair, wondering if she really should be talking about such an intimate topic with Mrs Fletcher. 'It's just that he seems to be very enamored of her. He visits her restaurant every time he goes into town.'

'Well, I wouldn't be too concerned. From what I know of Fanny, she is a woman who knows her own mind. And I don't think she would be interested in the likes of your Richard, or any other man, for that matter. I believe she is happy being able to run her own life without the help of a man.'

It was soon time for Mary Ann to get back to prepare dinner for Richard. She left Mrs Fletcher's company feeling somewhat reassured about Richard's relationship with Fanny. But more importantly, she had someone she could call on to help with the birth of her baby.

Chapter Twenty

Mary Ann, Moonlight Flats, 1859

Mary Ann woke to a sharp pain. She lay there cradling her stomach. Was the baby finally ready to come? She was so scared, having no idea of how to give birth to a baby. Her mother had told her little except that she must accept the pain and that she would feel great joy when the baby finally arrived. Sometime later, Richard woke beside her.

'I think the baby is coming,' she said.

Richard looked at her in astonishment. 'Are you sure?'

'I really don't know, but I think so.'

'I will go and get Fanny to help you. She will know what to do.'

Mary Ann felt a stab of annoyance. Despite Mrs Fletcher's assurances, she had become quite jealous of Richard's close relationship with Fanny Finch. He talked of her constantly every time he returned from a trip into Castlemaine. She was sure that he had a special regard for her, even though he tried to reassure her when she voiced her doubts. She was not sure why she had such strong feelings, but the jealousy always bubbling beneath the surface made her restless and irritable when she thought of Fanny. In any case, she knew she needed the help of a strong woman to get through this. The pain was becoming intense, with contractions coming every few moments now. She smothered the feeling of jealousy twisting in her chest.

'That is very thoughtful of you. But I have asked Mrs Fletcher to help me with the birth. She is much closer, after all. Could you please go and ask her if she can come?'

Richard looked concerned. 'You arranged this without consulting me?'

Mary Ann did not want to argue now. Richard was obviously feeling put out that she didn't think Fanny an appropriate person to attend the birth of his child. She was not going to bow to his wishes this time. She drew a deep breath and squared her shoulders.

'She offered, Richard. She knew that there was no one else who I could rely on.' Mary Ann held her breath as another pain gripped her and Richard was jolted into action. He jumped out of bed and pulled on his breeches and a shirt.

'Very well, I will go to her immediately.'

It wasn't long before he returned with Mrs Fletcher.

'Well, my girl. Your time has come,' she said, glancing at Richard, who had followed her into the bedroom.

'Get some water boiling, Richard, and leave the rest to me.'

Mary Ann looked at Mrs Fletcher, smiling thankfully. 'Thank you for coming, Mrs Fletcher. I don't know what to do.'

'Don't you worry about that. The baby does and will come of its own accord when it is ready.' Another contraction ripped through Mary Ann and she cried out through gritted teeth.

'It won't be long now,' said Mrs Fletcher encouragingly.

Through the long day Mary Ann laboured until, as the sun was setting, decorating the sky with a blaze of red and orange, an angry squall sounded. The baby girl took her first breath.

Mrs Fletcher wrapped her in a blanket and placed the tiny bundle into Mary Ann's arms. Mary Ann looked at her newborn with delight, but also with growing fear. How could she look after such a tiny human? This tiny scrap of a thing would be totally reliant on her. Mrs Fletcher fussed around, making Mary Ann comfortable and tidying away all signs of the birth.

'Shall I bring Richard in now?' she asked.

'Oh yes please, he will have been pacing. He will want to see his daughter.'

Richard strode into the room and beamed at Mary Ann. He moved slowly towards the bed, seemingly anxious as to what he would see.

'Richard, we have a daughter,' said Mary Ann, unable to contain her happiness. Richard stared down at the baby and gave his wife a quick kiss. He reached down and touched the baby's head, then moved towards her hand. The tiny fingers wrapped themselves around his finger.

'She must have a name,' said Richard. 'What shall we call her?'

'I have been thinking that I would like to name her for my mother, so I thought Ann would be nice.'

'Ann it is then,' said Richard. 'I will leave you to rest now.' And he left the room without another word. Mary Ann stared after him. Why had he left in such a hurry?

Chapter Twenty-One

Richard, Moonlight Flats, 1861

Richard just couldn't bring himself to care for the baby girl. Mary Ann was struggling to cope with the newborn and he did nothing to help. He spent more and more time at the mine, so he didn't have to think about it all too much. But the guilt still gnawed at him. Why couldn't Mary Ann have given birth to a baby boy? Then he would have been truly happy. She had made him a father. But a daughter. It was not what he hoped for.

One evening, not long after Ann's birth, Walter looked at Richard with concern. The day was drawing to a close and the sky was darkening 'Shouldn't you be getting home to your family?' Richard didn't know what to say. He couldn't bear to tell his friend that he was avoiding them.

'I'll head home soon,' he said with a wave of his hand, trying to dismiss Walter's comments. But Walter would not be deterred.

'What's going on? You have a bonny new baby and a hard-working wife who loves you. You should spend more time with them.'

'Leave it, Walter.' His voice was low and controlled, but he could feel his anger building with an almost frightening calmness. 'It's none of your business.'

'You may not think so, but I am getting fed up with you moping around all the time.' He paused and drew a breath. Richard could see his friend was struggling to maintain his temper. 'I'm your friend. I'm trying to help. Go home to your family.'

Richard glared. 'Alright, that's enough. I'm going.' Richard's anger cooled as he walked home. Walter was right. He was not being fair to Mary Ann or to his baby daughter. He loved Mary Ann and did not like what these feelings of anger and guilt were doing to their relationship.

He arrived home just on dark. He smiled at Mary Ann, but she did not return his smile. The baby was crying and Mary Ann rocked her gently, doing her best to comfort her.

'Where have you been? It is very late. You are always coming home in the dark lately. Surely you don't need to be at the mine this late.'

Anger bubbled up again as Richard listened to his wife's complaints, but he pushed it down, knowing that he had to try harder. 'I'm sorry Mary Ann.'

It was all he could offer, but he saw her face soften. She was a loving wife and it pained him that he was hurting her.

'Richard, is anything wrong?'

'What do you mean? What could be wrong?'

'It is just that you are never home and you don't seem at all interested in your daughter.'

'Nonsense, Mary Ann, you are her mother. I work hard at the mine all day. You can't expect me to take care of the baby as well.'

'No, I don't. That's not what I mean. Sometimes I think you don't even really like her. You never hold her or pick her up when she is crying.'

Richard was silent. How could he tell her what was really wrong?

'Please talk to me. I know something is wrong.' Slowly, he came to the conclusion that he needed to open up to her, even though he knew it would hurt her more.

'She's a girl, Mary Ann.'

'What? Of course she's a girl. What do you mean?'

'I had my heart set on a son.' There, he had finally said it. But he could see that his candid admission had hurt her. She stared at him despairingly.

'I know a son would be preferable to most men, but I did not know you felt so strongly. You should have told me.' Tears rolled down her face as the baby continued to whimper in her arms.

'I really am sorry. But don't you see? I need someone to carry on the family name. We are all alone in Victoria, without any family. I want to build a family name that people can respect.' He could see the effect his words had on her, but that was how he felt. At least he had told her now.

She sighed deeply. 'We can have more children, Richard. I am sure we will have a son next time.'

Mary Ann had returned to helping at the mine, winding the windlass, whilst Ann slept in a cradle beside her. His wife's strength and willingness to support him in everything he did, did nothing to lessen his feelings of guilt.

Ann had grown quickly and was soon toddling around the mine, with Mary Ann constantly chasing her. Finally, she told Richard that she could no longer work at the mine and keep Ann safe. Besides, there was plenty to do at home. .

Richard's feeling of guilt lessened as he got to know his daughter. Ann was a precocious little tomboy who wanted nothing more than to follow her father around and copy his actions. At first, he had tried to avoid her approaches, but he had to admit she was a persistent little thing and soon he realised he did, after all, love the little girl. She would try to help him with jobs like collecting the wood. Richard loaded up a small basket with kindling so that she could carry it into the house.

One evening, as they sat relaxing after a long day, Mary Ann turned to Richard with a look of concern. He had tried to be more sympathetic to her feelings over the last few months and he felt their relationship was finally starting to heal.

'What's the matter? You look worried.'

'Oh Richard, I am not sure how to tell you this. But I have been feeling unwell for some weeks now. I think I am pregnant again.'

At hearing those words, Richard swept her up in a hug and spun her around. Ann ran around their legs, chuckling. 'But that is wonderful news.'

Mary Ann beamed at him, and he was glad that his reaction made her happy. If only she would have a boy this time.

The months went by all too slowly for Richard. He longed for a son to be born.

Finally, Mary Ann went into labour. Mrs Fletcher was again there to assist. After a labour of seven hours, Mrs Fletcher ushered Richard into the room. Honestly, this bossy woman annoyed him. This was his home. He didn't need her to tell him what to do.

He looked at Mary Ann and saw that she was gazing at the baby lovingly. But as she realised he had entered the room, her look turned to one of desolation. She looked at him pleadingly.

'Richard, we have a daughter.'

Richard could not hide his disappointment and after staring at the baby for a moment and giving Mary Ann a quick kiss, he left the room. But not before he saw the look of contempt on Mrs Fletcher's face. She really was maddening. It was none of her business.

He saddled his horse and headed into town. Needing to console himself with a drink, he headed straight for Fanny's restaurant. He saw her as soon as he entered, talking to a group of rowdy miners. He ordered a drink and sat down at a table. After some time, Fanny approached.

'Hello there, Richard. To what do we owe the pleasure of your company this early in the day? '

'Mary Ann just gave birth to another daughter.'

'That is lovely news, so why the glum look?'

'Oh Fanny, surely you can understand that I want a son. I need an heir.'

'Why Richard I am surprised at you. You often talk of your daughter, Ann, and it seems to me that you love her dearly. There will be more children.'

Richard felt his shoulders tense. He just wanted to wallow in self-pity. Why did Fanny have to point out his faults? But he knew her well enough. He should have known that she would have little sympathy in this case.

Chapter Twenty-Two

Mary Ann, Moonlight Flats, 1861

M ary Ann cried bitter tears as Richard left the room. Her new daughter was so precious, but she was devastated to have disappointed Richard again. Mrs Fletcher's disdain for Richard's attitude was clear on her face. Mary Ann badly wanted to support her husband, but she felt quite unable to do so. Despite her obvious feelings about Richard, Mrs Fletcher displayed her usual kindness and tried to cheer her.

'Mary Ann, you must dry your tears. Richard will come around just as he did with Ann.'

Mary Ann was not so sure. But one thing was certain, if the baby's father would not be there for her, Mary Ann knew she must give this new baby all her love and attention. She dried her tears and smiled down at the tiny baby.

'What shall we call you? I think Emily is a good name for you.'

'That is indeed a lovely name,' said Mrs Fletcher.

As soon as the baby was settled, Mary Ann suggested that Mrs Fletcher should go home. She didn't want the older woman there when Richard returned. She sat waiting for him. Ann was upset that he was not there to kiss her goodnight. But Mary Ann had eventually settled the toddler and she was finally fast asleep. Little Emily was sleeping peacefully in her arms, blissfully unaware of the tension between her parents.

It was late when Richard finally returned. It was immediately obvious that he had been drinking as he weaved in through the door. Mary Ann looked at him and her emotions bubbled in her stomach. Why did it have to be like this? She loved Richard, but she was tired and her patience was thin.

'Where have you been?' she asked, trying to relax so as not to wake the baby sleeping in her arms.

'Where do you think I have been? Drowning my sorrows, of course.' His harsh words were slurred.

'Have you been at Fanny's place?'

'I have.'

'Oh Richard, why do you have to spend so much time with that woman?'

'She is a good friend. She gives me good advice and I like her.'

'Are you sure that is all it is? Perhaps you would prefer to have her as your wife.' She cringed as the ill-advised words fell from her lips and she realised she wasn't sure she wanted to know the answer. But she was struggling to control the anger that was causing the tightening in her throat, making it impossible to speak calmly.

'Don't be ridiculous. If you must know, she had no sympathy for me. She knows I want a son and told me that if I was patient, we would eventually have a son.'

'At least she shows some sense there Richard, but I still don't like that you spend so much time with her.'

Richard gave her a chilly look and left the room. When Mary Ann entered the bedroom he was asleep, fully clothed. She settled the baby in the cradle beside the bed and prepared for bed herself. As she took a final look at the tiny newborn before getting into bed, the tears once again slid down her face. This should have been such a happy day.

Chapter Twenty-Three

Mary Ann, Moonlight Flats, 1865

Ann was six years old when Mary Ann again found herself pregnant. After Emily, she had given birth to another daughter, Elizabeth, just last year. Mary Ann despaired that she would ever be able to give Richard a son. She dearly loved all her daughters. They gave her more joy than she ever thought possible. But as each daughter was born, Richard became more withdrawn. Had he fallen out of love with her? Surely, they could not let the lack of a son break the strong bond they had built before the girls were born. They had been through so much together. But Richard did not seem to be able to get past the fact that Mary Ann had been unable to give him a son. He spent more time at work and less time at home with his family. Despite the anger and sadness she felt at his coldness towards her, Mary Ann wanted more than anything to give her husband a son. Having finished washing the dishes, she wiped her hands on a towel and stared out of the window as the sun sank low on the horizon. She thought sadly about the last few years, which had not been kind to the struggling family.

The mine had been abandoned. Richard had not been able to make a living and pay the costs associated with the crushing machine he shared with the other miners. He had no choice but to close his mine and find alternative work. There was not much available that suited him. As the mining boom receded, new industries grew up in the town and he was fortunate to secure a job at the Castlemaine Gasworks. This was another reason for Richard's unhappiness. He had always worked for himself and did not take kindly to taking orders from his new bosses. It reminded him too much of his convict days. The work was dirty and hard, and the days were long. However, Mary Ann wondered whether the long days suited Richard, as he did not seem to want to be near his family.

To add to their woes, his wage was barely enough to support their growing family. Mary Ann had to stretch every meal so that they had enough to eat. She couldn't help but think back to her childhood when her father had lost his bailiff position and poverty had haunted her family, hunger a constant companion. Determined that her girls would not suffer the same fate, Mary Ann spent every moment she could in the garden, digging and planting, to ensure they had fresh fruit and vegetables. She also lavished her attention on the old goat and the chickens as their contributions to the food supply were vital. The goat provided them with fresh milk each day and Mary Ann scalded the milk to make butter. Four chickens were penned in a small enclosure and provided a steady supply of eggs.

Her patience had also been sorely tested when Richard had grieved so openly after Fanny Finch died the previous year. He had been devastated. It seemed to Mary Ann that he cared more about this woman than his own wife and children. But she knew she shouldn't blame Fanny. She wasn't entirely surprised at the attraction that her husband had for her. She was a formidable woman and as Mary Ann had gotten to know her better, she had herself found her kind and always willing to help anyone who needed it, especially the small female population of the town. In fact, Mary Ann had read in the Castlemaine paper of how Fanny had witnessed a woman being attacked by a man and dragged him off her. She was not one to be messed with. But sadly, she had died in the Castlemaine hospital after not receiving proper care for inflammation of the lungs.

Mary Ann's thoughts were brought back to the present by the sudden flutter of movement in her womb. Her hands flew instinctively to her stomach, as if to protect the baby. She was scared. What if she had yet another daughter? Surely this child would be a son. As each day passed, she grew more worried. Richard had taken no interest in her pregnancy, and she was sure he believed she was not capable of producing a son.

It was a cold grey morning when she went into labour. Richard had risen early and left for the gasworks as usual. As the day wore on and she knew the time was getting closer, she called Ann.

'Ann, can you please go to Mrs Fletcher and ask her to come here?'

'Yes, mother. But do you mean I should go on my own?' Mary Ann could see that Ann was pleased, although a little confused, that she was to be allowed to run off on her own to Mrs Fletcher's house. Ann had been there many times with Mary Ann and her sisters, so she knew the way very well. Normally, Mary Ann would never have let Ann go off on her own. But right now, she saw little alternative. She needed Mrs Fletcher to be with her as she had been for her other births.

'Yes, Ann. But you must run all the way and not stop until you get to Mrs Fletcher's house.'

She breathed a sigh of relief when Ann flew back into the house ahead of Mrs Fletcher. The older woman bustled in after Ann, directing Mary Ann to her bedroom to lie down.

'Where is Richard?' she asked. 'I shall send for him.'

'No, please don't,' pleaded Mary Ann in a low voice. 'I don't want him here. I don't want to see the look on his face if we have another girl.'

Mrs Fletcher frowned.

'Well, that is a very sad state of affairs.' But she said no more and went to check on the children. The girls were playing happily under the watchful eye of Ann, who seemed to understand that something important was happening and she would need to look after her sisters. Mrs Fletcher gave her a reassuring smile and proceeded to prepare lunch for them before rejoining Mary Ann in the bedroom.

The baby came quickly and was born in the early afternoon. Richard had not yet arrived home. Mrs Fletcher let out a cry of triumph.

'Well, it will serve his lordship right, not being here for the birth of his first son.'

'It's a boy?' said Mary Ann, trying to push herself up with her elbows to see the tiny child as Mrs Fletcher wrapped him in a warm blanket.

'It is indeed. A fine young fellow he is too.' At that moment, the tiny baby started to cry in the loudest voice Mary Ann had ever heard from one of her newborn babies. She slumped back on her pillows as Mrs Fletcher placed the baby boy in her arms. As with all her children, she immediately fell in love with the tiny boy as he clutched at her finger, and she put him to her breast.

That night, Richard arrived home late, as usual. Mrs Fletcher had stayed on to look after the girls and give them their tea. Mary Ann was so very lucky to have such a good neighbour as Mrs Fletcher. By now she was out of bed sitting by the stove, her daughters gathered around her cooing at their baby brother, when Richard came in.

She saw the scornful look Mrs Fletcher gave her husband.

'Thank you, Mrs Fletcher, for all you have done today, but my husband is home now. You should go home. We will be fine,' said Mary Ann. Mrs Fletcher didn't look very impressed at being so summarily dismissed, and Mary Ann gave her a guilty smile. She wanted to speak to her husband and did not want Mrs Fletcher judging him.

Richard had stood by the door, looking bewildered at the scene that confronted him.

'Why didn't you send for me?' he asked as he noticed the baby in her arms. Mary Ann could contain the news no longer.

'You have a son, Richard.' Mary Ann had mixed emotions when she saw Richard's face light up with surprise and delight. If only he had shown such delight at the birth of his daughters. Richard seemed lost for words as he moved towards Mary Ann and the baby. He looked at the tiny bundle tightly swaddled in a warm blanket.

'Really Mary Ann, we have a son?'

'Yes Richard, we finally have the son you have always longed for.' Mary Ann was happy for Richard, but she could not forgive him for his attitude towards his daughters. She put her feelings aside. This was a precious moment and she wanted it to be a happy one.

'What shall we call him?' she asked. 'I think he should be called after his father. Richard junior.' Richard could not hide his delight at Mary Ann's suggestion. He looked at his wife with renewed admiration.

'I think that is a fine idea,' he said, glowing with pride. 'May I hold him?'

Mary Ann passed the tiny bundle to his father and watched as Richard gazed at his son as if he was somehow different to their previous babies. Well, of course he was a son, but he was also another member of their growing family, just as her girls had been.

Chapter Twenty-Four

Mary Ann, Moonlight Flats, 1867

Richard grew quickly and soon became known as little Richie. He was a quiet, cheerful baby, when he was well. But he was a sickly child. The girls were robust and rarely sick. But Richie was always coming down with some ailment or other.

Mary Ann worked hard in their home, cleaning and cooking for her growing family. They had dug a well, so they had better access to water.

'Come girls, we need to collect some water.' Mary Ann worked the pump to fill three buckets. Each of the girls picked up a bucket and carried it to two big tubs near the house. Little Richie toddled around, getting in the way.

'First, we need to put the ashes in, then you can pour your buckets in.' After a day or two, the murky water from the well would be clear. Once the tubs were full, it was time to gather water for the garden.

The vegetable garden was at the rear of the house. It had been hard work preparing the soil in the early days. Although they had grubbed out many of the larger rocks when they built the house, the ground was still rocky and hard. But over the years Mary Ann had managed to get rid of all the rocks and condition the soil with plant matter so that the vegetables now grew strongly. The girls filled watering cans to water the plants.

The children were playing happily in the yard whilst Mary Ann worked in the vegetable garden. But dark clouds were looming and soon large drops of rain started to fall. Suddenly the sky opened up and the rain poured down in torrents and in minutes, they were all drenched.

'Richie, come in out of the rain,' called Mary Ann. 'Quickly girls, before you get soaked. Richie will catch cold again if he gets wet.'

As Mary Ann dried Richie's hair, Richard arrived home.

'How did you get so wet, my boy?' He glanced at Mary Ann, who looked at him guiltily. 'The rain came out of nowhere. I got the children inside as quickly as I could.'

'You really should have been watching more closely.' He picked up his son and hugged him tightly. 'And where are my girls? Have you been good today and helped your mother?' He sat down in his comfortable armchair and the girls gathered around, laughing and talking all at once.

Ann, although still the tomboy of the family, clamoured to tell her father her news. 'I baked a cake today. Mother said we could have some after tea.'

Circumstances had improved for the family and there was much laughter and joy in their home. Richard was doing well at the Gasworks and had been appointed as a supervisor on an increased wage. They had everything they needed for the first time in years. A scullery and an extra bedroom had been built onto their stone house, this time from timber. But the heart of the home was still in the stone living room and laughter rang out at all times of the day.

On Sundays, they all attended the service at the local Lady Gully church. Mary Ann dressed the girls in pretty ankle-length dresses, their hair curled in ringlets and decorated with bows. Curling the girl's hair was a Saturday night ritual, so they looked their best for Sunday. Richie was dressed in a jacket, over his ruffled shirt and knee-length breeches with long socks. His tiny feet were shod in button up boots.

It had been a long week for Richard. Now that he had a supervisor's position, his days were longer. When he arrived home late on Friday evening, Mary Ann, as usual, had a hearty meal waiting for him. The girls were happily playing for a change without fighting. Richie, now just past eighteen months old, was toddling around the living room.

'Daddy is home,' said Ann gleefully as she spied Richard coming down the road. She was a bright young girl, now eight years old, learning to read and write at the school she attended with Emily in Moonlight Flats. She loved to peer out the window each evening to watch for her father. When he was at home, she still shadowed him everywhere he went.

Ann raced out to greet her father as he came through the gate and up the path towards the front door. He grinned at her as she ran to him. He picked her up and whirled her around. Mary Ann watched on as Richard laughed and greeted Emily and Elizabeth. Then his eyes were drawn to his son. He swooped down and picked up the small boy who laughed and gurgled happily as he pulled at his father's beard.

'How has my boy been today?' he asked the bright-eyed boy. In return, he got a few mumbled words that, to his delight, sounded like 'dada.' Mary Ann smiled as Richard planted a quick kiss on her cheek before turning his attention back to his son. The girls returned to their play and Richard sat down at the table, with Richie perched on his knee.

'How was your day, Richard?' asked Mary Ann.

'Long and hard, as usual. But we have got everything under control at the Gasworks now, so next week I should not have to work such long days.'

'That is good news. Perhaps we can take some time off and go to the dance at the hotel tomorrow night?'

'Hmm, that sounds like a grand idea. Perhaps I can let the workers go a bit early tomorrow. I am sure they will all have some entertainment that they would like to attend on a Saturday evening.'

Mary Ann was pleased. Since Richie had been born, she had little time for any leisure activities, so she looked forward to seeing some of the locals who had become their friends. She suspected she was pregnant again but had not yet told Richard. Now that he had his boy, informing him of another child on the way did not create so much anxiety in her. But this would be their fifth child. The family was becoming very large, and she wasn't sure that having another mouth to feed would please Richard.

The next day, Richard went off to work and Mary Ann spent the day preparing good clothes for them all to wear to the dance that night. She heated the heavy iron on the stove and pressed all the clothes so that her family would look clean and neat.

Richard arrived home in the early afternoon and the family prepared for their big night out. It was not often they got to socialise, so this was quite an occasion.

The hotel was not far away, just at the end of their road. It was only a mile or so to walk. The family set off in high spirits, with Richie gurgling happily, sitting on his father's shoulders. The girls ran ahead, laughing gaily. Within no time, they reached the hall. Gas lights shone in the dusk as the sun set behind the hotel. It was a festive scene with people coming from all around to enjoy a night of dancing, eating and drinking.

'Oh Richard, thank you for allowing us to come tonight,' said Mary Ann. 'I think we will have a wonderful time.'

'You deserve a night out, my love. You've been working hard lately,' Richard said jovially. Mary Ann was surprised; she often felt he didn't notice her efforts. It felt good to be appreciated, knowing that he understood that he was not the only one who contributed to the family. Her smile was radiant and the evening became even more enchanting.

Stepping into the hotel, they handed over their admission. The proprietors had obviously invested considerable effort in decorating the room for the occasion. Fresh sprigs of eucalyptus and vibrant native wildflowers were strung up alongside multi-coloured bunting adorning the rough wooden walls and dangling from exposed timber beams overhead.

The lively tunes of a group of local musicians filled the air with an infectious energy. A burly gentleman played a merry tune on his fiddle, while another man blew heartily into a wooden flute. The third member of the band was an older woman whom Mary Ann didn't recall ever seeing before. Her hands danced over the keys of an accordion. Their boisterous melodies echoed through the crowded hall.

The room was teeming with familiar faces – miners, farmers and shopkeepers alike. As they wove through the crowd, many voices rang out in hearty greetings towards them.

'Evenin' Evans family!' called Richard's friend Walter, from his spot by the fireplace.

'Good to see you here,' chimed in Mrs Fletcher as she balanced a squirming toddler on her hip. Mary Ann recognised the toddler as belonging to another of her neighbours. They responded warmly to each greeting.

At one end of the long rectangular hall, stood a table that looked ready to collapse under vast amounts of food. Freshly baked loaves of bread lay next to dishes overflowing with roasted meats; jars of homemade preserves were placed to accompany scones. People were eagerly helping themselves to generous portions.

Mary Ann carefully unfolded the cloth covering her woven basket and revealed her contribution: potted meat sandwiches with tangy homemade pickles. She added them to the table, a modest addition to the abundant feast. Her mouth watered at the delicious scent emanating from the table and she realised in her haste to make sure everything was ready, she had forgotten to eat since breakfast.

There were lots of families present and children ran everywhere in between the legs of the adults. Ann, Emily and Elizabeth were soon running around with friends and having a wonderful time. The dancing began as the man playing the fiddle announced that the first dance would be a quadrille. Richard put Richie down on the floor and, sensing his chance to escape, he immediately toddled off.

'Look after your brother, Ann.' Waiting just a moment to ensure that Ann was following the toddler, he grabbed Mary Ann by the hand and led her to the dance floor, where they joined another couple to make up the dance formation. Mary Ann was delighted. Richard was rarely in the mood for anything other than work, let alone dancing.

A social occasion such as this was also a rare chance to catch up with news of their friends. Richard spent time with some of the men at the bar whilst the women sat around sharing news and gossip.

All too soon, it was time to go home. The children were tired. Elizabeth had fallen asleep under a chair and Richie snuggled in his mother's arms. They gathered the family together and headed for home. Mary Ann carried Richie whilst Richard carried Elizabeth. Annie and Emily were still in high spirits, but Mary Ann felt sure they would be asleep as soon as their heads hit their pillows after such a wonderful and invigorating evening.

Once the children were all tucked up in bed, Richard and Mary Ann sat by the fire.

'Well, that was fine entertainment. Did you enjoy yourself?' asked Richard, taking a sip from his tea.

'It was lovely, Richard. I am so glad we went. But did you hear the news?' Mary Ann's face suddenly clouded with worry. 'One of the ladies told me there is an outbreak of measles in Castlemaine. Two children have died already.'

Richard's brows knitted in a frown. He hadn't heard. The men were inclined to talk about work and business, whilst the women's talk turned more to children and family.

'That is terrible news, Mary Ann. I hope no one at the dance was infected.'

'I know, that thought occurred to me as well. But surely no one would come to the dance if they were unwell.' Yet, as she voiced her thoughts aloud, she was overcome by nagging fear and doubt. She supposed such events were part of the reason that infections spread so quickly.

Mary Ann's fears were well founded. Only four days after the dance, Richie developed a fever. He whimpered quietly, lying on the tiny daybed Mary Ann had fashioned for him in the living room so that she could keep a close eye on him. She felt his forehead, hot under her hand. He was burning up. She lifted his shirt and saw the angry red spots all over his chest and back. He had the measles. She was sure of it. Already she had heard of more children dying of the disease in the last few days. That could not happen to her baby boy. She must get a doctor. But she dare not leave him. Her heart pounded as she tried to decide what she should do, all the time her fear mounting.

When Richard returned from work that evening, Mary Ann rushed to meet him. 'Richie is very ill. He has a terrible fever.' Richard felt the small boy's forehead. His voice was strangled, barely more than a whisper as he looked at his son. 'He's burning up. Why didn't you come and get me straight away? He needs a doctor.'

Mary Ann cringed. 'I couldn't leave him.' Richard's whole body trembled as he sat down looking at his son, tears welling in his eyes. 'This is bad, very bad. I will go for the doctor.'

Richard left immediately. Mary Ann grew more fearful as Richie's condition deteriorated. She bathed his burning forehead with cold cloths, constantly dipping them into a dish of cold water and wringing them out to try to make him more comfortable.

Richard was gone for a long time but eventually he reappeared with the Doctor. Mary Ann thought the Doctor looked tired and pale. The outbreak of measles had been going on for days now and everyone was in need of his services.

'Yes, there is no doubt that little Richie here is suffering from measles,' said the Doctor. 'But unfortunately, there is little I can do. You must just try to keep him comfortable and make sure that he has sufficient hydration. Sweetening his drinks may help.'

Over the next few days, Richie's condition worsened. Soon the girls were also covered in angry red spots. Richard did not go to work for an entire week and did not leave his son's side. Whilst Mary Ann could not control her anger that he again paid little attention to the girls, she was glad of his help. It was true that the girls were not as sick as Richie.

Throughout the long days and nights, Mary Ann and Richard nursed Richie and the girls. But it seemed nothing they did helped poor little Richie and his condition continued to worsen. His hot little body became limp and lethargic. He could not keep anything down.

After a week, the girls were feeling better, although the angry red spots still covered their faces and bodies. But Richie was not recovering in the same way. Mary Ann felt faint with exhaustion, but she knew she must keep going for the sake of her children. She would not give up on Richie. He must pull through.

Richard's face was haggard as his glazed eyes stared at Mary Ann. 'I am going for the Doctor, there must be something else he can do.'

Mary Ann was doubtful. She would have preferred that Richard had stayed to help her look after the children. But she, too, was hopeful of a miracle and so did not object to Richard's proposal. After some time, Richard again arrived with the Doctor. He came into the room and first checked on the girls.

'They are doing fine.' He felt their brows and nodded. 'Yes, I am sure the girls will all recover.' Mary Ann let out the breath she had been unaware she was holding. Thank goodness the girls would be alright. The doctor continued. 'Now I will see the boy.'

As soon as he looked at Richie, Mary Ann could tell that he would not be as confident in his diagnosis, but she was unprepared for his next words. He gave them both a worried look.

'I am sorry, but there is nothing more that can be done. You must just try to keep him comfortable. But I doubt he will see out the night.'

A hollow cry escaped from Mary Ann's lips. Richard turned on the doctor, his eyes blazing with rage. 'No, you can't give up on him. He seemed much better this morning. He must recover. We cannot lose him. There must be something you can do.' Mary Ann reached for his arm, trying to calm him. He jerked away from her. She feared his anger, and the thought of losing her darling Richie drained all the strength from her body.

There was sympathy in the doctor's eyes. 'I am really sorry, Richard, but I don't think the boy can possibly recover. His decline over the last few days is obvious. I have to go. I have other patients.' With that, he nodded to Mary Ann and left the house, closing the door gently behind him.

Richard was furious, his voice low and harsh. 'How could you have let this happen, Mary Ann? It was your idea to go to the dance. I am sure that is where he picked up the disease. And you should have called the doctor straight away.' Mary Ann was distraught and cowered under the wrath of her husband. She knew it would do no good to argue with Richard. Perhaps it actually was her fault.

Richard took one last look at his son before he headed for the door.

'Where are you going?' asked Mary Ann.

He did not answer but slammed the door as he left her to deal with all her sick children on her own again.

Richard did not return as darkness fell. Mary Ann sat by her son's bed applying cold cloths to his forehead. She watched as the sky darkened and the stars began to appear. Thankfully, the girls had fallen asleep peacefully, looking so much better today. It was just her and Richie trying to get through the night. Richie did not make it to daybreak. In the early hours of the morning, he took his last laboured breaths. Mary Ann could not believe he was gone. She felt a crushing weight descend on her as she picked him up and cradled him in her arms. The diarrhea had taken its toll and his poor, wasted body was as light as a feather. She could feel his tiny bones poking through his once chubby little body. As tears poured silently down her face, she felt like her heart had shattered into a thousand pieces.

Richard came home, after being away for several hours. He found Mary Ann still sitting with Richie cradled in her arms. The girls were huddled together on the settee crying softly, not knowing what to do as their mother was so distraught she had barely noticed when they had climbed out of bed and come to find her.

Richard took Richie from Mary Ann's arms. He berated her through clenched teeth.

'Look what you have done. My boy is dead, he is gone, and we can never get him back.'

'I am so sorry,' Mary Ann sobbed, gazing beseechingly at her husband. 'You know I would never intentionally do anything to hurt the children.'

'And yet you have.'

Richie was laid to rest in a tiny grave in the Campbell Creek cemetery on June 20, 1867, five days after his death. As they lowered his coffin into the grave, Mary Ann reached for her husband instinctively, knowing however, that he would shrug her away. She wondered if he would ever forgive her.

Chapter Twenty-Five

Mary Ann, Moonlight Flats, 1868

Mary Ann felt a tiny flutter in her womb. She was anxiously hoping that she could give Richard another son. But she was fearful. She hadn't told Richard yet. How she wished he did not place such importance on having a son. *What if she had a girl*? She, of course, would love another daughter, just as much as a son. But she knew Richard was likely to push her further away if she bore another daughter. He had been silent and morose since Richie's death, still blaming her. The girls had tried to engage him in their play, but he had pushed them away too.

As Mary Ann knelt to pray each night before bed, she asked God to grant her wish that this baby would be a boy. She still missed Richie every single day, after all it had only been two months since his death. Another baby would never replace him. She knew she had to rise above her grief so that she could nurture the tiny being growing within her.

As she began to show she knew she would need to break the news to Richard. It surprised her that he hadn't already realised. But then he had barely looked at her since the death of her darling boy. Finally, she summoned the courage to talk to him one evening when he seemed in a better mood than he had been of late.

'I need to talk to you.' She fell silent, not able to go on. Richard looked at her, the contempt evident on his face.

'Well, go on, what is it you want?' Mary Ann's mouth was dry as she swallowed and tried to go on.

'I..... I have something to tell you. I hope you will be pleased.'

'Oh, for goodness sake, get on with it Mary Ann.' Her face grew red as she blurted it out.

'I am having another baby.'

'What? Really?' said Richard as a smile slowly spread over his face, lighting up his eyes. It was the first time Mary Ann had seen him smile in weeks. Even his daughters, whom he could have no reason to blame for Richie's death, had not been able to make him smile.

'Yes, it is good news, isn't it?' said Mary Ann doubtfully, careful not to say anything to anger Richard and spoil the moment. But Richard's smile soon faded and she could read his thoughts. She knew he was thinking this would probably be another girl.

'Yes, it is good news, Mary Ann.' But he rose from the table and left the house. She knew he needed time and space to process his thoughts. But at least he had seemed pleased to begin with. This must be a boy, thought Mary Ann.

The days became hotter as spring moved into summer. Emotions were strained between Mary Ann and Richard. But Mary Ann kept her hopes up. She worked hard in the garden and spent time with the girls, teaching them to read and write, all to take her mind off her approaching confinement. But despite trying to keep busy she could not help becoming more anxious as the baby's arrival drew near. One particularly hot day in January, Mary Ann's contractions began; bearing down on her as relentlessly as the scorching sun in the cloudless blue sky. Mary Ann tried to occupy her mind by getting outside and sitting under the gum trees that ringed the stone cottage. Occasionally she would rise and walk around for a bit and then settle back in the chair. The girls chatted happily, playing around her feet.

'Ann,' said Mary Ann. 'Can you please run to Mrs Fletcher and ask her if she will come.'

'Why, what's wrong?' Ann, now nine years old, liked to think she was very grown-up. She bossed her two little sisters and sometimes made them miserable. But she doted on her mother and was never far from her side. Mary Ann wondered how much Ann noticed Richard's coldness towards her and whether she tried harder to make Mary Ann happy. If this was true it was an awful burden for the young girl to bear. Mary Ann knew she needed to try harder to heal the rift between herself and Richard for the sake of her growing family.

'There is nothing wrong, I just need a visit from Mrs Fletcher.' As Ann ran from the house, Mary Ann said a silent prayer. *Please let this one be a boy.*

Mrs Fletcher arrived and helped Annie into bed.

'Are you sick, mummy?' asked Elizabeth. At four years old, Elizabeth was a serious little person, and Mary Ann knew she was a bit of a worrier.

'No, my little princess. Mummy is fine. I just need a rest.' She smiled at her three precious daughters. 'You can all go outside to play so long as you promise to stay inside the yard.' The frown did not leave Elizabeth's face, but she took the hand that Emily offered and they went into the yard with Ann.

Richard arrived home from work, fortunately earlier than most days. Mrs Fletcher came out from the bedroom when he arrived.

'What's going on? Is the baby coming?' he asked. Mary Ann could hear the concern in his voice from her bed.

'She is doing well, Richard. It won't be long now,' answered Mrs Fletcher.

And sure enough, before the sun had started to dip below the horizon, the cries of a baby rang out. The girls rushed in from their play outside wanting to know what was happening. It wasn't long before Mrs Fletcher came out of the bedroom.

'Has mummy had another baby?' asked Ann.

'Yes, she has. You can go in now.'

Mary Ann was propped up in her bed smiling broadly, the tiny bundle held close to her. Richard hung back as the girls rushed over to peer at the new baby. 'It's a boy, Richard,' she called over the heads of the girls who were clamouring to see the tiny creature.

A huge smile spread over Richard's face as the realisation came to him that he had another son. He strode over to the bed and looked at the tiny baby. Mrs Fletcher had been fussing around but now decided that Richard and Mary Ann needed some time to themselves. She bustled the girls from the room. Richard sat on the bed beside Mary Ann and took the baby from her. 'I want to call him Richard,' he said. Mary Ann looked at him trying to understand what he was thinking. With already two Richards she did not want to use the name again.

'This baby is not a replacement for Richie. He will be his own person. What would he think as he grew up if he was named after his dead brother? He might feel second best.'

She had already given some thought to names. She took the tiny bundle from Richard's arms and rearranged his wrappings as she spoke, not looking directly at Richard.

'Why don't we call him William, after your father?' Richard was thoughtful and getting up from his chair, he started to pace.

'I don't want Richie to be forgotten.' Mary Ann was still a little afraid to look at Richard.

'Of course he won't be forgotten Richard. He was our first-born boy. We will always love him. But don't you think it is unfair to your new son to be named after his brother simply because he is no longer with us?'

Richard sat down and his face softened as he leaned over and gently brushed the baby's forehead. 'Perhaps you are right. William is a fine name for him. I am sure my father will be delighted. We must write and tell him.'

Mary Ann relaxed. She had not wanted to fight with Richard and was pleased that he had agreed with her. He rarely took her side in any argument.

Chapter Twenty-Six

Mary Ann, Moonlight Flats, 1872

Relations between Richard and Mary Ann significantly improved in the years after William's birth. The arrival of another son seemed to soften some of the tensions between them. As their family grew, so too did the bond they shared.

By 1872, the family had expanded to include five children. Their three daughters were a continued source of delight to Mary Ann and they now had two healthy sons. Frederick, the youngest, had been born in 1870.

Mary Ann flourished in her role as a mother, doting on her children and finding purpose in caring for them. It helped that Richard had grown into fatherhood, softening towards his brood, now that he had two sons.

Yet despite the warmth emanating from the family and their happy home, Mary Ann couldn't shake her persistent worry about Richard's discontent with his job at the Gas Works. She could sense the growing frustration at the monotony of the work and saw the weariness in his face when he returned from work each day.

'I am tired of working for other men,' he said one evening, as the couple were sitting by the fire. 'Since I became a free man, I have always been my own boss. Working at the Gasworks does not suit me.'

Mary Ann sighed and shifted in the chair. She was pregnant again and the baby growing within her was causing her a lot of morning sickness. She did not feel at all well with this pregnancy, which annoyed her no end as all her other pregnancies had been relatively easy.

'But what can you do? There aren't that many opportunities.' Mary Ann had an ominous feeling that Richard had some plan in mind that would mean changed circumstances. They had done well on the supervisor wage Richard was now earning. Surely, he wasn't going to put all that at risk again.

'Don't worry. I'm not going to leave my job at the Gasworks, although I hate it there. But I am going to apply for another mining license.' Mary Ann did not know what to say. She was glad that he would not be leaving the Gasworks, but this would mean he might never be home if he started a new mining venture as well.

'But won't that mean you will be terribly busy? You work too hard now.'

'Now Mary Ann, I know it will be hard to begin with, but I know I can do it. And if the new mine takes off, I can leave the Gasworks then.' Mary Ann was not convinced but as usual she knew there was little point arguing.

'Very well. It appears you have made up your mind.'

'Indeed, I have. The application has already been lodged. It is called the Try Again Company and I am sure it will be worth our while. I have a good feeling.' Mary Ann tried not to let her disappointment show, but she was worried. She had her hands full. Now she would be dealing with all the children alone whilst Richard tried to make a new mining venture work.

But Mary Ann really needn't have worried. Each week Richard seemed intent on starting work on the mine but something always prevented him from making a start. His friend Walter had been pleased when Richard had told him about the new endeavour. He too had gone to work in another job. But, like Richard, he was a miner at heart and promised to help with the new venture. Yet as the winter drew on, not a stone had been turned.

William had grown into a happy but wild four-year-old. Mary Ann was never able to take her eyes off him or he would be up to some mischief or other. And now Frederick at age two was starting to toddle around trying to follow his brother. She struggled to keep up with both of them and relied on the girls to help out. Ann, in particular, at age thirteen was a sensible girl and a great help to her mother. Mary Ann felt Richard had spoiled William, letting him get away with his little pranks and not reining in his high spirits.

She could not forget the time that William had fallen out of a tree. Richard was supposed to have been watching him.

'It's perfectly alright Mary Ann, don't fuss. He is not hurt.' But Mary Ann had not missed the look on Richard's face as the boy had fallen and lay dazed on the ground for a minute or two. It was only when he realised William had not been seriously hurt that he had relaxed.

'Yes, he is alright this time, but you shouldn't encourage him.' Mary Ann had been angry and implored Richard to be more watchful.

But William was not to be discouraged. He continued to get himself into all sorts of scrapes. Mary Ann was grateful that Ann also tried to keep a careful watch on him but he was constantly on the move.

Now, as Mary Ann cradled her swollen belly, heavy with their seventh child, she was bone weary. She needed a break from the constant noise and chaos of her offspring.

'Ann, take the others and go outside and play. But make sure you keep an eye on William and Frederick.' She turned to William and issued a stern warning. 'You are not to go out of the yard. And no climbing trees. Do you hear me?'

'Yes Ma,' said William with a cheeky grin.

'Go on, off you all go and play. Don't take your eyes off the boys, Ann.'

As the children ran outside gleefully, Mary Ann sighed. She trusted Ann to keep an eye on the younger children. Surely, she could just lay down to rest for just a few minutes. She yawned as she made her way to the bedroom and lay on her bed.

She hadn't meant to fall asleep, but she awoke with a start sometime later, having no idea how long she had slept. Alarm filled her head. Where were the children? She rose clumsily from her bed and rushed outside to check on them. They were playing happily in the yard, but as she looked around, she realised William was nowhere to be seen.

'Ann, where is William?' Ann's eyes darted to all corners of the yard.

'He was here just a minute ago,' Ann looked at her mother fearfully. She knew she would be in a lot of trouble if William had wandered off. Mary Ann stared crossly at her eldest daughter. She knew she was being unfair, but she couldn't help being angry with Ann.

'I told you not to take your eyes off him. Quickly we must find him.' Ann had tears running down her face as she ran off to try to find William, looking in all the places she knew he may have been hiding.

'William, where are you?' called Mary Ann. 'Come here at once.'

After a few minutes, it was clear that William was not in the yard. Mary Ann was becoming frantic.

'Ann, run to the mine. Tell your father what has happened. Quickly. Go now!' Fortunately, it was Sunday, Richard's day off from the gasworks. He was at the site of the new mining lease with Walter. They were finally starting to investigate the sinking of a shaft. Ann would be able to reach him quickly. Ann turned her tear-streaked face to her mother imploringly.

'I'm sorry, Mother.'

'Never mind that now, just go.'

It was not long before Richard, Walter and several other men from the mine came running towards the house.

'What's happened?' asked Richard.

'It's William, I can't find him anywhere.' By this time Mary Ann was totally panicked and sobbing so hard she struggled to get the words out.

'When did you see him last?' Mary Ann tried to pull herself together so that she could answer Richard. Richard would find him in no time.

'Ann was looking after him. I had to lie down to rest. I was exhausted.'

'What? Do you mean to say you left him alone while you slept?'

Mary Ann could not look at Richard. 'Please can we talk about it later? We need to search for him.'

Richard scowled at her, his eyes flashing with anger. The men from the mine witnessed this scene between husband and wife with embarrassed looks. Walter stepped forward.

'Richard, calm down. This will never find the boy,' he said. Mary Ann breathed a sigh of relief as the tension was diffused slightly.

'Yes, of course, you are right. The rest of us will start looking. Will you go into town and round up some more men to come and search?'

'Of course.' Walter strode off and saddled Richard's horse to ride into town.

Mary Ann gathered the children and took them inside where they all sat waiting for news. Mrs Fletcher appeared in the doorway.

'Oh, my dear, are you alright?'

'Thank you for coming Mrs Fletcher.' Mary Ann had tried to maintain her calm for the sake of the children, but at the sight of Mrs Fletcher, she crumbled. All the children were crying quietly. She knew the older girls had heard the cautionary tales of little children getting lost; their parents warning them never to stray too far from home. They knew that some lost children never returned. The grisly tale of the three boys from Daylesford who had never come home was in everyone's minds. They knew of the dog bringing his master a small boot complete with the foot still inside. The bodies of the boys were found huddled together in a tree trunk. What if William never came home?

Mrs Fletcher put the kettle on and made the children something to eat. Whilst they sat around the large kitchen table eating, Mrs Fletcher put a cup of steaming tea into Mary Ann's shaking hands.

'Now, now Mary Ann, you mustn't fret so. It is not good for the baby. The men will find William.'

'Richard is so angry with me. And rightfully so. I should never have laid down. I only meant to rest for a couple of minutes. But I fell asleep. I don't even know how long I was asleep. William could have wandered off a long way. He is such a scamp. He would think it a fine adventure. Until he got hungry of course.' Mary Ann smiled and then a small giggle escaped from her. She was becoming hysterical.

Mrs Fletcher held her close. Mary Ann dissolved into tears yet again. She wondered what was happening to her little boy. He would be scared and hungry. They must find him soon.

Chapter Twenty-Seven

Richard, Moonlight Flats, 1872

Richard and the rest of the men from the mine started to spread out calling William's name. Soon cries of coo-ee were echoing throughout the bush. Word spread quickly in the small community. It was not long before Walter returned with a group of men and a full search party had been organised.

It was a fear that haunted most of the adult population. A tragedy like this could befall any one of them; children could so easily disappear in the thick, unforgiving bush. Not to mention that the ground was pitted with deep mining holes that would swallow up a small child.

'How could Mary Ann allow this to happen?' Richard and Walter were tramping through the bush. Walter searched his friend's face.

'Really Richard, you can't honestly blame Mary Ann for this, can you? You know how adventurous William can be.'

'All the more reason never to let him out of her sight. She left Ann to look after him.'

'She has been looking exhausted lately, so you can't really blame her for needing to rest.'

Richard just frowned. Despite his friend's plea for Mary Ann, he could not forgive her. He knew in his heart of hearts that he was being unfair, but right now he was too angry and worried to admit to that. He called William's name loudly as they continued to thrash through the dense bush.

More residents joined the search over the course of the day. A search headquarters was set up at the Sebastopol hotel. Men came from Castlemaine and all the surrounding districts. Soon there was a horde of men searching every acre of the thick bush that surrounded the Evans' home. The women folk set to work filling containers with fresh water, making soup and baking fresh bread to feed the hungry searchers.

Hour after hour they scoured the bush making as much noise as they could. The fading sunlight filtered through the gum trees casting long shadows as night approached. The searchers began to light lanterns, which cast an eerie glow through the bush. Nocturnal creatures stirred. Each noise made Richard's heart leap hoping it might be William, only to have his hopes dashed. Richard felt hopeless, his throat raw from shouting. There was no sign of the boy anywhere. Fear gripped him as he began to imagine that they would never find his son.

'You mustn't give up Richard. We will find him,' said Walter trying to lift Richard's drooping spirits.

'He will be hungry and thirsty by now,' said Richard. 'Anything could have happened to him.' Neither of the men wanted to voice their concern that William may have fallen down one of the abandoned mine shafts.

'I will never forgive myself, or Mary Ann for that matter, if something terrible has happened to him.'

'Come now Richard, let's not think the worst. There is still time to find him before darkness falls.'

But as the sun sank below the horizon, Richard struggled to keep his belief that they would find the boy.

Just as all hope seemed lost, one of the searchers came running up to Richard.

'We found this snagged on a bush. Is it from William's clothing?'

Chapter Twenty-Eight

Mary Ann, Moonlight Flats, 1872

Mary Ann and the children remained at the house. As much as Mary Ann wanted to join the search, she knew someone needed to be there in case William returned of his own accord, but as the day stretched on, hope lessened. Mary Ann looked up as the door opened.

'Have you found him?' Richard was home, surely that meant they had found William.

'No, I have just come home to pack some food and then I will be off again.' He did not make eye contact with Mary Ann, and she could see the anger and despair blazing in his eyes.

'There is no sign of him?' Mary Ann was desperate for some news.

'One of the searchers found a piece of fabric that looks like it is from his breeches.'

He held out the small scrap of fabric. Mary Ann grasped it and held it to her nose. 'Yes, it is definitely from his clothes. Surely this means he can't have gone too far.'

Mrs Fletcher packed food for Richard, and he left again without another word. Mary Ann was again reduced to tears.

'Come Mary Ann, we must get the children ready for bed,' said Mrs Fletcher. Mary Ann raised her head and looked into the scared eyes of her four children. She realised with a start that she had barely paid any heed to them since William had disappeared. Ann must be feeling so guilty. Mary Ann felt her protective instinct come to the fore.

'Of course, come children. You must get to bed now.'

'But what about William?' wailed Elizabeth. 'We can't go to bed until he comes home.'

Mary Ann tried to convey a confidence she did not feel. 'You must get some sleep. I am sure they will find William soon. There are lots of people out looking for him. No doubt he will be here when you wake up.'

While Elizabeth and Emily got ready for bed and Mrs Fletcher changed Frederick's nappy and tucked him into his cot, Mary Ann whispered to Ann.

'This is not your fault.' Ann looked at her mother gratefully, but tears rolled down her cheeks and the anxiety that she had been feeling was evident. Mary Ann felt remorseful that she had been so self-absorbed that she had let Ann suffer all day without her support.

'But it is my fault, I should not have let him wander off. I should have watched him more closely.'

'Nonsense, you know what your little brother is like. He has no fear and is always distracted by any small thing. He probably just chased a butterfly. It is my fault. I should not have left you alone for such a long time. You mustn't worry, Ann. Everything will work out.' As she said these words, she was transported back to the words her mother had said to her all those years ago when desperate poverty had meant that they had to pack up their home and move to a new town. Her mother had told her that no matter what happened they would always have each other. But what if William never came home. They might not always have each other. She tried to dispel her negative thoughts as she hugged Ann tightly. 'But now you must go to bed. I am sure the men will find William soon.'

Once the children were all tucked into bed, Mrs Fletcher made Mary Ann a cup of tea. She put a plate of food on the table in front of her. Mary Ann looked at the food realising that she had not eaten all day. She must try to eat, she had to keep her strength up. As she took a nibble of the meal, she turned to Mrs Fletcher.

'I can't thank you enough for being here to help me. I am quite at my wits end. Goodness knows how the children would have managed if you had not been here. But you must go home now and get some rest too.'

'Oh no, I am not leaving you like this. I will wait until Richard returns. He will eventually have to come home to rest.'

The two women were dozing on the settee when Richard finally arrived home in the wee small hours of the morning. Mary Ann awoke with a start when she heard the door open.

One look at Richard was enough to tell her that there was no news.

'I am going to sleep for a couple of hours and will go back out to continue looking at daybreak,' he said and without a further word he left the room. Mrs Fletcher rose from the settee.

'I will leave you to get some rest now, Mary Ann. But I will be back first thing in the morning.'

'Thank you so much,' said Mary Ann wearily as she closed and bolted the door behind her good friend. She must try to get some rest for the sake of the other children and the tiny being growing inside her.

Mary Ann stirred as she felt Richard get out of bed. She was bleary-eyed with lack of sleep. The sky was getting lighter, but the sun was not yet up.

'Are you going back out to search?' she asked.

'Of course.' But that was all he said as he pulled on his breeches and buttoned his shirt. Mary Ann just wanted him to talk to her. She felt totally alone in her anxiety about her missing child. But he was obviously in no mood to talk, at least not to her. She could still feel the anger burning in him.

She dragged herself out of bed and followed him into the kitchen where he grabbed a piece of dry bread and a pannikin of water before heading out the door to rejoin the search.

Mary Ann put the kettle on to boil and made herself a cup of tea, then sat listlessly on the settee to wait for news. The tea grew cold and was still sitting on the table when the children came tumbling into the room. She heard Frederick begin to whimper in his cot and went to collect him.

'Has William come home yet, Mummy?' Her youngest daughter, Elizabeth, looked at her hopefully as if William would have just walked in the door this morning.

'No, but your father and everyone else are still looking. I am sure they will find him soon.' She tried to sound confident but knew by the look on Ann's face that she had failed.

'I'm hungry,' wailed Elizabeth. Mary Ann looked at a loss. Ann stepped in.

'Come on Elizabeth, you too Emily. We will make Mother some breakfast.' Mary Ann tried to smile thankfully at Ann. But she rose from the settee and settled Frederick back into his cot and went to help the girls to get breakfast.

Soon after they had eaten bowls of steaming porridge, there was a knock at the door. Mary Ann started up hurriedly, but it was only Mrs Fletcher. Mary Ann frowned.

'Oh, I am sorry Mrs Fletcher, but I was hoping it was someone with news.'

'I quite understand dear, and I am sorry to disappoint you. Did you get any sleep?'

'A little, please come in.'

For the rest of the day, Mrs Fletcher bustled around the house feeding everyone and generally helping out.

The search continued all that day and into the next with no sign of William. Richard was becoming more and more morose and had still not conversed with Mary Ann. He came home, accompanied by Walter, as the sun was setting on the third day of the search.

As they entered the cottage, Walter whispered to Mary Ann. 'I convinced him to come home to rest for a while.'

The two men sat at the kitchen table eating some stew, which Mrs Fletcher had prepared. Mary Ann sat with them and listened to their stilted conversation.

'I don't know where else we can look,' muttered Richard, looking completely defeated.

'We will find him, Richard,' said his friend. 'You must not give up hope.'

'But it has been so cold overnight, and he has no food or water.'

'The police have coordinated the search in the last couple of days so we are much more organised now. We are making sure that we cover every inch of ground. I am sure he will be found soon.'

Just as the sun was setting, casting long shadows across the stone cottage, a cry rang out from the bush nearby. Everyone in the house heard the noise and looked at each other for a moment, too stunned to move.

Richard and Walter ran from the house, closely followed by Mary Ann, Mrs Fletcher and the children. Poor Frederick, asleep in his cot, was momentarily forgotten.

They saw a group of men running towards them through the bush. William was cradled in the arms of one of the men. Mary Ann was fearful as she approached William. He looked limp in the man's arms. Was he alright? Oh, dear God, please let him be alright.

As the two groups converged, Richard reached for his son. Mary Ann looked at her son in his father's arms. 'Oh, thank the heavens,' her voice choked with emotion.

'Found him by the creek, bit scared but none the worse for wear,' said the man who had been carrying William. Mary Ann looked at William in the arms of his father. His face was grubby and covered with scratches.

'Quickly, bring him inside Richard.' Richard carried the boy inside and he drank thirstily from the pannikin of water that was presented to him. Mary Ann took her son from his father and hugged him tightly. 'You must never run away again. You had us worried sick.'

William looked at his father fearfully. He must have known he would be in trouble for running off when Ann and the girls were not looking.

Richard's stern face softened as he looked at his son in Mary Ann's arms. 'It's all right, William. We are not angry, although you should not have run off. We are just pleased to have you back. We didn't know what had happened to you.'

His sisters gathered around, their faces a mix of tears and joy. 'Thank goodness you are home William,' said Ann.

Richard went back outside to thank the searchers, still gathered in groups in the yard. They wandered off looking pleased with themselves. The ale would flow tonight at the Sebastapol Hotel. He shook hands with Walter.

'I cannot thank you enough for everything you have done.'

'It was nothing more than anyone would have done. I am just very pleased that William is home again and appears to be unharmed. I will be off now. I could use a drink and then a good night's sleep, as I am sure you could too,' he finished as he turned to leave and join the others at the hotel.

The cottage was soon bustling with activity as Mary Ann and Mrs Fletcher fussed around in the kitchen dishing up bowls of the hot stew which Mrs Fletcher had prepared that day. As soon as the meal was served to the joyful family, Mrs Fletcher took her leave.

Mary Ann went with her to the door. 'You are a good friend. I could not have gotten through this without you. Thank you.'

'Nonsense, but now I will leave you to your family.' She gave Mary Ann a quick hug and hurried off towards home.

Frederick was stirring in his cot, disturbed by all the commotion. Mary Ann picked him up as the whole family sat down to eat, saying a quiet prayer in her mind, thankful that William was now sitting at the table wrapped in a warm blanket and noisily slurping his stew.

Chapter Twenty-Nine

Mary Ann, Moonlight Flats, 1872

Following William's adventures in the bush, Richard was even less inclined to get the new mine up and running. Mary Ann felt he did not really trust her to look after the children. It irritated her that as soon as he returned from the Gas works each evening he would spend time with the children and often questioned them about what their mother had been doing each day. But time was running out. The licence was likely to be revoked if mining did not begin soon.

'What is happening with the mine, Richard?' Mary Ann and Richard were sitting at the table, having finished their evening meal. The children had gone outside to play in the last dying rays of the sun. Richard looked at her with something like disdain.

'What do you mean, what's happening? You know nothing has happened. I have not had time to do anything, what with the Gasworks and looking after you and the children.' Mary Ann ignored the reproach in his voice. She understood he was still angry, but she was also growing impatient.

'But Richard, I know you received a letter about it last week. Won't they revoke the licence if you don't do something soon? You know you could rely on Walter to come and work with you again.'

'Well, yes, I know Walter would help. And the licence could be revoked given that it is now over 6 months since it was granted. But what am I to do, Mary Ann?'

Mary Ann spoke tentatively. She didn't want to upset Richard. He was so annoyingly touchy on the subject of the children lately.

'You know I am perfectly capable of making sure the children are cared for if you want to spend some time at the mine.'

'I do know that, Mary Ann, but after what happened to William, I still feel anxious about something happening to them.' Richard rose from his chair and paced the room. 'I don't know what to do. Working at the Gasworks for the rest of my life is not what I want, but I can't see how I can make a go of the mine. I think I will just have to let it go.'

Mary Ann's fears were well based. As November came along and the days were lengthening, Richard received notification that he must return the lease at once. The licence was duly revoked and Richard faced the prospect of continuing to work at the Gasworks. Mary Ann knew this would not be an option he would readily accept, so she was not surprised when early in 1873 he decided to try again.

'I am going to lodge another application for a mining license. I am determined to make a go of it this time.'

Mary Ann was losing patience with Richard's grand schemes, which lately never seemed to amount to much. But she knew it was useless to protest.

'If that's what you want, Richard, then go ahead. But please talk to Walter and make some plans to start work on the mine.'

'You must not doubt me. You do not understand business. I know what I am doing. In any case, if I get the lease, I can sell it to a more cashed up company if I decide not to work it.' Mary Ann said no more.

It was not long before Richard received word that his application was unsuccessful. He was glum as he told Mary Ann.

'I guess it is because many of the deep shaft mines have not done very well. Quartz mining for gold is not that profitable here, like it has been in other mining towns.'

'Perhaps it is more likely to be because you did not work the previous lease.'

Richard glared at her angrily, scoffing at the idea that it had anything at all to do with him. Mary Ann thought it wiser to say no more. But she was not surprised that, before a month had passed, he came to her with yet another plan.

'You remember we were able to mine slate for our floor from the land of the original lease? Well, I have gathered a group of investors, and we will set up a slate mining company. It will be called the Castlemaine, Sandhurst and Melbourne Slate Mining

Company. I will be a major shareholder.' Richard sounded very proud of the ambitious name and his plans for the new venture.

'I beg your pardon?' said Mary Ann. 'What do you mean? Where will you get the money from if you plan to be a major shareholder?'

'Don't panic, I don't need to put up all the money up-front. There are eighteen other shareholders. Most of us have promised to buy 1500 shares at the price of 10 shillings each.'

Mary Ann was horrified.

'But that is £750! Surely it is not wise to invest that much in something that is unproven.'

'You're not listening. We won't have to come up with that to begin with. I am hopeful that mining can commence immediately and we can begin selling the slate. The additional payment of the shares would only be called in if needed.'

'Richard, I understand the value of gold. But how can slate be valuable?'

'It is being used all over already for flooring and roofing. I have even heard of a fine mantelpiece being fashioned from slate. There is definitely a market. It is quite exciting.'

This did sound rather hopeful to Mary Ann. Perhaps this could be the break they were looking for. In any case, she had no further say in the matter and soon Richard was working in the slate quarry.

Chapter Thirty

Mary Ann, Moonlight Flats, 1880

Despite Mary Ann's doubts, Richard and the other shareholders soon had the slate quarry producing well, with the slate being distributed all over Victoria. Richard had been able to leave his job at the Gasworks and was back to his usual high-spirited self. Eight years had passed providing a welcome respite from the hardships that had plagued them in the early years of their marriage, the death of their first-born baby boy, the commotion caused by William being lost in the bush and the constant struggles of making a living. Mary Ann and Richard's bond had once again become strong and continued to grow. Three more children, Rosa, Albert and Lily had been born. They were now a big, happy family numbering ten. The company was thriving and Richard was happier than ever. Once again they had everything they needed.

Sitting in her comfortable chair by the fire, Mary Ann's needlepoint lay forgotten in her lap as she pondered their now comfortable life. The old stone home had continued to expand to make room for the large family and they had replaced the original bark roof with shiny zinc. The combination of the stone walls and the slate floor kept the rooms warm in winter and cool in summer.

Mary Ann cherished having all her children still living with her in their busy home, but she knew that one day they would have to leave and start their own lives. Ann was now twenty-one and Mary Ann supposed she must marry and move away soon. She couldn't help but feel a sense of sadness at the thought. But she was proud of the strong bond that they shared and she believed she played an important role in keeping them all close. Family was everything to her. She loved them all dearly and protected their bond fiercely, despite the intermittent challenges she and Richard faced in the past in their occasionally tumultuous relationship.

Her heart squeezed as she thought of the family she had left behind in England. Although she wrote often, she received few replies. She missed them all dreadfully and longed to see them again, but as each year passed, it seemed less and less likely that she would ever return to England, even for a visit.

As for Richard, he worked hard to provide for their family. However, Mary Ann couldn't shake off worries about his health. He had been so unwell lately, suffering from a persistent cough, which left him breathless for long periods. Mary Ann was growing more concerned for him and, after a particularly bad attack, she decided it was time to talk to him again. She had tried several times to convince him that the cough might be serious.

'You should see a doctor. That cough is awful.'

'It's not that bad,' he said. 'It's just the dust from the mine. The coughing clears my chest.'

'But Richard,' Mary Ann began.

'No, leave it Mary Ann. I am fine. I don't have time to be running off to some quack who won't be able to do anything for me anyway.'

Over time, as Richard continued to work hard, his cough persisted. Mary Ann felt sure it was getting worse.

Chapter Thirty-One

Ann, Melbourne, 1880

Ann was nervous. It was time to tell her mother. She had been thinking about her future for months now. She was 21 years old and was still living at home with her parents. There must be more to life. On occasions, she and her sisters accompanied their mother on trips to the city. Melbourne was thriving in a golden age and she wanted to be part of it.

As she helped her mother chop vegetables for their dinner in a rare quiet moment when the rest of the family had deserted the kitchen, she decided it was time to broach the subject. 'Mother, I want to do something with my life.'

'Oh really, Ann,' said Mary Ann, continuing to slice the carrots.

'I am serious Mother.' Ann's knife stilled as she realised that her mother was not paying attention. Mary Ann looked up.

'Yes, Mother, apart from my family, there is nothing here for me in Castlemaine. I am 21 years of age and I want to do more with my life. I love you all dearly, but I want more. The man of my dreams is out there somewhere. I want to have what you have, a big, happy family. Melbourne is such an exciting city.

You know that from our trips. Surely you can understand me wanting to live there and have new experiences.' She could tell that she now had her mother's full attention.

'Well, that is quite a speech, my dear. But surely you want to stay close to your family. Family is no small thing, you know. We have always been very close. Wouldn't you be lonely without us? You can't just run off to the city on a whim.'

'I am not doing this on a whim, Mother. I have been thinking about it for ages. There was an advertisement in the Argus for a nanny. I am going to apply for the position.'

'You must think about this. What will your Father say?'

'I am sure Father will support me. He knows how much I want this.'

Ann and her father had grown particularly close over the last few years. She had felt his coldness sometimes in her early childhood, but that had only made her more determined to please him and make him happy. Lately she had taken an interest in the mine and had helped him with the bookkeeping.

'I beg your pardon. You mean to say you have spoken about this with your Father?' Mary Ann gave her a sad look and Ann could see that she was disappointed.

'I am sorry I haven't mentioned it to you sooner. But Father and I have talked about what I should do. I love you mother, but you have so much on your hands that I sometimes can't find a moment to talk.'

Mary Ann turned away and Ann was sorry that she had obviously upset her mother. But she wasn't about to change her mind.

After a moment, Mary Ann returned to chopping the carrots. 'Very well, Ann. If this is what you really want, of course I won't stand in your way. It's just that you have always been my rock through everything. I will miss you.'

Ann could see how emotional her mother was, so she wrapped her arms around her, but she was pleased that she seemed to have gotten her mother's grudging approval. She wanted both her parents to be happy for her, not just her father. She was confident that, when she got used to the idea, her mother would see that this was a wonderful opportunity for Ann.

'We better get this stew on the stove. We will have the hordes looking for their dinner soon.'

Ann wrote the letter to apply for the position and waited impatiently for a response. A few days later, a letter arrived. She was to go to Melbourne to meet the family and if they liked her, she would be considered for the job.

Ann dressed carefully in her best day dress. She liked the dress. It was fawn, silk-trimmed with cream lace. The buttons ran from the small collar right through to below her waist and it had a stylish tiered bustle at the back. After arranging her long dark hair into a bun at the nape of her neck, she added a hat, embellished with a ribbon. A pair of soft kid gloves completed her outfit.

Looking at herself in the mirror, she was pleased with the effect. Her hazel eyes sparkled, framed by dark lashes, her lips curved into a gentle, contented smile.

Richard drove her to the station in the buggy so that she would be in time for the first train of the day. As she sat on the platform at the Castlemaine railway station waiting for the train, the excitement bubbled inside her. This was the first time she had travelled to the city unaccompanied. Once she reached Spencer Street station, she needed to find transport to Fitzroy, where the family lived. Her father, wanting to assure her safe travel in the city, had provided her with sufficient money to hire a private carriage. She asked a porter at the station for help. He smiled at her as he directed her to a nearby carriage stand where she hired a carriage.

Feeling triumphant that she had managed to navigate the hustle and bustle of the city, she finally arrived at her destination at the appointed time. She stared in amazement at the house, wondering if she was sufficiently equipped to work in such a wealthy home.

The Gertrude Street home was an impressive sight on the wide, tree-lined street. The two-storey mansion, built from warm sandstone, had tall, narrow windows topped with decorative trim. A wide verandah wrapped around the front and side of the house, held up by cast-iron columns with decorative ironwork. The gardens were neatly maintained, with trimmed hedges, blooming flowers, and a fountain. The front doors, made of polished mahogany, featured stained-glass panels catching the bright sunlight.

Ann paused to draw a nervous breath before she raised the shiny brass door knocker and tapped it three times. She did not have to wait long before the door was opened by a well-dressed servant.

'Hello, I am Ann Evans,' said Ann, trying to sound confident and assured.

'Won't you come in? Mr and Mrs Granville are expecting you.' He led her through the grand entrance hall with its high ceilings and a chandelier sparkling overhead. A sweeping staircase led to the upper floor. He showed her into a beautifully appointed parlour, which had a pleasant scent that Ann could not place. Was it perhaps lavender? She tried not to stare at the ornate fittings, large mirrors and heavy curtains. The walls were lined with portraits of dignified looking men and women who Ann assumed to be ancestors of the family.

'Miss Evans to see you, Madam, Sir,' announced the servant.

'Please come in, Miss Evans. Take a seat,' said a woman who appeared to be not much older than Ann. 'My name is Adelaide Granville and this is my husband.'

'I am pleased to meet you both,' said Ann. Another servant, dressed in a full-length black dress with a pristine starched white apron and mob cap, came in carrying a tea tray. She carefully poured tea for everyone.

'Thank you, Kate,' said Mrs Granville, as the servant left the room. Once they were all seated with a cup of tea, the interview commenced.

'Have you any experience looking after young children Ann?' asked Mrs Granville. Ann smiled.

'I am the oldest of nine children, so yes, I have had plenty of experience.'

'But this will be a bit different, don't you think? Looking after someone else's children.'

'Oh yes, I can see that it will take some time to get to know your children, but I am sure that I will soon grow to love them as if they were my own family.' Mrs Granville smiled and turned to her husband, who gave a slight nod.

After they had chatted for a while, it was time to meet the children. Mrs Granville rang a bell and the servant called Kate brought them in. As they entered, Ann surveyed them. There were three of them, two girls, and the oldest was a surly-looking boy. She had already been told their ages ranged from two to eight years old. Mrs Granville rose from her chair and took the hand of the smallest girl.

'Now children, this is Miss Evans. Please say hello.' The children replied with a chorus of hellos.

'This is Sophia,' said Mrs Granville, indicating the toddler whose hand she held. 'And this is Caroline and Edwin.' She nodded towards each of the children in turn.

Ann rose from her chair and came closer to the children. She bobbed her head to the girls and shook Edwin's outstretched hand. They seemed polite, well-behaved children.

'I am very pleased to meet you all.'

Mrs Granville gave the servant a nod and she led the children from the room. There were a few more questions and the conversation continued for some time, but eventually they offered Ann the position.

'Oh, that is wonderful. Thank you. I am sure I can provide good care for the children.'

'You will have a three-month trial, so we will soon see,' said Mrs Granville with a smile. Ann thanked Mr and Mrs Granville and took her leave.

She decided to walk back to the station. It was not such a long distance and she had time before the train left. She was glad that she had been successful in securing the position, and as she made her way, she began to skip along happily, until she suddenly remembered that she was a refined young woman who had just become a nanny. She held her head up high and continued walking in what she hoped was a sedate and elegant manner.

When Ann arrived home late that evening, Richard was waiting for her at the Castlemaine station. She chattered excitedly, describing her day to him on the journey home, telling him she had been successful. But as they approached the cottage, Ann fell silent. What would her mother say? She knew her mother did not want her to leave home, but Ann was determined to follow her dreams and move to Melbourne where she could start a life of her own. Of course, she would miss her mother and her family, but she hoped more than anything that her mother would be happy for her. When they arrived, Mary Ann was sitting by the fire darning socks, pulling them over the wooden darning mushroom that held them firm as she sewed. Ann went to her mother and gave her a hug.

'I got the position.' Ann could not contain her joy despite her nervousness at what her mother's reaction might be. 'I start on Monday.'

'That's very soon, Ann,' said Mary Ann, setting down her mending. 'Are you sure about this? Do you really want to leave home so quickly?'

'Yes Mother, you know I do. I have been thinking about this for a long time. There is so much to see and do in the city. I feel alive there. It feels like such an adventure and Mr and Mrs Granville are just delightful. The children seem well behaved.'

'But Ann, it seems so impulsive,' said Mary Ann.

Richard frowned. 'Really, aren't you happy for Ann? She is a grown woman now and she should be making her own way in the world.'

Mary Ann sighed. 'Yes, you are right, of course.' She turned to Ann. 'Of course I am pleased for you, darling. It is just that I will miss you so much, as will your brothers and sisters.'

'I know, Mother, but I won't be gone forever. I can come home for holidays. Now that the train is running to Castlemaine, the trip doesn't take so long.'

'Perhaps we could take the occasional trip to Melbourne, Mary Ann,' said Richard.

'Yes, of course. That would be nice.' But she didn't look convinced.

Ann spent the next few days packing. As the day of her departure grew nearer, she wondered if she was making the right decision. Apart from her own siblings, she had little experience with any other children. Living in that big house with such a wealthy family was daunting. She was not at all sure she could live up to Mr and Mrs Granville's expectations. On Sunday, Richard and the boys loaded her trunk into the cart and Ann pushed all her doubts aside as she hugged her mother tightly. They both had tears in their eyes. Emily and Elizabeth also clamored for a hug. Richard helped Ann into the cart, then jumped up and grabbed the reins. All the younger children were yelling their goodbyes as the buggy moved off. Ann was so excited to be off on her adventure, but she could see the sadness in her mother's face, which in turn made her feel sad. But they were soon on their way to the station and the family was left behind. Ann's spirits soared.

Richard unloaded Ann's trunk and found a porter to load it onto the train.

'Well, my girl, this is it. Your big adventure,' his voice carried a mixture of pride and caution. 'Be careful in the city and don't take any risks. Remember, it is not like the country. There are plenty of scoundrels about, you know. And make sure you come home for a visit whenever you can. Your mother will want to see you.'

'I know Father, I will be careful,' said Ann impatiently. She hugged her father tightly. 'Goodbye Father.'

As Ann found her seat, the train whistle pierced the air. Leaning out the window, she waved to her father. With a lurch, the train began its journey, the rhythmic bump of the wheels against the tracks a soothing backdrop to Ann's racing thoughts. Settling into her seat, she released a contented sigh, the thrill of embarking on her adventure coursing through her veins like a fast-flowing river.

As the journey continued, Ann thought of her parents at home. They had often talked of their own journey to Australia from far off England. It must have been so much harder for them, given that they knew that, in all likelihood, they would never see their families again. Ann's adventure was nothing in comparison. She could return to her family with ease should her new life not turn out as she hoped.

Chapter Thirty-Two

Mary Ann, Moonlight Flats, 1882

Mary Ann was busy in her garden. Normally the hard work required to keep the plants producing well, and the feel of the earth on her hands, calmed her. But today she had so many things on her mind. Ann had been gone for nearly two years now, but Mary Ann still missed her terribly. Of course, her house was still overflowing with seven of her children still living with her and Richard. Sometimes she felt guilty that she missed Ann so sorely when she was so blessed with her other children still being at home. But things were changing and Mary Ann did not like what she knew must eventuate as all her children decided their own fates. She would prefer to keep them all under her wing forever.

Ann was the only one of her children who had so far left home, although she hoped Emily would marry the nice young man she was stepping out with. As he was a local man, Emily would not be too far away if she married him. Mary Ann liked him very much so she waited hopefully for them to announce their engagement. Elizabeth was a different matter. Mary Ann was not sure she would ever marry.

William and Frederick had both insisted on leaving school last year and now worked at the quarry. Mary Ann would have preferred that they had stayed on at school a bit longer, but with Richard being so unwell, she was glad that they were able to help out. The three youngest children were doing well at Mr Lord's state school. In fact, Rosa had won a prize. Mary Ann smiled at the thought. Unfortunately, Albert was a little wild and often got himself into trouble. Her baby girl Lily had just turned five and gone off to school for the first time this year.

Mary Ann thought back to her recent visit to Ann. Emily and Elizabeth accompanied her on the train trip to Melbourne. They met Ann in the teahouse in the Block Arcade in Collins Street. It was then that she had told them her news.

'I have met someone,' she said, lowering her eyes. Emily and Elizabeth shrieked and gave her a surprised look.

'What? Tell us more, quickly,' said Emily. Mary Ann sat quietly looking on and listening carefully as Ann went on. 'His name is George. He is very handsome and I like him very much. I met him when Kate and I, you know, the scullery maid I have told you about, were coming home after our Saturday off. We were nearly run over by two runaway horses. He and his friend offered to escort us home.'

'Oh my goodness,' said Elizabeth. 'What a romantic way to meet.'

'I have been seeing him on my days off and I even went to a ball and danced with him.' Emily and Elizabeth giggled. 'Oh, if only I could find a man who would dance with me,' said Elizabeth.

Mary Ann had remained silent until now. 'It does sound very romantic, Ann, but what sort of man is he? What does he do for a living?'

'Now Mother, you must hear me out. He is quite a bit older than me and has been married. He has two children.'

Mary Ann was shocked. She could not believe that Ann had fallen for an older married man. Ann continued speaking quickly, before Mary Ann could find her voice to say anything. 'His wife died some time ago and his children are delightful. Please Mother, just be happy for me. When you meet him, you will like him, I am sure.' But there were more shocks to come.

'There is one more thing I must tell you. He did something foolish in England before he came to Australia. He was working as a postal official and stole an envelope with a small amount of money. His family was very poor and he was only stealing to try to help them. He changed his name when he came to Australia so that he could put his criminal past behind him.'

It really was too much. Mary Ann wanted better for her daughter. Of course, she hadn't met the man yet, so she supposed she should reserve her judgement. Surely Ann would not be foolish enough to take up with a dishonest man.

Suddenly she collected herself, remembering that in fact her own husband had a criminal background. It was so long ago now that it barely, if ever, entered her thoughts. His background was just a distant memory. She had no right to judge this poor man so harshly when she understood all too well how hard it had been in those days in England.

Thoughts of her husband brought her back to the present as she dug a section of the garden ready for a new planting.

She was increasingly worried about Richard. He was still very unwell. In fact, the doctor said that his condition was not improving. But he continued to work in the slate quarry, which Mary Ann suspected was not helping his illness. Mary Ann wished Richard would rely on William and Frederick more heavily and take some time off.

But she had her concerns about the boys as well. Neither of them seemed keen on working with their father at the quarry. Only yesterday she had listened to how annoyed they were with him. They had come in from work early, leaving Richard to finish the day's work.

'What are you doing home from work so early? And where is your father?'

'He is still at the quarry,' said William.

'Why aren't you both there helping him?'

'He told us to go home out of his way,' said Frederick.

'What do you mean?'

'Oh, Mother, he is impossible,' said William. 'He is always telling us off for the smallest thing. It seems we cannot do anything right.'

'Why do we have to work at the quarry?' said Frederick. He glanced at his brother, looking for support. Mary Ann was losing patience.

'Of course, you have to work at the quarry. You left school so that you could work with your father. You know how unwell he is. He needs your help.' Frederick just scowled. But William continued. 'Mining is dying out. The slate will not last forever. I want to do something else. Father would not have to work if he sold the quarry and we went to work somewhere else to earn money for the family. You can't want him to keep working, can you Mother?'

'Well, I do wish he would slow down, but you know he will never agree. Let that be an end to it. Your father will be home soon and I don't want him thinking that you have other plans.'

Chapter Thirty-Three

Mary Ann, Moonlight Flats, 1882

M ary Ann was anxious. A letter had arrived from Ann some time ago. Today was the day that she was bringing her betrothed to meet the family.

Gertrude Street, Fitzroy

25th January 1882

Dear Mother,

I am sorry it has been so long since I have written. I hope you are all well and that father is not too much worse. It was good to see Emily and Elizabeth when they visited last month. Such a pity that you were not able to come to Melbourne with them, but I know you are worried about father.

I have wonderful news. I have told you about meeting George. You will never believe it, but he has asked me to marry him and I have accepted. I know you would probably prefer that I waited to find a man more my age. But he is so kind and generous. And so handsome. I know you will like him. You know he had a slightly chequered past in England but since he has been in Australia,

which is 20 years now, he has proved himself to be a well-respected
citizen. He works hard and is convinced that he can support me as
his wife.

Now that we are betrothed, I have asked him to come with me
to Castlemaine to meet you all. We will arrive on the train on
Saturday, two weeks from now.

I have missed you and everyone terribly, so I am looking for-
ward to seeing you all very much.

Your loving daughter

Ann.

Mary Ann had risen early to complete some chores before
Richard and the children woke. When the kettle boiled, she
made a cup of tea and took it into him.

'How are you feeling this morning?' Mary Ann placed the
cup of tea in his shaking hands as he sat up in bed. It was
Saturday. The previous evening, she had convinced him he did
not need to go to the mine today and that he should be here to
meet George.

'I am fine thankyou, Mary Ann, you mustn't fuss.' But the
simple act of talking started a coughing fit. Mary Ann quickly
took the cup from his hands until his coughing subsided. She
tried to smile as he again took the cup from her and sipped the
tea.

'You haven't forgotten that Ann is bringing George to meet
us today?'

'No, of course I haven't. I am looking forward to meeting the
man who could tame our Ann.'

'Well, once you have finished your tea, you must get up and get ready. They will be here directly. I will go and see to the children now, if you are alright.'

Mary Ann went to wake the rest of her large family.

Soon, everyone was ready to welcome Ann and her fiancé. Mary Ann watched on as William hitched the horse to the cart. She was pleased that he had grown out of the mischievous ways of his early childhood and was now well settled. When he was not at the mine, he spent all his time with the horse. He was well practiced and the old mare who had served them well over many years stood still as William whispered in her ear to keep her calm, so the process was complete in under ten minutes. He set off to meet the train from Melbourne at the Castlemaine station.

'I'll be back before you know it,' he shouted to his mother as he flicked the reins and the horse moved off.

Mary Ann waited anxiously until she heard the sound of the horse's hooves and the rattle of the cart on the rough rocky ground outside the house. Her family all spilled out the door, keen to be first to greet Ann and wanting to get a look at her husband to be. Mary Ann and Richard followed more sedately and watched on as George helped Ann down from the cart. William unhitched the cart and started to brush down the old mare.

As Ann jumped down, she turned to her brother.

'Thank you for picking us up, William. I must say I was surprised to see you. I had been expecting father to pick us up. You are so grown up and handled the cart beautifully.'

William beamed with pride. Since childhood, and after William had been lost in the bush, Ann had barely taken her eyes off him, becoming his chief protector. Mary Ann knew Ann felt responsible for William running off that day, which was partly her fault, as she had not reassured Ann as she should have. But the whole situation had resulted in William and Ann becoming very close.

Ann's siblings quickly surrounded her, wanting to hug her and welcome her home. Soon it was Mary Ann's turn to hug her oldest daughter.

'Oh Ann, I have missed you so much. How are you?'

'It is so good to see you, Mother. I have missed you too. I am wonderful, thank you. It is lovely to be home.'

Richard stepped forward and embraced his daughter, glancing warily over her shoulder at the man whom she had brought to meet them.

'Father, this is George. George, this is my Father, Richard,' said Ann.

As Richard and George greeted each other and shook hands, Mary Ann looked on. Ann had said that he was older, but Mary Ann was surprised to see that he was actually old enough to be her father. But she had to admit he was a handsome man still and seemed very charming and polite.

'It is a pleasure to meet you both,' George smiled confidently as he glanced around at Ann's brothers and sisters. 'And your family. Ann has told me so much about you all.'

Soon the whole family sat down at the table ready to enjoy the meal, which Mary Ann had prepared with help from Elizabeth and Emily. A tantalising aroma emanated from the roast lamb and vegetables as the steaming dishes were placed on the table. The dishes were passed around, allowing everyone to help themselves. For dessert, there was an apple pie spiced with cinnamon.

Mary Ann watched on as Richard and George seemed to get along well and chatted amiably. Richard seemed to like George, so perhaps she needed to soften her opinion and be happy for Ann, rather than worrying about George being too old for her daughter.

'What is your occupation, George?'

'Actually, nothing in particular. I turn my hand to anything that is offered. But, rest assured, I manage well and will provide Ann with a comfortable home.'

Richard frowned slightly at this. Mary Ann, eager to keep the conversation amiable, responded.

'Yes, I am sure that is true. Have you made wedding plans? When will you be married?'

Ann looked at her mother, obviously startled that her mother had gotten to the point so quickly. 'We plan to marry in August.'

George nodded. 'Yes, we will be married in St Patrick's cathedral.' Mary Ann was pleased that they intended to marry in the cathedral. It was such an imposing building, even though it was not yet finished. It would make a lovely backdrop for the special day.

'I do hope you will all be able to come to Melbourne for the wedding,' said Ann excitedly as she spooned another serve of apple pie into George's bowl. 'Perhaps you could even stay for a day or two. There is a very reputable boarding house in Fitzroy.'

As they finished the meal, Richard asked George if he would like to see the quarry.

'I would like that very much. I am surprised there is still so much mining going on in the area. After all, the gold rush has been over for decades now.'

'That is true, but we are not mining gold. We have shares in a slate quarry and as you would be aware, there is a tremendous demand for this material for roofing and flagstones. We have done very well over the years.'

As the two men set off to the mine, Mary Ann pulled Ann aside.

'He is older than I imagined, Ann.'

Ann, who had obviously been expecting this, had her justification prepared. 'Well yes, he is forty-four, but age means nothing really. He is a good man and he works hard. I love him and I know he will be good to me.'

Mary Ann squeezed her daughter's hand. 'I am glad, Ann. So long as you have thought this through. You know you will be expected to look after his children.'

'I know, but they are well brought up children and William is nearly grown. And Ann is such a sweet little girl and I think she has taken to me. She misses her mother dreadfully.'

Ann had to return to her nanny duties that evening, so soon it was time for her and George to get back to the station to catch the evening train. Once again, William hitched the horse up to the cart and the family waved them off.

'I hope she is making the right decision.' Mary Ann wiped at the tears welling in her eyes as she waved.

Richard put a comforting arm around her shoulder. 'I feel he is a good man. I think she will be happy.'

Mary Ann was surprised that he was taking Ann's betrothal so calmly. He was not so happy to see Emily stepping out with her beau. Perhaps George's mature age sat better with her husband than it did with her.

Chapter Thirty-Four

Ann, Melbourne, 1882

The wedding took place on August 16, 1882. It was a cold and blustery day. But nothing could dampen Ann's spirits as she woke on her wedding day.

Mary Ann and the rest of the family had travelled to Melbourne on the train the previous day and were staying at a boarding house. Ann's employer had graciously allowed Ann, her mother and her sisters, who were to be her bridesmaids, to dress at their house.

Mrs Granville had been delighted when Ann told her of her plans to marry.

'Oh Ann, that is wonderful. I think George is a splendid match for you.' Ann smiled gratefully at her employer. Her marriage would mean that she could no longer work for Mrs Granville, so she had been nervous about breaking the news.

'Thank you, Mrs Granville. It means a lot to me that you approve of my decision to marry.'

'Well, of course I do. Every young girl should have the opportunity to be happily married. But we shall miss you. The children have grown very fond of you.'

Mary Ann, Elizabeth and Emily arrived at the Granville residence early to prepare for the wedding. The girls helped Ann to pile her hair up into an elaborate hairstyle high on her head held with jewelled hair pins, which would be perfect for the floral head dress and tulle veil.

'Are you sure this is right for you, Ann?' asked Mary Ann.

'Oh really Mother, you must stop doubting me. I know what I am doing. It is the day of my wedding. Please, just be happy for me.'

'Of course. I'm sorry. It is just so important to me that you are happy.'

Ann could tell that her mother was anxious as she watched on while Elizabeth and Emily helped Ann dress in the stunning satin wedding gown, fastening the buttons at the back. The high-necked bodice was decorated with fine embroidery and cinched in at the waist. Long sleeves ballooned slightly before tapering in at the wrist. The neckline and cuffs were trimmed with lace. It had a full skirt with a small bustle. Elizabeth carefully picked up the lacy, full-length veil, which was attached to a headpiece embellished with dainty flowers. She pinned it in Ann's hair.

'Oh Ann, you look so beautiful. I really am very proud of you.' Ann returned her mother's smile as she dabbed the expensive 4711 perfume, which George have given her as a wedding present, behind her ears and on each wrist. She slipped her feet into white satin slippers and picked up the white kid gloves that would complete the outfit.

Emily and Elizabeth were also effusive in their compliments. Ann felt beautiful. Once she was dressed, Mary Ann opened a velvet jewellery case.

'This will be your something borrowed, my darling girl.' She took out a string of pearls and fastened them around Ann's neck. 'They belonged to my mother. She had so few nice things, so I was astounded when she gave these to me as your father and I were heading to Australia.' Ann fingered the pearls as she stared at herself in the full-length mirror.

'Thank you, they are just stunning. I will take great care of them and return them to you as soon as I am married.' Ann's eyes welled as she hugged her mother tightly.

The time came for the wedding party to assemble at St Patrick's cathedral. All the family were there. Mary Ann sat in the front row with all of her family, except for Richard, Emily and Elizabeth who would walk down the aisle with Ann. Some of Richard and Mary Ann's close friends from Castlemaine had also travelled to Melbourne to attend the wedding. George's two children sat on the other side of the church with some of their departed mother's family. George stood at the altar with his two friends, who would stand up for him. The front ten pews were decorated at each end with garlands of flowers. Flowers also adorned the altar. The cathedral was an elaborate building, providing an awe-inspiring venue for the wedding.

Suddenly the pipe organ struck up the wedding march and the huge sound filled the church. Ann felt nervous as she started walking slowly down the long aisle with her hand clasping

Richard's elbow. Ann locked eyes with her mother and was gladdened by Mary Ann's smile. Ann had never been so radiantly happy.

After the ceremony, the guests enjoyed a sumptuous wedding breakfast at a small hall near the cathedral.

The following day, Richard and Mary Ann and the rest of the family were to travel home. Ann and George waved goodbye.

Ann had kept an awful secret from her family. She was four months pregnant when she and George married. They spent time together at his home when his children visited their mother's family. She had not meant to allow him to seduce her before the wedding, but he won her heart, and she could not resist him.

It wasn't as if she and George had not planned to marry. They had even set the date before Ann realised she was pregnant. But now that they were married and the baby was due in January, she knew she must tell her family. Her mother would be shocked.

Although she had been nervous telling George about the pregnancy, he was very understanding and actually had been pleased. This was a surprise to Ann because she wasn't even sure he would want more children at his age. In fact, they were both thrilled in the lead up to the wedding. But now she must tell her mother. She would write her a letter. It might seem like the easy way out, but she did not have the courage to visit her mother to tell her the news in person. This would be the best option and would give her mother time to come to terms with the situation before Ann had to face her. She felt fairly certain her father would be angry too, so hopefully her mother could make him understand that she and George were happy about the impending birth.

Chapter Thirty-Five

Mary Ann, Moonlight Flats, 1882

Mary Ann was content with life. The slate quarry continued to provide a good living for the family. All her children were well. The only thing that she was really concerned about was Richard's continuing poor health. If only he would slow down and leave more of the work at the quarry to William and Frederick. Although they were still very young, they were strong and healthy. Mary Ann knew that they could take on a lot of the work if Richard would only take some time off.

Mary Ann did enjoy the occasional trip into the township when the younger children were at school. Today seemed a perfect day to make the trip. Trips to Castlemaine were not a common occurrence, as the family was quite self-sufficient. They had the goat for milk and Mary Ann scalded the milk to make butter. She still grew all their own vegetables in a plot at the back of the stone cottage. Occasionally, they killed one of the goat's kids for meat. But that was a very limited supply, so meat usually had to be purchased in Castlemaine.

She wanted to cook a special meal for Richard to celebrate his 56th birthday. The mail had not been collected recently, so she would also be able to stop by the Post Office. She dressed carefully, donning a bonnet to keep the sun off and prepared for a trip into town to purchase a leg of lamb from the butcher. Although she was not as adept at hitching the horse to the cart as William was, she was able to perform the task well enough if the old mare was willing to stand still. Emily was very fond of the old horse, so she helped by holding her still and keeping her calm. Soon, Mary Ann was climbing into the cart.

'You will remember to do a load of washing and prepare some vegetables for the roast whilst I am gone, won't you?'

'Of course, we will make sure everything is done,' said Emily. 'We are quite looking forward to a family meal.'

'And I will bake a cake for Father's birthday,' added Elizabeth.

Mary Ann smiled at her girls. She was not looking forward to when they would both leave home. She waved a cheerful goodbye and flicked the reins.

A letter from Ann awaited her at the Post Office. It had been a long time since Ann had written, so she was eager to read her news. She decided to have some tea at the little cafe that she sometimes visited and read the letter.

'What can I get you, Mrs Evans?' asked the young waitress.

'Just a pot of tea thank you. Oh, and perhaps just one of those little apple cakes.'

As she waited for the tea to arrive, she broke the seal on the letter and took out the folded paper within. As she started to read, she gasped.

'Is everything alright Mrs Evans?' asked the waitress who arrived with her tea just at that moment.

'Yes quite, thank you,' replied Mary Ann. But everything was not, in fact, alright. She was quite shocked by the news in Ann's letter.

25th September 1882

172 Fitzroy Street

Fitzroy

Dear Mother

I hope you are all well. George and I are both well. We have news. I am going to have a baby. I know it is soon. In fact, the baby is due in January. I know that will come as a shock to you, mother, but I can't tell you how happy I am. I love George's children very much, but to have a baby of my own fills my heart with joy. We had already decided to marry, so it is really of no consequence.

I am so excited I can barely think of other news. But I must add something, I suppose.

Melbourne is flourishing. It is such a vibrant city, although many are calling it Smellbourne, because it really is quite smelly. George and I take the children to the Botanical Gardens sometimes. The gardens are quite beautiful at this time of year.

George is still working hard at his job and we are doing well financially. I have been able to get some new dresses made so I will look presentable during my confinement.

George says I mustn't travel, although I would love to come to visit you all. I miss you so much. Perhaps you could arrange a trip

*to Melbourne. I hope you do not think too badly of me, Mother. I
really am happy and so is George.*

Sending love to everyone

Your loving daughter

Ann.

Mary Ann arrived home, hesitating about telling the girls.
Richard needed to know first. She was not sure how he would
take the news. He liked George, but she feared that this news
would shatter that good opinion. Once they were alone in their
bedroom that night, she decided she could not contain the news
any longer. The weight of the secret had become unbearable.

'I have had a letter from Ann,' she blurted out, despite her
efforts to remain calm. Perhaps if she remained positive, she
could convince Richard that the news was not so dire.

'About time,' he said gruffly, his words punctuated by a harsh
cough. 'We have not heard from her for weeks.' His pale, drawn
face caused Mary Ann to hesitate.

'What does she say?'

Deciding now that she had raised the subject, she could not
put off telling Richard any longer, despite his ill health, she took
a deep breath. 'Well... she is going to have a baby.'

'That is good news, isn't it? Why do you look so troubled?'

Mary Ann's hands shook as she replied. 'It appears the baby
was conceived before they were married.' Seeing his look of
surprise, Mary Ann added quickly, 'Ann assures me that George
had already proposed before she realised she was pregnant, so
they were always going to be married.'

Richard's face contorted with anger. 'That does not excuse their behaviour. How could they be so irresponsible? Show me the letter.'

Mary Ann handed him Ann's letter. He unfolded the letter, fumbling with his reading glasses. As he began to read, his face grew redder and his laboured breathing became shallower.

'Richard, you must calm yourself. Getting angry is not good for your cough. They sound happy. Surely we should support them.'

'I am sorry, Mary Ann. I cannot support such irresponsible behaviour.'

Mary Ann felt her own anger rising. This was exactly the reaction she had feared. Now she realised the time until the baby was born would be filled with conflict unless she could convince Richard that he was being unreasonable. She would be torn between the love for her eldest daughter and her duty to her husband.

At first, Mary Ann had been shocked by the news herself, but unlike Richard, she was quickly able to put her disappointment behind her and looked forward to the birth of her first grandchild. She knew Ann would make a wonderful mother. They had glowing reports from the Granvilles about how well she had cared for their children. She just hoped that Richard would come around so that they could both enjoy the birth of their grandchild. But whether or not he did, she was determined that nothing would spoil it for her. She was going to be a grandmother.

As soon as Christmas celebrations were over for the family, Mary Ann prepared to go to Melbourne to be with Ann when the baby was born in January. As it was Ann's first child, Mary Ann wanted to ensure she was there in plenty of time in case the baby came early. She was worried about leaving Richard and the younger children for such a long period, but Emily and Elizabeth promised to take charge of the household chores and make sure the younger children were looked after.

She had visited Ann soon after they had received news of the impending birth and had been relieved that Ann looked well and that George was as attentive as ever. As she prepared to leave after her brief visit, she hugged Ann tightly and told her she would be back for the birth. Ann was relieved to know that her mother would be there for her.

'Thank you, Mother. I must admit to being rather nervous and it will be good to have you here. I only wish you could stay longer this time, but I know you are worried about Father.' Mary Ann had chosen not to reveal Richard's displeasure about the impending birth to her daughter.

William took Mary Ann into the station, so she could catch the train to Melbourne. As she waved him goodbye, she gave him a quick hug. 'Please look after your Father. He has been quite unwell lately.'

'I know, but he seems determined to soldier on.'

'Yes, he is being very stubborn, but please try to get him to slow down a bit. You and Frederick can manage the quarry.'

'We can, of course. I will do what I can. Please don't worry. We will look after everything. You just worry about Ann.' Mary Ann smiled. She got onto the train and found herself a seat and waved to William as the train pulled out of the station. William had grown into a sensible young man. She was very proud of him. She settled back in her seat, determined not to worry too much about the rest of her family. Ann was her priority for the moment.

The trip was uneventful, although the weather was warm and by the time she reached Melbourne, she was hot and tired. She was glad to see George waiting patiently when she alighted from the train. She hurried over and hugged him.

'Oh George, it is so good to see you. I have been rather anxious to get here to make sure that Ann is alright.'

George smiled teasingly. 'Really, Mary Ann, don't you trust me to look after her?' In the short time that George had been a member of their family he had certainly endeared himself to Mary Ann and they had quickly become close.

'Of course I do. But I am her mother. You must humour me. I need to see for myself.'

'Then come. I have the buggy ready. Let's get home as quickly as possible.' George picked up Mary Ann's bag and they hurried towards the hitching rail where the horse waited patiently for them. George threw Mary Ann's bag up into the buggy and helped her up. He jumped up and took up the reins. Soon they were travelling down Collins Street at a brisk pace.

Ann was sitting under the verandah at the front of the elegant two-storey terrace house, fanning herself with a colourful silk fan. She struggled to her feet as she saw the buggy approaching.

George did not have time to get around to help Mary Ann before she climbed down herself and threw herself into Ann's outstretched arms.

'I am so glad you are here, Mother. The time is getting close now. I can feel it.' Mary Ann held Ann at arm's length.

'Let me look at you. You do look well enough. But there is at least a month to go, so let's hope this little baby has no plans of hurrying into the world yet. How do you feel?'

'I feel quite well, just a little tired. But George has been look-ing after me.' She turned to George and gave him a quick hug and kissed him on the cheek. Mary Ann smiled. The approach-ing birth had obviously done nothing to dampen their fondness for each other.

'I must tend to the horse, Ann,' said George. 'Take your mother inside.' He flicked the reins and turned the horse and cart down the side alleyway towards the stables at the rear of the house.

Mary Ann looked around her. George and Ann were obvi-ously very happy in this lovely home. Its pitched roof and bay windows were offset by elegant wrought iron lacework.

'Do come inside, Mother. We will have tea. Ann Beatrice has made some scones.' Just at that moment George's daughter, Ann Beatrice, came hurrying out of the house. She was affectionately known by both her names now to distinguish her from Ann. She didn't seem to mind at all.

'Hello Mrs Evans. How nice to see you.'

'Hello Ann Beatrice, it is lovely to see you again.' Ann Beatrice smiled and led the way into the house. Ann linked arms with her mother as they entered.

Mary Ann glanced around the elegant entrance and peered into the parlour to the right of the entryway. It was a welcoming space furnished with comfortable sofas upholstered in rich fabrics, a marble fireplace, and shelves lined with family photographs and books.

'Can you please show Mother where she will be sleeping, Ann Beatrice?' said Ann.

'This way,' said Ann Beatrice, skipping down the passage ahead of Mary Ann who followed her up the polished wooden staircase. She was delighted when Ann Beatrice showed her into a comfortable room. Lace curtains covered the multi-paned windows and the floor was carpeted. Mary Ann gazed at the beautiful antique furnishings. George must be doing well. The house appeared to be well appointed.

'There is water in the jug if you wish to freshen up,' said Ann Beatrice, closing the door as she left the room. Putting her bag down on the bed, Mary Ann poured some cool water into the washbasin. After freshening up, she went downstairs to join the rest of the family.

Ann insisted Mary Ann sit in the parlour whilst she and Ann-Beatrice made tea. The young girl carried in a big plate of scones with cream and jam. George joined them and ate his fair share of the fragrant scones. Mary Ann took it all in, grateful that her daughter had such a loving family around her.

Ann had been quite correct when she said the birth felt close. Mary Ann had only been with them for three days when Ann's labour commenced. Everyone was anxious knowing that there was still a month until Ann's due date.

Ann had engaged a midwife to attend the birth, but given the early labour, the midwife called in the local doctor as well. It was a long and painful labour. After thirty-six hours, Mary Ann was becoming concerned. Ann was exhausted. The doctor had left Ann in the capable hands of the midwife, who still seemed confident that everything was going as it should. Mary Ann was not so sure.

'Don't you think we should call the doctor back?' she asked.

The midwife sniffed, looking at Mary Ann with disdain. 'I think I know what I am doing.'

'Of course, but it has been a long time and I am worried that Ann is not coping well.'

'She must expect a bit of pain.'

Mary Ann felt her heartbeat quicken as her anger rose. She went to find George, who was pacing the hallways downstairs. When he saw Mary Ann coming down the stairs, he turned to her expectantly. But his face fell immediately when he saw the look of concern on Mary Ann's face.

'What's wrong? Is Ann alright?'

'I don't know. I really don't think so. She seems so exhausted and weak. I suggested we should call the doctor again, but the midwife would not hear of it. But I think we really should.'

'I will go now.' He hurried to the hall stand and put on his hat and coat and was out the door before Mary Ann could say anymore.

Soon the doctor arrived and George showed him up to Ann's room. As the doctor hurried to Mary Ann's bed, George peeked nervously into the room. Mary Ann was more worried than ever. Ann was pale and looked awful. George was drawn to her bedside. He held her hand and whispered quietly to her.

'You should leave now, George. I need to examine your wife.' George reluctantly left the room on the doctor's instructions to resume his pacing in the downstairs hallway.

Not long after the doctor arrived, the tiny baby was born. He was a perfectly formed baby boy, despite being over a month early. But Mary Ann knew he was too small. She was worried when George was called into the room to meet his son. He was so pleased, but at first he didn't seem to realise that the tiny baby was struggling to breathe. Ann herself was barely conscious when the baby was laid in her arms. His first cries were weak and quiet.

'Oh Mary Ann, what am I to do? Is Ann going to be alright?' said George.

'The Doctor thinks she will be fine. He has given her a tonic. With rest she should recover.' Mary Ann looked at her daughter, pale against the white linen of the bed. The tension in the room rose as the doctor watched the tiny baby carefully. Eventually, he turned to George.

'I am sorry, there is nothing more I can do. I think he was just born too early. I don't think he will survive much longer.' George's face drained of all colour. Mary Ann could not believe what she was hearing. Her first grandchild was not going to live. How could that be? She went to George, who sat holding his wife's hand as she slept fitfully, unaware of the drama unfolding around her. 'I am so sorry, George,' she said, resting her hand gently on his shoulder. Tears slid down her face. She was devastated, but felt she had to be strong for Ann and George. The doctor took the tiny baby from Ann's arms and placed him in the cot that had been prepared for him. George could not even look at his son. Mary Ann left him to comfort Ann and went to sit by the baby's cot. She stared at his tiny features and watched as his chest barely rose. It wasn't long before the doctor whispered quietly that the baby was gone. He had died without a further whimper. Mary Ann sat staring at him for a long moment, trying to drink in all his features so that she would remember every tiny little thing about his face. The doctor broke the news to Ann that her baby had died, but she did not seem to comprehend. George was inconsolable. Tears welled in his eyes, and he moaned softly. Mary Ann felt her heart would break for her daughter. Memories of having lost little

Richie all those years ago came flooding back. She was overcome with grief.

Ann slept for several hours after the baby passed away. When she awoke, some of her colour had returned. Mary Ann looked at her with sympathy.

'George, I am so tired. But where is the baby?' George grimaced. Despite the Doctor having already informed Ann of the death of her baby, she seemed not to have taken in the news.

'Ann, I am so sorry, but the baby has died. He was too small and weak to survive.' Ann tried to lift herself off the pillows but immediately collapsed backwards.

'What do you mean? George, bring me my baby.'

'Ann, it will do no good. He has died.'

'That can't be true. Bring him to me.'

Mary Ann cringed at the anguish in her daughter's voice. She wondered how Ann would deal with the overwhelming grief that would fill her days from now on.

George saw no alternative other than to show Ann the proof that he was gone. He motioned to Mary Ann, who gently picked up the tiny boy and placed him in Ann's arms. She gazed at his tiny perfect body, holding his limp hands. After several moments, she began wailing. Mary Ann loosened her hold on the baby and took him from her arms. She laid him back in the crib and returned to Ann's side. She held one of Ann's hands whilst George held the other. Together they tried to comfort the devastated new mother, who would not have a baby to raise.

Mary Ann knew it would take many months for Ann to fully recover from the trauma of losing her first born. But Mary Ann had the rest of her family to consider so, after four weeks and with a heavy heart, she prepared to return to Castlemaine. She hugged her daughter goodbye and watched as tears once again sprang to Ann's eyes. She turned to George.

'George, you must take care of her. I know you are hurting too, but please do your best to lift her spirits.'

'Of course,' said George, the grief clear on his face. He was barely coping himself. 'You know I will try to help her get over the loss. But it is going to take time.'

Chapter Thirty-Six

Mary Ann, Moonlight Flats, 1884

I t had been two years since Ann's first baby had died so tragically. Mary Ann visited frequently over that time to try to help Ann come to terms with her loss. Finally, Ann was starting to recover, but it had taken a long time. The news was not so good for Richard. His condition was continuing to deteriorate. The doctors told him he must get away from the slate quarry. The dust was not good for his lungs. Each morning when he awoke, he would cough violently for several minutes, barely able to breathe. Mary Ann hated to see him like this and tried everything she could to make him realise he must give up his work. As she was making his sandwiches and packing them into his lunch tin, she decided to try again.

'But you know I can't, Mary Ann. There is too much to do. The quarry will not survive if I am not there to ensure the smooth running.'

'But the boys can help. William and Frederick can work the mine. And Walter has always been such a loyal friend and worker. I am sure he will continue to help.'

'Mary Ann, don't you realise the boys do not have their hearts in it?'

Mary Ann stopped spreading dripping on the bread she was preparing for his lunch. She looked at her husband sceptically. 'I don't believe that, Richard. The boys work hard.'

'That's what they tell you. They are only boys, Mary Ann. They could never run the mine. And it seems Frederick is determined to become a bootmaker. He has no genuine interest in the quarry at all.' Mary Ann finished packing his lunch and handed it to him with a sigh.

'Perhaps you are right. But you cannot keep going the way you are.'

Richard leaned down and kissed Mary Ann on the cheek. 'You must not worry, my love. I can keep going until William is old enough to take over.'

Mary Ann forced a smile as he left the house. But her thoughts had gone to Frederick. She really must talk to him. She had no idea that he wanted to become a bootmaker, of all things. Where had this idea come from? But for now, she had a busy day ahead.

She put on her bonnet, ready to leave the house. She hitched up the horse to the buggy and set off for Castlemaine.

Shopping complete, she headed for the post office, hoping there would be a letter from Ann. She was pregnant again and her baby was due in April. Mary Ann knew she was anxious following the birth of her first child. Sure enough, the letter was there.

Dear Mother and everyone.

I hope you are all well. I am feeling quite well. Much better than my last confinement. I feel confident this baby will be born strong and healthy.

Mary Ann paused in her reading of the letter, wondering if Ann really was confident. She felt sure that Ann would be very anxious. Her time was approaching and Mary Ann decided it was time to make arrangements to travel to Melbourne to be with her.

The letter continued on with other snippets of news, assuring her family that all was well and that George and the children were looking forward to the birth.

That evening, she read the letter to Richard and voiced her concerns.

'I am worried about her. She seems sure this second birth will be without problems. Really, there is no reason it should not be. But I can't help worrying that something will go wrong again.'

'I am sure you are worried about nothing, but if you are so concerned, you should go to her as soon as possible.'

Mary Ann was pleased that he was keen for her to go and made immediate plans, but she was also worried about him. 'Are you sure you will be alright whilst I am gone?'

Richard's faced darkened. 'I will be fine. I am sick of hearing that you think I can't manage.'

'It's not that. I just worry about your cough and you insist on continuing working too hard.'

'Enough Mary Ann. Stop carping and worry about your daughter.' Mary Ann turned away, hurt by Richard's harsh words.

Nevertheless, a few days later, she arrived at Ann and George's new home in Cardigan Street, Carlton. They had moved home after the birth of the first baby and Mary Ann wondered if the memories had been too painful there. Ann rushed from the house to meet her.

'Oh Mother, it is so good to see you,' said Ann as Mary Ann hugged her daughter tightly.

'I am very glad to be here. You are looking well, my dear.' She turned to hug George and he took her bag into the house.

'I am feeling quite well. But of course, I am a little anxious now that the birth is so close.'

Despite her own foreboding, Mary Ann tried to reassure her. 'I am sure everything will be alright. You must relax and prepare for the birth.'

The baby was born two weeks after Mary Ann arrived. He gave a lusty cry soon after entering the world, and everyone breathed a sigh of relief. George and Ann were besotted with the new baby.

'We must call him George,' he announced. Ann seemed content with that, although Mary Ann wondered if she was just too exhausted to object after the long and difficult birth. He soon became known by both his christian names, George James, to avoid confusion.

The baby's first weeks were surrounded by love and the delight of his parents. But Mary Ann was concerned that they were blind to the fact that he might not be thriving as he should be. As new parents, she supposed that this was only natural. She stayed on for several weeks helping Ann to look after baby George, but eventually she knew she must go home to the rest of her family. However, as she packed her things, she couldn't help the ominous feeling that had seeped into her bones whilst caring for the tiny baby. She hated to leave when she was not sure that George James would be alright. She could not bear the thought of anything happening to him, knowing how much he meant to Ann and George and how devastated they had been at the loss of their first child.

The drone of cicadas filled the air on the stifling late summer afternoon. Mary Ann sat on the garden bench under the old oak tree, sweat beading her forehead, fanning herself with her handkerchief. The weather had been unbearable for weeks now, with no reprieve. The setting sun painted the sky with hues of pink and purple, but the beauty was lost on her.

She was feeling completely depleted and this news from Frederick did not help. It seemed there was nothing to be done. Frederick had made up his mind and no matter what was said, he was not giving up on his dream of becoming a bootmaker. He had been offered an apprenticeship and it seemed he would take up the offer. She looked up as the door slammed and Frederick emerged, fidgeting with the edge of his work shirt. He took a seat beside her, his eyes darting nervously to hers, then looking away. 'I start tomorrow, Mother. I have accepted the apprenticeship.'

Mary Ann reached out and took his hands in hers. 'Is there nothing I can do to change your mind, Frederick?' her voice breaking up. 'You know your father is not well. He needs your help at the quarry.'

Frederick's jaw tightened, determination flickering in his eyes. 'I am sorry, Mother, but I won't change my mind. There's no future for me there. William will stay on at the quarry and inherit father's share when he is gone. I need to make my own way.'

Mary Ann flinched. 'Please don't talk of your father not being with us. If only he would stop working so hard he might have a chance to recover.'

Frederick's gaze softened, concern etched around his eyes. 'I know he is looking quite ill most of the time. I do worry about him, but I don't think me staying at the quarry would make any difference. He shows no signs of slowing down. The way he ignores the doctor's advice and keeps pushing himself from dawn to dusk; it seems he is determined to work himself to death.'

Mary Ann's eyes widened and her voice was sharp with reproach. 'Frederick! Don't be impertinent. You should not speak of your father so disrespectfully.'

A mixture of defiance and embarrassment flashed across Frederick's face. 'I am sorry. I don't mean to upset you. But nothing I can do will make any difference. I am going to start my apprenticeship tomorrow and nothing you can say will change my mind.'

Mary Ann looked at her son, noting the determined set of his jaw. She knew she must admit defeat and give Frederick her blessing.

'Very well. If you have made up your mind, then I wish you well.'

Frederick's face lit up with a smile as he hugged his mother. She returned his smile and thought back to the day her brother Charles had started his apprenticeship as a shoemaker. 'I don't think I have ever told you, but your Uncle Charles, my brother back in England, is a shoemaker. He went to live with the man he was apprenticed to. I felt a great sadness as I felt his leaving was ripping our family apart. At least you will still be living here with us. That I can be thankful for.'

'I promise I will make you proud.' They sat together watching the colours of the sunset fade.

As Frederick stood to leave, her mind drifted to other worries. She had been worried about George James, Ann's delightful baby boy, for some time now.

George James had always been rather a sickly baby and now he was getting teeth. Ann's recent letters had been full of concern for her baby. He was only ten months old. Mary Ann wondered if it would be possible for her to go to Melbourne to see for herself how the baby was faring. But she was also worried about Richard.

Mary Ann rose early on another stifling hot day, once again to try to get Richard to take some time off, but of course he had headed to the quarry with William. Frederick had gone off full of excitement at the prospect of starting his apprenticeship. He was only fourteen years of age. Mary Ann wondered whether he really knew his own mind. She hoped he wouldn't regret his decision. But she dismissed this worry with the thought that he could always go back to working at the quarry.

The three youngest children had been bundled off to school with packed lunches and dragging feet. Rosa wanted to leave school, as many young girls did when they reached the age of twelve. But she was a bright young thing, so Mary Ann hoped she could convince her to stay at least another year or two.

Mary Ann cleared the breakfast dishes and filled the copper with another load of the never-ending pile of washing that filled a large part of her days. She lit the fire under the copper to boil the water, dumped the clothes in and began agitating them with a long stout piece of wood.

She heard the front gate open, so she left the washing to walk around to the front of the house. As she turned the corner, her heart sank as she saw it was a postal representative. This could not be good news. They didn't have a postal delivery this far out of town. The mail had to be collected from the Post Office. It must be a telegram. Telegrams usually meant bad news. Mary Ann drew a deep breath as she approached the young man. She knew he would know the contents of the telegram as he would have transcribed the message as he listened to it come down the line. Mary Ann searched his face for a clue as to what the telegram might contain. But he gave nothing away.

'Good morning, Mrs Evans. Telegram for you.' Mary Ann took the small piece of paper.

'Thank you.' It was all she could manage to say. The young postal worker gave a small nod before getting back on his bike and peddling away.

Mary Ann could contain her anxiety no longer. With shaking hands, she opened the telegram and read.

'George James has died. Ann is distraught. Please come. George.'

The devastating news hit Mary Ann like a physical blow. An anguished cry escaped her lips as her legs gave way beneath her. She crumpled to the ground, her body wracked with violent sobs. 'No,' she cried. 'Not again, please God, not again!'

Her mind reeled, unable to process the cruel reality. Her precious daughter had lost another child. She had to go, had to be there for Ann.

Emily burst from the house, her eyes widening in horror at the sight of her mother collapsed on the ground. 'Mother!' she cried, rushing forward. 'What on earth has happened? Are you unwell?' She took the telegram from her mother's hands and read the dreadful news. Turning back to the house, she called to Elizabeth. 'Come quickly Elizabeth, something terrible has happened.'

Mary Ann knew she must go to the quarry to tell Richard. Emily and Elizabeth dragged her to her feet. Pale and shaking, she took the telegram from Emily and read the ominous words again. Tears poured down the faces of all three women. Mary Ann knew it would take all her strength to make the trip to be by her daughter's side as she dealt with yet another tragedy. Why hadn't she been there? She could only imagine what her daughter was going through. If only she could be there to comfort her. She summoned her strength and hurried to the quarry. Richard looked up from his work as he saw her approach.

'Mary Ann, what on earth are you doing here? What is wrong? What has happened? You look like you have seen a ghost.'

Mary Ann could not hide her sorrow.

'It's baby George,' she started to sob uncontrollably, and handed the telegram to Richard. He quickly read the sparse words and the colour drained from his face.

'Oh dear god, how will Ann bear this? You must go to her at once.' Richard passed the telegram to William, who had emerged from the quarry at the sound of his mother's distressed voice.

'Come Mother, I will come home with you and help you get ready and take you to the train.'

'Thank you, William.' Richard gave Mary Ann a brief hug. 'I will come home with you too.'

'Perhaps you could travel to Melbourne with me, Richard?'

'I think that is a good idea, Father,' said William. 'I can look after everything here.' Mary Ann felt sick. She wished that she could have been there for her daughter. As it was, it would be hours before they could get there.

Richard and Mary Ann boarded the train to Melbourne. Mary Ann sat twisting a tear soaked handkerchief in her hands. How much longer? She needed to be with her daughter now. There had never been a longer train ride.

George greeted them at the door when they arrived at George and Ann's Carlton home. 'Ann has not been able to leave her bed.'

'What on earth happened?' asked Richard.

'His teeth were coming through and the doctor said that was the major cause of his illness. He has been terribly unwell for the past four days with vomiting and diarrhea. There was nothing the doctor could do.' Mary Ann hugged George and felt the big, strong man slump against her. She guessed he had been trying to be strong for Ann.

'Can we come in? I need to go to her.'

George looked startled, realising that they were still standing at the front door.

'Of course, I am sorry. Come in. She is in her bedroom. Please go up. She needs to see you both.'

They mounted the stairs and Mary Ann knocked quietly at Ann's door before entering the darkened room. When Ann saw her mother and father, she began to wail. She sounded animal-like in her grief, keening and sobbing as she tried to tell her parents what had happened.

'Shoosh, Shoosh,' whispered Mary Ann as she held her daughter close. 'George has told us what happened.'

'My poor darling baby, why did this have to happen? I didn't look after him well enough.'

'Nonsense. I know you looked after him with all your love. You cannot blame yourself.'

As Mary Ann held Ann, wondering if the sobbing would ever subside, a hollow numbness spread through her body as if all emotion had been drained from her, leaving only a cold emptiness. Richard sat on the other side of the bed looking like he would rather be anywhere but there. Mary Ann looked pleadingly at him, although she knew there was nothing he could do. His pain would also be too hard to bear. How were they all going to deal with yet another devastating loss in their family? They would have to lay another tiny baby to rest. Her own grief at losing her baby, Richie, all those long years ago, became raw all over again.

Ann had often confided in Mary Ann how much having a family of her own meant to her. Ann wanted a big boisterous brood, just as she herself had. Mary Ann felt a stab of almost physical pain as she wondered whether her daughter's longed for family dream would ever be realised.

Chapter Thirty-Seven

Richard, Melbourne, 1884

R ichard did not know how to comfort his wife and daughter. His daughter's keening continued for long periods and Mary Ann's eyes were red and swollen from constant tears. George was also visibly heartbroken. Richard paced around the house like a caged lion, as the grief-stricken house tried to come to terms with the loss.

Strangely, he couldn't help but feel guilty. He wondered whether he was being punished in some way, for the anger that had surged through him at the news that Ann had conceived a baby out of wedlock. He had been devastated when her first baby boy had not lived past his first day, feeling in some way responsible for the loss. When George James was born Richard had been smitten with the tiny boy. His very own grandson. Now George James was also gone and guilt continued to gnaw at Richard.

The funeral was devastating. The whole family travelled from Castlemaine. It was a dark, overcast day. Seeing his second grandson being lowered into a tiny grave beside his brother all but broke Richard. How could they move on from this second loss? He knew that Mary Ann would also be thinking of their own devastating loss when little Richie had died all those years ago. All those terrible memories came flooding back.

He and Mary Ann stayed on in Melbourne for a time. But he badly wanted to get back to the quarry. Was he being selfish? Perhaps he just felt the need to escape the sombre atmosphere of the Baker family home. He wasn't sure, but what he did know was that he needed to get back to work. Although he had to admit that his coughing fits had subsided somewhat and he was feeling better, having had little to do for the last few weeks once the funeral was over. He knew Mary Ann was right, that he should slow down, but right now he needed work to help him forget his grief.

'Come, Mary Ann,' said Richard, gently placing a hand on her shoulder. 'Let's go for a walk.' He hoped the fresh air would do her good. The grief the family had experienced had been like an earthquake and it was as if they were still trying to sort through the rubble. Richard did not feel able to deal with the weight of it any longer. He needed to escape and somehow find his way back to normal. He wanted Mary Ann to feel better, but didn't know how to make that happen.

'I don't like to leave Ann.'

'That's all very well, but you need to look after yourself.'

Mary Ann sighed. 'Very well, but only a quick walk.'

Richard frowned. He was becoming impatient. Together they walked down the tree-lined street. Richard breathed deeply, glad of the fresh air.

'We really should be getting back home,' he said. 'Ann seems to be coping better now and she has George and Ann Beatrice to look after her.'

'I know you are right, but I can't bear to leave her.'

'It has been a terrible time for all of us, but you know we can't stay indefinitely.'

'I didn't say anything about staying indefinitely, but I can't leave yet.' Mary Ann's voice had become shrill. Richard balled his fists at his side, trying to keep his temper under control.

'I have to get back. I can't leave all the work to William and Walter.'

'How can you be so uncaring? All you think about is that quarry. What about your family?'

'That is not fair,' Richard's voice rose to match Mary Ann's. 'Our family has to eat. The quarry is important.' Mary Ann just glared at him and quickened her pace.

When they returned, Richard was pleased to see that Ann was up and dressed. She still looked pale and fragile, but it was promising that at least she felt able to leave her bed. As the family sat having afternoon tea, making a pretence of eating the scones that Ann Beatrice had baked, Richard wondered how to broach the subject of their departure. Perhaps he should talk to George first.

Later in the day, he followed George to the stables under the guise of helping him groom the horse. Whilst George removed the dust from the horse's coat with a stiff brush, Richard combed through its mane and tail.

'We need to be getting back to Castlemaine,' said Richard.

'Of course,' replied George. 'I know that Mary Ann is worried about Ann, as am I. But the children and I can take care of her. You should get back to the rest of your family.'

Richard was relieved when, as they were eating dinner, George brought the subject up.

'Ann, you know that your mother and father must get back to the rest of the family soon.'

Ann looked startled. Richard frowned, paying careful attention to Ann's trancelike state. He supposed this would not help Mary Ann to make the decision that it was time to leave.

'Oh dear, yes, of course you must get back. I didn't mean for you to stay so long. How long has it been?'

'Are you sure you will be alright?' asked Mary Ann.

When Ann paused, George spoke up. 'You know how much we have appreciated you being here. But I will make sure that Ann is well looked after and if we need you, perhaps you can come back again.'

To Richard's relief, Ann nodded in agreement. Although Mary Ann still seemed hesitant, she eventually relented and agreed that it was time for them to head back home to Castlemaine.

Chapter Thirty-Eight

Mary Ann, Moonlight Flats, 1887

As the years went by, Mary Ann was finding it hard to care for her large family as well as Richard, so in some respects, she was glad that neither Emily or Elizabeth had married yet. As well as helping out around the house, they provided Mary Ann with welcome female company. The fact that they had not yet married did, however, cause her some concern. They were both getting to the stage when they could be seen as spinsters. Emily was twenty-five and Elizabeth was twenty-three. Fortunately, they had both found good, dependable young men and both had plans to marry soon. She thought back to her own decision to marry Richard. Not that she had a choice. At the time, she had not been in love with Richard, and she felt fortunate that she had come to love him dearly with time. He had given her a big happy family and despite the many trials of their marriage, they had a good life together. She wondered if her daughters were truly happy and in love, worried that they had settled for good and dependable men, rather than men who they truly loved. Whatever their reasons, they had made their decisions and she was glad for them and hoped they would be happy.

But just at present, she was pleased to have them around her to help her care for Richard and take on some of the household chores. Rosa, Albert and Lily were still at school. She was pleased to have convinced Rosa to remain at school, but she knew that this would be her last year. She was now fourteen years old and declared that she would not be going back once this year was over.

Richard's health continued to decline. By the end of 1886, he was no longer able to work, a reality that had devastated him. Once a proud and independent man, he now had to rely on Mary Ann and his daughters to provide all his basic needs. One morning, as he struggled to get out of bed, Mary Ann gave him a worried look.

'Wouldn't you be better off staying in bed?'

'I am tired of being in bed,' he grumbled. His patience was wearing thin and Mary Ann had to be careful what she said to him or he would fly into a rage, leading to awful coughing fits.

Mary Ann also had to deal with the younger children, who did not understand that their father was ver unwell. Lily was only ten years old and was often brought to tears by her father's bad moods.

'Your father does not mean to be angry with you,' she said to Lily after one such occasion when her father had growled at her for waking him up.

'I was trying to be quiet. He is so grumpy. I'm always making him angry.'

'It's not your fault. You must be patient. You know he is very unwell and in a lot of pain. Remember how grumpy you can be when you don't feel well?' Mary Ann smiled at her youngest daughter, feeling sympathy for her having to live with the current situation, which they all faced.

Mary Ann was also worried about their financial situation. Since Frederick had left the quarry, William and Walter had kept it running. But William was becoming jaded. Extracting and splitting the slate was hard work and Mary Ann knew he envied Frederick having the chance to escape to a different occupation. Even though he had always put his family first, she wondered how much longer William would stay on at the quarry.

Mary Ann sighed. Having finished her breakfast, she got to her feet. There was no point in continuing to ruminate over her problems. She should get to work. The washing wasn't going to do itself.

'Elizabeth, can you fetch your father's breakfast tray please?' said Mary Ann. 'I do hope he has been able to eat something.' When Elizabeth returned to the kitchen, she wore a worried expression and the tray had not been touched.

'Mother, I think you should check on Father. It seems he has not been able to eat anything this morning.'

Mary Ann had been anxious for days now. Richard was not at all well. She went into the bedroom to find him struggling to breathe. It was the worst she had seen him. His skin was grey, his breathing rapid and shallow. His eyes were wide and darted to her face as she entered the room.

'Richard, my darling, are you alright?' she asked, not sure she wanted to hear his answer. In fact, when he tried to speak, a bout of choked coughing took hold of him. Mary Ann thumped him on the back.

'I am going to send for the doctor.' She hastily left the room.

'Elizabeth, can you please ride into town and see if you can find the doctor? You are right, your father is much worse this morning.'

'Of course, Mother. I will go immediately.' She raced out the door and called the old horse, who took the small piece of carrot that she offered to entice her to come quickly. The mare stood patiently as Emily put on the rug and then threw the saddle over her broad back and tightened the cinch around her belly. She was an accomplished rider and was soon galloping into town.

Mary Ann watched her go before heading back to sit with Richard. She took a basin of warm water and a cloth to mop his brow, which was sprinkled with dots of perspiration, hoping that this might provide some comfort. She helped him to sit up and propped him up with pillows so that he might be able to breathe more easily. But there seemed little she could do. Her thoughts raced wildly, jumping from one terrifying possibility to the next, unable to focus or make sense of the chaos in her mind as fear took over.

Before long, the doctor arrived. He was a small, intense man, always immaculately dressed, who looked at Mary Ann over the top of his spectacles. He had been attending to Richard for many weeks and they had become friends. Carrying his leather bag into the bedroom, he examined Richard closely for some time before he spoke.

'Good morning, Richard. How are you feeling this morning?' Richard's breath was shallow and wheezy. He tried to talk, but the very effort of trying to say a few words left him obviously exhausted.

'Not too good, Doc,' was all he could manage.

The doctor took out his stethoscope and asked Richard to take a deep breath. As Richard attempted this, he had another coughing fit, which lasted some minutes. His lips were blue and his face contorted as the coughing eased.

Later, in the living room, the doctor looked at Mary Ann kindly.

'You must prepare yourself, Mary Ann. He will not last much longer. I am sorry, but he is dying. There is very little more I can do.' A sharp twisting sensation gripped Mary Ann's stomach and she began to weep quietly. Emily made tea and bought her mother and the doctor a cup. The doctor looked in on Richard one more time before he took his leave.

'Oh, what am I to do?' Mary Ann was still weeping. Elizabeth and Emily hugged her, their own grief evident as the tears rolled down their cheeks.

'I am so sorry Mother, I don't know how we will all manage without Father,' said Emily.

It was only a matter of days before Mary Ann watched her husband of thirty years take his last laboured breath. It seemed there was no end to the tragedies her family must endure. Her one goal over the many years since she had been forced to leave her family in England had been to hold her own family together and yet her darling Richie had died; she had lost two grandchildren and now she would be left to manage without her beloved husband. It was too much to bear.

Soon the whole family had gathered to mourn the loss of their father, including Ann and George, who had travelled from Melbourne. Funeral arrangements were made and memories of the patriarch of their large family flowed around the table. Friends and neighbours visited providing food and comfort for the grieving family. The quarry was silent for the time being with Walter joining in the family's grief.

The morning of the funeral dawned with dull sunshine. Winter was coming to an end and the vibrant yellow of the wattle trees heralded the coming spring. The family dressed in dark mourning clothes and watched on as the coffin was loaded onto the undertaker's cart. The family then climbed into the several carts that would take them to the Campbell's Creek cemetery.

The funeral was well attended, as Richard was a well-known and respected member of the community. His friend and partner Walter spoke of him in glowing terms in his heartfelt eulogy. When the service was over, Mary Ann hugged Walter. 'Thank you for your kind words. I know how much Richard meant to you. You were his first friend in Victoria and you have been faithful to him all this time.'

'Friends such as Richard are not common in this harsh land. I will miss him very much.'

After the funeral, family and friends returned to Mary Ann and Richard's stone cottage where they held the wake. Stories were told of Richard's adventures in the colony where he had lived for over forty years, the greater part of his life. No one mentioned Richard's convict past, something that Mary Ann was grateful for. It was, after all, only a very small part of who he was and he had been an honest man since he had arrived in Australia.

Ann and George stayed on for a time after the funeral, which was a great comfort to Mary Ann and the rest of the family. Ann had been blessed with another son, Thomas, who was now a strong and healthy two-year-old and she also brought her newborn daughter Kathleen, who also seemed to be in good health. George was obviously obsessed with his new family and spent all his time caring for his wife and children during the visit. Despite the grief of losing her husband, Mary Ann was delighted to meet her first granddaughter and spend time with Thomas. She was able to bury her overwhelming grief for short periods when spending time with these new family members.

The days were long now that Richard was gone. All of a sudden Mary Ann found herself with a lot of time on her hands, especially after Ann and George had gone back to Melbourne. Having been used to devoting so much time to her sick husband she now wondered what to do with herself. It had been such a pleasure having her two grandchildren to dote on for a time. She missed them all, now that they had returned to their home. Only six weeks had passed since Richard's death and Mary Ann's grief was still raw. She felt like she was in the dark, with no idea where she was going, trying to find her way in her new world. She was not used to being idle and often found herself reflecting sadly on Richard's death. At least she had Emily's wedding to look forward to and take her mind off her grief.

She was kneading dough for the bread, the steady movement as she worked the dough back and forward on the floured surface, calming her mind and numbing her thoughts, when William appeared at her side. He put his arm around her shoulder, hugging her to him.

'Really William, I am trying to work here.'

'You work too hard, Mother. Please come and sit with me for a moment.' Mary Ann could tell that William had something on his mind. So she set the dough to rest and wiped her hands. They sat on opposite sides of the table, looking at each other.

'I am sorry, Mother. I can't do this any longer,' said William.

She knew William was becoming restless and she held her breath, not wanting to hear his next words.

'What do you mean, William? Surely you are not going to leave me to try to run the quarry without your help.'

'I think we should sell the quarry. I have spoken to Walter and he might be willing to purchase Father's share. The business is doing well and there is plenty of demand for the slate.'

'And what do you plan to do?' she asked, feeling her anger rise despite knowing that she was being unfair. William had stayed on for much longer than he had wanted to. He had a right to live his own life.

'There are plenty of droving jobs around. I could see a bit of the country. I have saved enough money to buy a horse and all the kit I need.'

Mary Ann sighed. 'I can see that you have made up your mind. Although I do think you could have waited a bit longer after your father's death.'

'That is not fair, Mother. Frederick was allowed to go his own way. I know I could have waited longer, but an opportunity has come up and I don't want to miss it. Of course, I won't leave until we can sort out the sale of the quarry.'

Mary Ann needed to be alone. She left William sitting at the table and took a long walk in the bush. Tears flowed again, as they had many times since Richard's death. Her grief was overpowering, and she wondered how she would get through it now that William was also deserting her. The girls were both to marry soon. Frederick had married and had his own place in Castlemaine, although she was not sure how strong the marriage was. She felt that her family was falling apart. Of course, that was unfair on the younger children. Rosa, Albert and Lily would still be at home. But oh, how she would miss her oldest children.

After lengthy discussions and much soul-searching, Mary Ann and Walter came to an arrangement about the sale of Richard's share of the quarry.

'Walter, you have been such a good friend to Richard and even though he is gone, you are still here to help me out.'

'He meant the world to me, Mary Ann and I miss him every day. He saved my life all those years ago. It is the least I can do for my friend's family. Will you be alright without the income from the quarry?'

'I really don't know. At least I have the house and land. Perhaps if I invest the proceeds of the sale wisely, I will be alright. We will have to wait and see.'

Walter stood to leave and gave Mary Ann a brief hug. Now that they did not have the quarry in common, she knew they would see much less of each other and probably would eventually lose touch.

'I am always here if you need anything, Mary Ann. Please call on me if you are in trouble.'

Soon after the sale had been finalised, William packed up his kit in saddlebags, hung them on his new stallion and left for the drover's trail.

Mary Ann was devastated, despite knowing how much her son wanted this and how buoyant he was when he brought his new horse home. After all, he had waited a considerable amount of time in order to pursue his dream of droving and travelling the country up to North Queensland. She should be happy for him. She tried to smile as he said his farewells. But it was an empty smile. As he rode off, he turned and waved as his horse pranced around, longing to be galloping away. 'I will be back before you know it.' She hoped this was true.

Chapter Thirty-Nine

Mary Ann, Moonlight Flats, 1888

Emily's wedding was just days away. Mary Ann was looking forward to seeing her second daughter happily married. But without Richard to walk her down the aisle, there was an undercurrent of sadness. Over a year had gone by since Richard's death and the pain of grief still stabbed at her at the most unexpected times. She hoped William might make it home in time for the wedding so that he could stand in for Richard. He had written giving an address where he would be able to pick up a return letter from home on his droving trail, so Mary Ann had written hastily telling him that the wedding date was approaching.

She had driven the buggy into town weekly, hoping that a letter would come from him. Finally, she was rewarded. The letter said he hoped to be home in time for the wedding. He had been away many months and Mary Ann was excited to see him.

Several days later, Mary Ann and her youngest children, Albert and Lily, were sitting at the table whilst Mary Ann helped them with their sums. Lily was an outstanding student, and Mary Ann hoped she could convince her to stay at school for as long as possible. Opportunities were opening up for women and Mary Ann hoped her youngest daughter would do something special with her life. But she despaired for Albert. He was now twelve years old and was not in the least interested in his lessons. His behaviour had become worse recently, now that he didn't have his father to discipline him and he was always in trouble at school. He was out of control and she wondered what would become of him.

She looked up at the sound of horse's hooves on the rocky ground outside. Visitors were a rarity these days. Lily jumped up and ran to the window.

'It's William,' she shrieked, running outside to greet her brother. Everyone followed her out of the house and were all soon milling excitedly around William.

Mary Ann pushed her way through the other members of her family to wrap her son in a warm embrace.

'Oh William, you are home. How good it is to see you.' Tears ran down her cheeks as she surveyed the son she had not seen for many months. 'You look well. How tanned you are.'

'Hello Mother,' said William, extricating himself from his mother's arms. 'It is wonderful to be home. I have missed all you crazy lot.' They all talked at once, asking him about his adventures.

'Whoa, give me a minute. I have ridden a long way, and I will need to tend to my faithful horse before I can answer all your questions.' He took his proud stallion to the water trough and offered him a bucket of oats. After the stallion had eaten and drunk, William brushed him down.

'You are very attentive to that animal,' said Emily.

'He is my livelihood and probably my best mate, so he deserves the best. He has carried me faithfully over thousands of miles.' As he spoke, William stroked the stallion's nose and reached into his pocket for a piece of apple, which the horse snuffled gratefully from his hand.

'Come inside now William, you must be hungry. The girls have cooked a plum cake,' said Mary Ann, grabbing William's hand and leading him into the house. When they were all seated and enjoying afternoon tea, they clamoured to hear about William's adventures.

'Tell us where you have been.' asked Albert, his eyes wide. William swallowed his cake and started his story as everyone settled back to listen.

'I met the team in Bendigo. Then we headed up towards the Murray River, picking up herds of cattle along the way. Crossing the rivers was challenging, especially the Murray. It is wide and deep, so we had to search for a good crossing place. Once we found a place that we thought would be suitable, we roped one of the cattle and dragged him with a couple of horses into the river. Once the first one started to cross, the others followed. It took a couple of days to get all the stock across. Then we headed up along the Darling River through New South Wales and into Queensland.'

The family, particularly the younger members, were mesmerised by William's story.

'What did you eat?' asked Rosa, always fond of her food.

'There was plenty to eat. Don't worry. The cook drove ahead in a horse and cart, carrying all the supplies. He would pick a place for us to camp and when we arrived, he would have a hearty meal ready for us. When we were running short of meat, the boss would pay a visit to one of the stations along the way and we would have fresh meat and sometimes even fresh bread, which was a nice change from the damper.'

'How come you didn't get lost?' asked Albert.

'Well funny you should say that, because we had a horrendous storm one night and the cattle stampeded. One of the men got lost whilst we were trying to round up the cattle and we didn't see him for several days. Luckily, the boss knew a local tracker who found him and brought him back to the camp. Even though he was used to being in the outback, he had been scared out of his wits being out there alone, thinking he would never find his way back.'

The stories went on until it was time for bed. As they all said goodnight, Emily found a moment to talk with William. Mary Ann watched on as Emily hugged her brother.

'William, I am so pleased you have made it home in time for the wedding. Now that Father has gone, I was hoping that you could walk me down the aisle.' William grinned sheepishly. He missed his father, too.

'Emily, nothing would please me more.'

Mary Ann dressed carefully. It was six years since Ann had married and now finally, it was Emily's turn. Mary Ann was pleased for Emily but saddened to think that her daughter was finally leaving home.

It was a beautiful autumn day. Mary Ann gazed out the window at the three trees that she had planted all those years ago, when she and Richard had first arrived at Moonlight Flats. There was an oak, an ash and an elm, which were transformed into a vibrant display of autumn colours ranging from golden yellow to fiery oranges and reds. It was a sight that always filled Mary Ann's heart with nostalgia for her childhood home. She had lovingly tended these trees, carrying water from the creek to nurture them. Now they served as a poignant reminder of where she came from.

She turned to Emily, who was dressing in her exquisite silk wedding gown.

'Emily, dear, I am so pleased for you. I believe James is a good man and I am sure you will be happy.'

'Thank you, Mother. I love him very much.' Emily smiled at her mother. The loss of Richard was still felt deeply by both women, but this was a joyous occasion. They hugged each other tightly. Mary Ann felt a mixture of emotions swinging between happy and sad as she thought about another of her children leaving home to begin a new life.

Elizabeth came in at that moment.

'Come on you two, it is nearly time to go to the church.' Mary Ann smiled brightly at her. 'It will be your turn soon, Elizabeth.' Elizabeth was engaged to the handsome young Freddie, and her wedding was planned for the following year. Elizabeth smiled and gave her mother and sister a quick hug.

'I am so happy for you, Emily. This will be a wonderful day,' said Elizabeth. She handed Emily a pretty lace handkerchief with her name embroidered in the corner, below a little garland of bluebells. 'This will be your something blue.'

'Oh thank you Elizabeth, it is beautiful.'

Mary Ann opened the velvet jewellery case. 'And this will be your something borrowed.' She fastened the string of pearls around her daughter's neck and remembered the day her own mother had done the same for her. It was becoming a tradition for the pearls to be worn by the brides in the family.

The wedding ceremony was charming and a truly memorable event. Mary Ann watched proudly as her strong, handsome William walked his sister down the aisle. She fought back tears that threatened to spill, wishing that Richard could have been there. Of their nine children, he had only seen one of them wed, despite their thirty years of marriage.

Mary Ann's heart squeezed as she turned to see Emily approach the altar, and her gaze turned to James. She could tell he was nervous. He was a handsome young man and had waited patiently for this day. Emily, like all the family, had been distraught at the death of her father and had postponed the wedding, which had been planned for the previous year. James was a good man and had been kind and patient. Mary Ann felt he was a good match for her second eldest daughter.

Chapter Forty

Mary Ann, Moonlight Flats, 1902

'When I was in town today, I had tea with my friend,' said Elizabeth. 'She told me that she thought Frederick and his wife were having problems. She lives next door to them and has heard them arguing on many occasions. She said that Frederick stormed out late a few nights ago and she hasn't seen him since.' Mary Ann looked at Elizabeth in alarm. Elizabeth was helping her pour her freshly made jam into jars.

'That sounds a little far-fetched,' replied Mary Ann. 'They have only been married such a short time. Surely, they are not having problems already?' But as she spoke, she remembered how she had warned Frederick that he was rushing into the marriage. He married young against her advice and at the time she worried that the marriage might not last.

'Well, I don't know. My friend is not usually one to gossip. But I suppose she doesn't really know what is going on.'

Mary Ann sighed, keeping her hands busy, covering the jam jars with circles of parchment paper and tying them firmly with string. When he had opened his own shoe store the year before, Mary Ann was so proud of him. She hoped that this was a sign that he was making a go of things and that he could make his marriage work. This news of Elizabeth's was another problem that she didn't want to think about. Surely it was all just rumours, and if there were rifts in their relationship, she hoped Frederick would be able to work them out.

But it was not long before the problem reared its head again. Mary Ann could not believe what she had heard. She entered the kitchen, slamming her basket down on the table. She had just returned from town and the news was everywhere. Frederick was leaving his wife. She had been too angry to visit him whilst in town and had hurried home to try to ease her mind. How had he allowed this to happen? It was fortunate that there were no offspring from the marriage. And that was not all. Apparently, he had been seen at the hotel, drinking late into the night with Christina Loder.

Mary Ann had not seen Frederick for some time and realised, with a start, that he had been avoiding her and the rest of the family. Mary Ann decided it was time she took things into her own hands. She would go to his shop and confront him.

The town was busy as she secured the horse and cart at the hitching rail. She smoothed her full skirt and straightened her bonnet, before giving the horse a rub on the nose and heading towards Frederick's shop. The bell jangled as she entered and Frederick's head rose from his work. She saw the guilt written all over his face as his eyes swept the room, looking for a way to avoid this meeting.

'Hello Frederick,' said Mary Ann. 'It has been a while since you visited, so I thought I should call in on you.'

'Hello Mother, it is good to see you,' said Frederick fidgeting with his pen. Mary Ann decided to get straight to the point.

'I hear you have left your wife?'

'Well, yes, I'm sorry to say it, but we were just not well suited.'

'And I suppose you are suited to that woman, Christina? What are you thinking? This is not the way I brought you up. You must go back to your wife and resolve your differences.'

Frederick tapped the counter nervously, his voice raising slightly as he answered. 'I can't. It is done. She won't have me back. I have hurt her too badly.'

'It is not likely that you can make amends whilst you are still seeing that other woman. I know you have been seen together. You must stop seeing her.'

'You don't understand. We never meant for this to happen. But Christina makes me feel alive again. I was never happy in my marriage.'

Mary Ann's jaw clenched, her disappointment palpable.

'What of her husband and children? Have you thought about them? Surely you can see that this will create a scandal for both her family and yours. Your father would be turning in his grave if he knew.'

At that moment, their conversation was interrupted by a customer entering the shop. Mary Ann waited whilst Frederick glanced over a pair of boots for repair and gave the customer a price.

As the customer left the shop, Mary Ann turned back to Frederick. 'Frederick, I'm sorry that I was harsh, but what you have done has saddened me. I can't believe this is happening.'

'I am sorry too, Mother, but I cannot change my feelings. I am very fond of Christina and as there is no way my wife will have me back, then I think there is nothing to be done.'

'Oh Frederick, please just think about what I have said. No good can come of this situation.' With that, she turned and left Frederick to his thoughts.

Mary Ann could not control her anger, when some weeks later, she encountered Christina Loder in the street, walking towards Frederick's shop.

'Excuse me, I need a minute of your time,' Mary Ann called as she rushed to intercept the woman. It appeared that Christina knew exactly who she was because she tried to ignore Mary Ann and continue on her way. Mary Ann blocked her path.

'Hello Christina. I hope you are not on your way to visit my son?'

'I don't think that is any of your business,' retorted Christina, lifting her chin defiantly.

'That is where you are wrong, young lady. It is very much my business. You have destroyed my son's marriage. I would thank you to stay away from him before you do more damage.'

'I think he can make his own decisions. In any case his marriage was over long before I met him.' With a toss of her head, Christina pushed past Mary Ann, leaving her staring angrily after the aggravating woman. At least Christina decided not to enter Frederick's shop after all. Mary Ann knew Frederick would be angry that she had interfered, but she would do anything to protect her family, and she knew this woman would be no good for her son.

Chapter Forty-One

Mary Ann, Moonlight Flats, 1904

'Elizabeth, where is Frederick?' asked Mary Ann. 'I haven't seen him for weeks.'

Mary Ann was pleased to see Elizabeth. She saw too little of her oldest daughters these days. Of course, they had lives of their own. But it was wonderful when they took the time to drop in for a cup of tea and a chat, as Elizabeth had today.

'I was going to ask you the same question mother, I haven't seen him either and it seems his shop has been closed. When I was in town the other day, several people asked me why they couldn't buy boots.'

'Oh no! That is bad news indeed. To close his shop that he worked so hard to set up. I knew that woman would be his downfall.'

Mary Ann had tried to talk to him many times over the last two years, but he seemed determined to ruin his life. 'He has been avoiding his family and I hear he has been carousing with her at all hours of the night. But somebody must know where he is. Perhaps I should ask Mrs Fletcher. She usually seems to have her finger on the pulse of everything that is going on.'

Elizabeth grinned. 'You are not saying she is a gossip are you, Mother?' Mary Ann returned her smile. 'Well, maybe just a little. I haven't seen her for a while, so I will bake some scones and pay her a visit.'

After Elizabeth left, Mary Ann loaded up a basket with her warm, freshly baked scones and added a pot of cream and some of her homemade plum jam. She walked along the rough, dusty road towards Mrs Fletcher's small cottage. Mrs Fletcher had been a good friend to Mary Ann over many years, so Mary Ann felt obliged to visit her regularly. Her neighbour was getting on, and was not as spritely as she used to be. Besides, she was probably still Mary Ann's best friend after all the years they had known each other. Mary Ann knocked at the door and soon heard Mrs Fletcher's shuffling feet coming to the door.

'Oh, hello love,' said Mrs Fletcher as she opened the door. 'Do come in. And to what do I owe the pleasure of this visit?'

'Do I need to have a reason to visit my oldest friend?'

'No, of course not. It is lovely to see you. I think I can smell your delicious scones. I'll put the kettle on.'

Soon they were sitting at the table in Mrs Fletcher's comfortable living room, catching up with each other's news. The pot of tea, kept warm with a knitted tea cosy, stood between them. Mrs Fletcher poured tea into two delicate china cups and saucers and added milk from the matching jug. Finally, she added a spoon full of sugar to each cup and handed one to Mary Ann. They both helped themselves to a scone with lashings of jam and cream.

'It really is good to see you, Mrs Fletcher,' said Mary Ann, taking a bite from the fragrant scone. 'But there is actually something I wanted to talk to you about.'

'Oh, and what might that be?'

Mary Ann scanned her friend's face. They normally had no secrets from each other, so Mary Ann felt sure that Mrs Fletcher had an idea what Mary Ann wanted to ask her about.

'It's about Frederick,' she said, watching a frown crease Mrs Fletcher's brow. 'We haven't seen him for weeks. Have you heard anything about his whereabouts?' Mary Ann could tell that Mrs Fletcher was choosing her words carefully.

'I am sorry, Mary Ann. I have been pondering on how to tell you this news for some time. What I am about to tell you will not please you.' Now Mary Ann was really worried.

'Mind you, it is only gossip. I do not know whether it is true, but it is going around town that Frederick has taken off with Christina Loder. They both went missing around the same time. And you know, of course, that Frederick has been estranged from his wife for some time.'

Mary Ann felt the colour rising on her cheeks. She didn't know what to say.

'As I said, it is just town gossip, but it does seem strange that Frederick and Christina's husband had been fossicking together, apparently at Christina's insistence. And he and Christina have both gone missing at the same time. Word is that Christina has been staying out late frequently, much to her poor husband's despair. They have several children, I believe.

Tears welled in Mary Ann's eyes. What shame this would bring on her family if it was indeed true. 'This can't be true.'

'I really hope it is nothing more than malicious gossip. But you must be strong, Mary Ann. It is not of your doing. Frederick is a grown man and has made his own choices.'

It was not until three years later that Mary Ann discovered the truth. By then, she was relieved that all the gossip had died down. But there had been no word from Frederick in all that time. Now she could not believe what she was reading. Surely this could not be true. Christina Loder's husband, Oliver, had asked for a dissolution of his marriage and here it was plastered all over the newspapers. Frederick was even named in the scandalous article. Mary Ann stared in horror at the newspaper.

According to the article in the Mount Alexander Mail, Christina had conspired to have her husband adopt Frederick as a fossicking mate. Every Saturday, Frederick had taken the gold into Castlemaine to sell. Apparently, Oliver Loder was somewhat lame from an old knee injury, so was unable to do it himself. Christina would go into town to collect her husband's share of the money and not return home until very late. She was rarely home by midnight and would be seen in the company of a drunken man. Christina and her husband quarrelled often. Prior to Christina meeting Frederick, the couple were apparently quite close. On March 22, 1904, she had left their home with her youngest daughter, a girl of ten years of age, saying she was going to see the doctor. When she did not return home, Oliver had found that she had taken her own and her daughter's things and some linen, along with twenty pounds in cash.

Oliver Loder testified in court that Christina had said that the doctor recommended that she have some time away. Oliver had sold his plough for twelve pounds so that he would have the money for this holiday. The Saturday night before she went away, she came home at a quarter to twelve. He was in bed and they quarrelled again.

Mary Ann laid the newspaper down on the table. William, who was home after a prolonged droving job, looked at her with sympathy in his eyes.

'Did you know about this?' she asked him as tears rolled down her cheeks.

'No Mother, I had no idea, but Frederick had been quiet and withdrawn for some time before he left.'

'The article says that she left on the 22nd of March 1904. Was that around the time that Frederick disappeared?'

'As I recall, it probably was.'

'I should not have been so hard on him when he wanted to leave the mine. He had a right to make his own way in the world and I was cold towards him. I was so worried about how your father would cope without him. Perhaps if I had not been so hard on him, he might not have left.'

'Mother, you cannot blame yourself. Frederick is his own man. Nothing you could have done would have made any difference.'

'Oh William, what am I to do? This will start the gossip all over again. Everything has gone bad since your father died. What with this news and Albert bringing down the family's good name by being drunk all the time and frequenting hotels after hours.'

'That is a bit of an exaggeration Mother, and slightly unfair. Yes, Frederick and Albert have turned out to be rather bad eggs. But the rest of us have worked hard to keep the family afloat since father died.'

Mary Ann sat down with a heavy sigh. Despite working as a drover and being away from home a lot, William had always had his family's interests at heart.

'You are right, of course, William, although I wouldn't exactly say that my sons are bad eggs. They have just made some bad choices. I still love them as I do all my children.'

'Of course, Mother, I am sorry that I called them bad eggs. I am just angry that they both have caused you so much sadness and regret.'

'Well, I am sorry too. You have been a loyal son. I really do not know what I would have done without you these last ten years. You have been my rock.'

That evening as Mary Ann prepared for bed, she prayed for her family, including Frederick and Albert hoping that something might happen to bring them both back to her. She picked up a photograph from the dresser. The family photo, her most treasured possession, had been taken not long before her darling Richard had died. The faces staring back at her were frozen in time. With a soft kiss on the glass she returned it to its rightful place on the dresser. Then, pulling the covers around her, she lay down, the prayer still on her lips.

Chapter Forty-Two

Mary Ann, Moonlight Flats, 1935

Mary Ann sat in the garden of the home she and Richard had built all those years ago. She would turn 100 years old the very next day, and that momentous occasion caused her to reflect on her life and all that she had been through.

Ann appeared with a cup of tea for her. 'Thank you Ann. Could you do me a small favour and fetch the family photo from the dresser.' When Ann returned with the photo, Mary Ann gazed at it lovingly, tracing her finger over each member of her family in turn.

'Would you like some company mother?'

'No, I am fine thank you. You are busy with preparations for tomorrow.' As Ann returned to the house, Mary Ann's mind continued on its journey through her memories.

Her childhood had been happy despite the many hardships growing up in rural England, where the rich had all the privileges. She still felt that she had missed out on her teenage years by working at home on her lace making. It was strange how these childhood memories seemed to fill her mind more as she aged. It all felt like just yesterday. Her life with Richard had been long, with a lot of happiness, and she had many memories of their time together.

Mary Ann glanced out the window at her garden. Along with the trees she had planted to remind her of the old country, there was a small orchard of fruit trees including lemons, plums and apples. At this time of the year, the lemon tree was covered in blossom, and she wished she could go closer to smell the heavy citrus scent. But lately she just felt too tired for even the shortest wander in her garden. She marvelled at how they had gotten the trees to grow in the rocky ground. They were past their best now, but they had produced well since she and Richard had planted them all those years ago.

Mary Ann rubbed her hands together as she remembered the chafed hands and the aching back that were her constant companions during those early days when they had worked so hard together, to build a life for themselves. She could well remember when they had first arrived at Moonlight Flats, how she lived with Richard in a tent for many months until they built this stone home together. Her hands, now soft from her recent sedentary life, still bore the scars of carrying stones and winding the windlass at the mine. Her mind played tricks on her sometimes and when she looked at her hands, she still saw the rough, reddened skin of her youth. She thought back to building the house and later finding the squarest bits of slate from the mine to press into the mud for the flooring. For many years they made do with the bark roof before zinc had become available.

Now she thought of her own children and grandchildren. She had given birth to nine children. They had all survived to adulthood, except for her beautiful baby, Richie. She was thankful for the help of her neighbour and very good friend Mrs Fletcher through all those births and every other major event in her life since she arrived in this place. Poor old Mrs Fletcher had died twenty, or perhaps it was twenty-one years ago now. But she had been the best friend, and Mary Ann missed her greatly.

Mary Ann and her eldest daughter Ann had always been very close. She sighed as she thought that Ann's life had not always been blessed. Losing her first two children was devastating. She had wondered at the time whether Ann and George would be able to sustain their relationship through such hardship. Her own relationship with Richard had been sorely tested when Richie had died. He had been so aloof. But fortunately, both her's and Ann's marriages had survived the tragedies. Eventually, Ann and George reared six children and they had been the joy of Mary Ann's life. Ann's George had been a good man, but he had been gone for over 30 years now.

Mary Ann was glad that Emily had found a new husband after James had died so suddenly. She had married another James in 1901 and he was also a good man who cared for her and their children.

Her boys, apart from William, had been somewhat of a disappointment to her. As a child and young man, Frederick had always been a dutiful son. He had made a good business for himself as a bootmaker over the years and had contributed to the family's income when they needed it most, after Richard had died. But he had never returned after his shocking disappearance so long ago and she still grieved his loss. She would never have believed that he would desert his wife and family to run off with that Loder woman. But the evidence said otherwise. She had felt so terribly let down when the news hit all the papers. Now she had no idea where he was. Albert, well, he didn't bear thinking about. He had caused her many tears over the years. He was a drunkard and had found himself in court on numerous occasions, charged with drinking in a hotel after hours.

She was thankful that at least William had stayed true to the family. He had been there for Mary Ann when Richard died and was still there to this very day. He was no longer droving at his advanced age. Mary Ann was very proud of him.

She was so lucky her girls had all done so well for themselves. Elizabeth was happily married to Fred. Rosa had married and moved away. Although she didn't see Rosa very often, she wrote numerous letters and she sounded happy and content. Mary Ann's youngest daughter, Lily, was a spinster and happily so. She had gone off to Melbourne and loved city life as women were making a stand for equal rights. Mary Ann smiled at the thought of her youngest daughter. A feminist through and through. A tough woman of 58 years now, who knew her mind and would never be tamed by any of the young suitors who sought her out over the years.

Mary Ann had to accept that whilst she had tried to always protect her family and keep them close; it was an impossible task. Sadly she had all but lost contact with her family in England. Letters from the old country were few and far between. But despite this loss and the loss of her beloved husband, she still had a large and loving family, even though they were scattered all over Victoria. She loved each one of them with all her heart, even those missing from her life. And she knew that her family loved her, too. It was all she could hope for.

Weariness washed over her. Her eyes drooped and soon she was asleep and dreaming of the past.

The family was gathered at home. The house still stood proud after 75 years. Of course, it had undergone many changes and improvements, but the original stone that Mary Ann and Richard had collected still formed the foundations.

Grandchildren and great grandchildren played happily in the yard, enjoying cousin time. Mary Ann sat in a comfortable chair by the fire, where she could see out to all the activity in the yard. She wished she had half the energy of the children. But she was weary. Sometimes she wished she could just close her eyes and never open them again. But then she would remember all the good things that surrounded her. Family and fortune. Life had been good to her overall.

Suddenly, a shout went up.

'What is going on?' asked Mary Ann, worried that someone had been hurt. Ann looked out the window and turned to her mother in shock.

'It can't be.' Ann raced out the door with surprising nimbleness, considering her advancing age.

'Wait, what is happening?' Mary Ann was left in her chair. She certainly couldn't move as quickly as Ann. By the time she'd have gotten out of her chair, the commotion would likely be over. She waited patiently to see what all the fuss was about.

Before long, Ann came back inside, her arm linked through a man who bore a striking resemblance to her.

'Look Mother, look who it is!'

Suddenly, it dawned on Mary Ann.

'Is that really you, Frederick?' she asked, feeling uncertain and not wanting to get her hopes up.

'Yes, Mother. It is me.' Frederick looked at his mother sheepishly, not at all sure of the reception he would receive.

'Where have you been? How could you have put us all through this? We had no idea where you had gotten to. And now you think you can just turn up and say, "Yes, it's me" as if nothing has happened.' Frederick came forward, knelt before his mother's chair and clutched at her hand.

'I am so sorry, Mother. I never wanted to hurt anyone.' Mary Ann jerked her hand from his grasp. But then quickly took his face between her two hands and looked deeply into his eyes.

'You have some explaining to do, my boy.'

'Oh come Mother, it is your birthday,' Ann interjected. 'Surely explanations can wait. Frederick is home. The whole family is here now. We can truly celebrate.'

Mary Ann smiled at her ever-sensible daughter. Ann had never liked conflict.

'Very well, let us celebrate today, but you still need to explain yourself, young man.' She gave Frederick a stern look.

As all the members of the family got acquainted or re-acquainted with Frederick, the celebrations began in earnest. Cider jugs and teapots were constantly doing the rounds and the banquet, which the women of the family had prepared, was enjoyed by all.

At the end of the day, as the celebration wound down, Mary Ann felt a desperate need for some peace and quiet.

'Ann, could you please help me. I would like to go outside to sit for a bit.'

'But Mother, it's getting cold out now.'

'Please Ann, I can put my coat on and some blankets will keep me warm enough, just for a short time.'

'Very well, Mother, if you are sure.'

Mary Ann slipped on her coat with Ann's help and they went to her favourite seat in the garden, where the last rays of the sun could provide a little warmth.

'Thank you,' said Mary Ann as Ann spread a blanket across her knees.

'Would you like some company?' asked Ann.

'No, it has been a big day, I would just like to sit for a bit.' But she hadn't been there long before Frederick came to join her. She could see the guilt clouding his eyes.

'I am so sorry, Mother. I know I have caused you pain. I should never have left the way I did, without even saying good-bye. But I knew how angry you would be.'

'But why did you have to leave Frederick?' asked Mary Ann, feeling her chest tightening with the grief that his disappearance had caused. Frederick sighed deeply and was silent for a moment before he spoke. 'It was hard after Father died. I felt guilty that I had left the quarry, left him without my help. My marriage was never easy either. Although the shop did well, it was never enough for my wife. She always wanted more than I was able to provide. The pressure of it all just became too much. Christina offered me some respite. She didn't ask anything of me. She was having problems in her own marriage. Her husband was not well and was always on her back. We decided the best option would be to leave Castlemaine and make a new start. But it was a mistake. Christina and I soon went our separate ways. I wanted to come back then, but I felt too ashamed.'

Mary Ann's emotions were in turmoil. She was relieved to see her son again after so long, but she couldn't hide the anger she felt at the hurt he had caused and the deep sadness she felt at all the years they had lost.

'I can see that you are sorry. But your disappearance left such a hole in our family.'

'I know I don't deserve your forgiveness, but I am truly sorry, and nothing has given me greater pleasure than seeing you and the rest of the family again.'

Mary Ann turned to Frederick and hugged him tightly. 'It really is good to have you home. I miss your father every day and I know that I can never have my whole family back together, but having you here today has made me very happy.'

Chapter Forty-Three

Ann, Moonlight Flats, 1935

When Mary Ann did not appear the next morning, Ann went into her room.

'Are you alright Mother?' she enquired. 'You do look a bit peaky.'

'I expect it was just all the excitement of yesterday, but I do feel rather more weary than usual.'

'Perhaps you should stay in bed.'

'Nonsense, I will get up now.' But as Mary Ann tried to swing her legs over the side of the bed and sit up, she went white and looked like she was going to faint. 'Perhaps I will lie here just a bit longer.'

'That is a good idea Mother. I will bring you a cup of tea. What about a piece of toast?'

'Thank you my dear, that sounds lovely.' As Ann left the room, she saw her mother slump back against the pillows. Despite her determination, which had always been her hallmark, Mary Ann was unable to get out of bed that day. In fact she was bedridden from that day on.

Only two months later, on a cold day in May, Mary Ann lay on her death bed. All her children were gathered around her as her ragged breath tore at her lungs. She had developed pneumonia after falling ill not long after her 100th birthday. The doctor had been called and had been to the house several times over the course of the last weeks. But on his last visit, four days ago, he had informed the family there was nothing more he could do. Ann knew that Mary Ann had accepted that she would soon die.

'One hundred years on earth is enough for any woman,' she told her family proudly. All her grandchildren and great grandchildren had been ushered in to say their goodbyes. Mary Ann seemed confused as to which was which, there were so many of them.

'It was so hard to remember all their names,' she said to Ann when they were alone together. 'My mind is not what it used to be.'

Ann held her mother's hand as she lay taking short raspy breaths.

'I feel at peace Ann. Soon I will be with Richard again.'

It was only Ann who sat with her during the long night. The others had gone to their beds. She dozed on and off in the chair by her mother's bed. Suddenly she woke with a start, perhaps it was a premonition. Mary Ann had stopped breathing. Her face was pale but she was still warm to the touch. Ann did not hurry to inform the rest of the family but rather, pulled her chair in and sat close to her mother. She took her scarred, white hand

and bent over to kiss her mother's brow. Mary Ann looked so peaceful. Ann shed a few tears and said a quiet prayer. But she could not truly be sad. Her mother had been ill for longer than she would have liked. Ann was glad that her faith was strong that she would meet her beloved Richard again in the afterlife. Eventually Ann went to inform the rest of the family. Mary Ann took her last breath on May 4, 1935.

Acknowledgements

Every author knows that whilst we spend endless hours locked in our writing cave, in fact writing a book is far from a solitary pursuit. This book would not be what it is today without the invaluable contributions of many individuals.

Firstly and most importantly I would like to thank my editors, Kelly Rigby and Cecile Shanahan. Your dedication transformed my work from a manuscript into a fully formed story. I am deeply grateful for your patience and guidance.

My early beta readers gave me thoughtful feedback which, as always, was an important part of my writing process and was greatly appreciated. Thank you Hannah McCarthy, Sandra Wiles, Kylie Eklund-Denman and Wendi Kruger. Also to Heather Kelly whose careful proofread helped put the final touches on the story.

Historical fiction requires deep research which for me is a labour of love. As England was the setting for the early chapters of this book I needed to immerse myself in that time period. I read and took inspiration from classics written in Victorian

England including Hard Times by Charles Dickens and The Mayor of Casterbridge by Thomas Hardy.

The Castlemaine Historical Society were able to furnish a wealth of information about the branch of my family who inspired this story. Their commitment to preserving local history is commendable.

Once again, Douglas Thomson from High Voltage Studio has created a cover that captures the essence of the story. Thank you for your patience through several iterations.

Finally, thank you to you, my readers. Your support is my greatest motivation. During the challenging times when the story seems elusive, the thought that you will read my books keeps me going.

Authors Note

As with my two previous books, Conflict at Hanging Rock and Breaking Free, this book is a work of fiction inspired by real events and people. It is the story of a branch of my family who settled in Castlemaine, Victoria, Australia at the time of the 1850's goldrush.

Once again I have changed the names. However in this case I have kept the first names of many of the characters so they might be recognisable to anyone who knows this family well. All the dates are factual but there are some events which did not take place as far as I know, although they easily might have. I have also used my imagination and my knowledge and research of social history of the time to fill in some of the gaps where the facts are not available.

One particular example is the question of how Richard came to meet Mary Ann. She was only ten years of age when he was transported to Van Diemen's Land and yet ten years later he came back to England very briefly to marry her and take her back to his home in Castlemaine. How he knew of her and how they met remains a mystery so I have had to draw my own conclusion.

I like to include historical characters in my stories when appropriate. In this case I came across the story of Fanny Finch who was a well known and colourful character on the goldfields. She is thought to be the first woman in Victoria to vote, long before women's suffrage was achieved. Much has been written about her and the State Government of Victoria erected a memorial headstone on her previously unmarked grave in the Castlemaine cemetery in 2020.

I hope you have enjoyed this, my third family story. If you have, it would help me immeasurably if you could leave a review on your preferred platform.

Also By Pauline Wilson

Nineteen-year-old Annie finds herself incarcerated in the Kew Lunatic Asylum in 1894, her memories shrouded in a fog of confusion. She finds an unlikely ally in the Matron of the asylum who is determined to help her break free from her nightmarish reality. As Annie's journey to rediscover herself intertwines with the Matron's fight for justice, they must confront the darkness of a society that silences and oppresses women.

But in the depths of her despair, will the man she loves be there to support Her?

This emotional and powerful story exposes the abuses and mistreatment that were all too common in mental institutions in the late 1800s.

Robert Blayney thought his life was over. But a twist of fate landed him in Port Phillip clutching his ticket of leave.

Now he must make his way into the interior in the early days of European settlement. Soon the rest of his family join him on his farm. With the exception of his brother who is incarcerated in Van Diemen's Land.

As he becomes wealthy and his reputation as a gentleman grows, his desire to hide the secret of his convict past is thwarted by family conflict.

When the family feud comes to a climax, will Robert lose all hope?

Meanwhile, the growing community is struggling with a conflict of its own.

www.ingramcontent.com/pod-product-compliance
Lightning Source LLC
Chambersburg PA
CBHW030519120726
47904CB00005B/1535